NEED HIT SERGI. . . .

As powerful as the death agony of the channel whom Sergi had been escorting to Keon, the sensation of need roused Sergi instantly into his Companion's mode. He had never felt such a depth of need before.

A Sime entered the shrine—another weary traveler taking shelter from the storm, but this one sought more than a warm, dry place to spend the night. Sergi's overwhelming response meant that this newcomer was beyond thought, beyond stopping—a Sime more powerful than any Sergi had ever encountered, a killer stalking its prey, needing Sergi's life force to live!

ABOUT THE AUTHOR

Jean Lorrah is Professor of English at Murray State University in Kentucky. She met Jacqueline Lichtenberg through *Star Trek* fandom, and the two first combined their talents in *First Channel* and *Channel's Destiny*, which are also Sime/Gen novels.

It was with Jacqueline's encouragement that Jean created her own *Savage Empire* series, which has now grown to five novels, three in print and two in production at this writing. Jean has published a number of short stories, and is co-editor with Lois Wickstrom of *Pandora*, a small-press magazine of science fiction and fantasy.

Loving both teaching and writing, Jean occasionally has the opportunity to combine these disciplines by teaching creative writing. She remains as active in fandom as possible, attending several conventions every year. Like Jacqueline, she would like to know what readers think of her work, especially what they would like to see in later books.

AMBROV KEON
A Sime/Gen Novel

Jean Lorrah

*The Sime/Gen universe is an original
creation of Jacqueline Lichtenberg.*

DAW BOOKS, INC.
DONALD A. WOLLHEIM, PUBLISHER

1633 Broadway, New York, NY 10019

DAW Collectors Book No. 662.

First Printing, February 1986

1 2 3 4 5 6 7 8 9

PRINTED IN U.S.A.

Foreword

All my work in the Sime/Gen series must be dedicated to Jacqueline Lichtenberg, who is gracoius enough to let me come and play in her universe. It is a most exciting and appealing universe, and has inspired three fanzines which publish readers' comments and suggestions, as well as stories, artwork, and poetry. If you enjoy the Sime/Gen universe and would like to comment or find out more, Jacqueline and I can be reached through our publishers or c/o *Ambrov Zeor*, P. O. Box 190, Monsey, NY 10952. You may be sure your comments are read with great interest. If your letter requires an answer, please enclose a stamped, self-addressed envelope.

Both Jacqueline and I have been active in science fiction fandom for many years, and are firm believers in the interaction between readers and authors. Your comments are welcome!

Chapter One

The Mizipi River flowed smoothly in the late-summer stillness. No breeze stirred its calm surface. The heavily laden raft glided on the current with almost no guidance.

The river swung around a bend and flowed south once more, the broad surface of the water reflecting unbroken blue sky for as far as the man and woman aboard the raft could see. They drifted straight down the middle of river, and Morgan Tigue set his pole down. "We've got clear sailing now, Risa," he said.

Risa balanced her pole, twice as tall as she was, and laid it beside her father's on the raft. "I'll be glad to get home," she said, seating herself on a canvas-covered chest. "I loved the trading, but getting our goods home is just plain boring."

Tigue laughed, the hearty laugh of a man who enjoys life despite its hardships. "Be glad of boredom, Reesey—you don't really want to fight the Gen Border Patrol!"

Risa didn't protest the childhood nickname, although no one but her father could get away with calling her that. He was training her in the family business, and this had been her first trip out-Territory, their most successful trading venture yet. The raft was loaded with barrels of nails, coils of wire, plowshares, knives and axheads—perhaps raided from Gen Territory, but purchased at the huge East Market in Nivet Sime Territory. The only commodity more profitable than metal goods was Gens . . . but Morgan Tigue was no Genrunner, nor did he want his daughter to be one.

Risa knew there was more to her father's antipathy to Genrunning than its danger and quasi-legal status. He—and therefore she—had kin on the Gen side of the border. Lots of people did, of course, but not everyone had the strong family loyalties of the Tigues. Morgan Tigue had guided his own brother to the border when he established as a Gen. Risa would be expected to take brother Kreg, if—

No. She refused to consider it. Kreg must be Sime, like Risa and their father. Risa had changed over safely despite all their worry. So would Kreg!

As if to reassure herself, Risa stretched her arms, extending her handling tentacles to touch her fingertips. The tentacles, developed at changeover, normally lay sheathed along her forearms. Now they emerged from the openings at her wrists, two over the back of each hand, two under the palm, relieving the growing pressure on the laterals still sheathed on either side of each forearm.

"We'll be home by tomorrow morning," her father said, his selyn field—his life energy—meshing with hers as he used his Sime senses to gauge her state of need. "You're coming up short again," he said, unable to hide his concern. Risa could hear the unspoken words, "Just like your mother."

"I'm all right, Dad," she said firmly, deliberately hiding her discomfort. She was still in her first year after changeover; surely her need cycle would normalize eventually. Besides, this had been an active trip—there was nothing surprising in her needing more selyn than usual.

To take her mind off need, she examined her arms, freckled by the sun. Her bare feet were turning pink again; she pulled on socks and moccasins to protect the fair skin.

A broad-brimmed straw hat shaded her face. She should put on a long-sleeved shirt against the noonday sun, but it was so dreadfully hot—

In the far distance a small, ragged cloud scudded across the horizon, followed by two more. "Look, Dad—there's a breeze blowing on downriver."

"Good," he replied, leaning back against a crate. "I sure will be glad to get home."

"Kreg's taking care of things."

"He's a fine boy," her father agreed. "Growing like a weed."

Again words remained unspoken; Risa knew her father was worried that Kreg might turn Gen—might even have done so while they were away, and had no one to warn him or to guide him to the border—

She shoved the thought aside again, then wondered if it was a premonition. "Both your mother's brothers turned Gen," Tigue said as if in answer to her thought. "So did my brother Jerro. Figure the odds, Risa—Kreg'll change over. There's two Simes to every Gen in Sime families."

On the average, Risa thought. But all sorts of odd things ran in families; what if large numbers of Gens ran in theirs? After all, Gens were needed so Simes could live.

"It wouldn't be so bad if we *knew*, one way or the other," said Risa. "Then we could prepare—"

"Wait till you have children, Reesey. It's better not to know. Just love your family—that's important. You and Kreg grow up and find people to love, and give me lots of grandchildren. We'll have a whole house full of kids, like the family I grew up in."

As a child, Risa had always loved her father's stories of his four sisters and a brother—but now the stories took on new meaning. One of his sisters had died in changeover, another in childbirth. One had turned Gen and been caught and killed running for the border. His last sister, the only one of her aunts Risa could remember, had been murdered in a Gen raid . . . and his brother—even if he still lived—might as well be dead. Risa had known these facts for years, but since her changeover they weighed heavily on her heart.

"What's the good of family if you lose them all?" she asked—then was sorry she'd said it as through her Sime senses she zlinned the pain the question brought her father.

"Not all," he replied after a moment. "I've got you and Kreg—and I had ten good years with your mother. Loss is part of life, Risa . . . and you can't refuse to love people because someday you might lose them."

The breeze reached them. The raft lifted and dropped over little wavelets. Risa stood, easily balancing, letting the air cool her sunburnt skin. Now that she was Sime, her body healed such minor damage while she slept; she would have a deeper tan—and more freckles—in the morning.

She was grateful even for such minor advantages, for when she was a child exposure to the summer sun had meant pain, blistered skin, and peeling. At fifteen, still not changed over, she had sneaked away with others her age to swim in the river. Keeping up with her Sime friends, she had gotten such a severe sunburn that she suffered for days with raging fever. She could have died, she now knew—a stupid way to end a life. If she ever had children—

She supposed she would someday, and yet she couldn't imagine a man she could love the way her mother had loved her father, nor see herself with children of her own. So she changed the subject. "Maybe we'll make enough profit this year to buy that house you want, Dad."

"We won't live behind the store forever," he replied. "But investments first—we'll expand the business again now that you're grown up. You and Kreg will be rich someday."

When they were growing up, Risa and Kreg had hardly realized they were *not* rich. Most parents taught their children to read, write, and do simple arithmetic—

and that was that until a child changed over and might seek special training or an apprenticeship. But Risa and Kreg had been sent half-days to a small private school in Norlea, where they were taught history, geography, music, and etiquette.

Morgan Tigue believed that acting rich was as important as being rich. Their store might stock trinkets and flashy wares for the general run of customers, but the apartment behind the store was sparsely furnished, in the finest of quiet taste. The family wore clothes of the best material, in conservative cut that would remain in style for years. Before her death, Risa's mother had made all their clothes; now they were outfitted by a tailor who would trade services for first choice of Tigue imported goods at wholesale prices.

The wealthy bought at Tigue's, even though the store was on the waterfront, not in the fashionable high-rent district. Morgan Tigue carried the best of everything, from buttons to wagons—and boasted that if he didn't have it, he could get it in a month. Risa had never known him to fail.

He always talked about building a house, but always plunged his money back into the business. *I guess I'll have to buy that house for Dad someday,* Risa thought.

The river grew rougher. The scattered clouds thickened, and ragged-edged thunderheads followed from the south. "Storm brewing," said Risa, glad now to put on her loose-sleeved shirt as the air cooled swiftly.

"Let's tie up till it's over," said her father.

Risa agreed, for the raft, although sturdily built and adequate to its burden, was not very maneuverable.

Along here the river had no distinct shoreline. Winding channels on either side of the main current were separated by marshes or hummocks. No islands—nothing to secure the raft to. If that storm blew as wickedly as it was threatening, they should unload their heavy cargo onto solid ground and drag the raft ashore. But where?

Morgan Tigue scanned the east bank, part of their home Gulf Territory. The west shore was held by Gens.

The wind whipped at the water, veering the raft off-course to the west.

Risa and her father stood on the starboard side, their poles ready to push off from hummocks or sandbars. Balancing on the leading edge of the raft, they zlinned, Sime senses separating water from the obstructions they could not see.

The river was wide and shallow here. The two Simes vectored the raft into a clumsy southward course, heaving in unison to keep it from veering farther west.

They were augmenting, using selyn from their stored reserves for strength to fight the wind, but neither could go on that way for long. Southward progress slowed. Risa tried to peer ahead through the spray, longing to see an island, a bit of tree-lined shore—any shelter at all.

The misting spray churned up by the wind was joined by fat drops of rain, thunking onto the raft like stones.

The rain increased in force, driven sideways on the wind. Blinded, the Simes maneuvered by their special senses, toes gripping the raft through their moccasins.

As Risa heaved the raft off a sandbar, the wind shifted. The raft swung in an arc around the pole, almost pulling her overboard.

She lurched, staggered, let go of the pole and grabbed for it again. They dared not lose the ability to steer.

The rain was no longer drops, but sheets—a waterfall roaring over them. *It can't go on like this for long,* Risa thought. Such intensity had to blow itself out quickly.

It was dark as night now. The water rose in waves, river mingling with rain on the howling wind.

The river turned to mud as debris churned up from the bottom. The wind shifted again, now driving north, as if to push the mighty Mizipi backward!

The river fought back. The raft tossed and shook, the two people on board clinging to the ropes. Their poles washed overboard. They were helpless.

Risa could zlin her father's selyn field. He was on the

raft, not five paces away, and yet they dared not let go their precarious hold to reach for one another.

The wind howled and shrieked about them. Risa knew now what the storm was: hurricane.

Just the edge of a hurricane had hit Norlea when Risa was nine, tumbling trees and buildings, killing four people. Now she was being carried straight into the heart of such a storm. The only time she had ever felt so helpless before was at her changeover—but her father had been there to see her through. Now he was as helpless as she was.

The raft spun on the surging river—rebounded off a hummock—heaved over a white-capped wave. There was a sickening lurch. Risa felt the sturdy timbers twist beneath her, straining the lashings.

"Dad!" she shouted, the wind tearing the sound from her mouth.

She could zlin her father's steady field. Tigues were survivors!

The ropes holding their cargo snapped. The heavy tarpaulin whirled off into the wind as crates and barrels of metal implements fell overboard.

Another wave tossed them skyward. The remaining cargo flew up, landed with a slam—timbers split!

Risa's section of the raft dissolved beneath her hands and tentacles.

The raft swung away from her and back—her father was clinging to remaining timbers with one hand, reaching for her with the other.

Kicking madly, Risa reached toward him. His end of the timber broke free, pitching him into the water head-first.

More items poured off the raft. Heavy iron implements whirled like corks on the current. A crate of plowshares spilled into the water—one struck Morgan Tigue in the side, and Risa zlinned the sickening pain of breaking ribs.

"Dad! Daddy!"

The air was suddenly full of flying nails. Risa's father

was maddeningly close, swimming despite his pain. But selyn flowed from a wound in his leg. Any wound losing selyn like that would be pumping life's blood into the river—

With all her augmented strength, Risa fought the waves. "Daddy!" she screamed, her mouth filling with muddy water. His field was fading!

She came close enough to touch him with finger- and tentacle-tips. He was unconscious.

The wind howled mockingly. The last of her father's life force faded away. It was an empty body she clutched at. Then it was torn from her grip and swept away in the current. Dead, it provided no field for her to follow.

Waves washed over Risa's head. Survival instinct overcame her shocked grief, and she began to swim. A piece of raft bore down on her. Perhaps she could grab hold—

The wind was playing games. Risa reached for the raft. It swung away from her as she sank in the trough of a wave. Behind her, the crest carried crates of nails and axheads—the wave broke, raining down iron. Risa was aware only of screeching pain in head and left shoulder—and then nothing.

Risa woke to pain and terror. She didn't know where she was. When she opened her eyes she saw that she lay on solid ground, while her Sime senses told her she was being tossed violently with waves of heat and cold beating over her.

The conflict between her senses made her want to scream, but only a whimper emerged from between her chattering teeth.

Some rational part of her mind recognized her symptoms: psychospatial disorientation. Unconscious, she had been flung ashore far from where the raft had disintegrated. The Sime orientation she had developed at changeover—the sense that told her where in the world she was—had been disrupted.

Closing her eyes plunged her back into the river, as

if she must now experience at an accelerated rate everything that had happened while she was unconscious. When she forced her eyes open, she seemed to be suspended over an abyss, looking *down* into treetops and blue sky. Helplessly, she clutched at the muddy grass as the world changed colors and began to spin. Nausea shook her.

It went on and on. Darkness brought the storm back—or was it another sensory distortion? Rain pelted her. She tried to curl up to escape as it burned her with boiling drops, stung her with ice. The world spun again.

Finally the worst was over. It was dark and pouring down rain, but the wind had lessened to ordinary force. If she could trust her time sense, it was just after midnight.

She knew where she was now: in Gulf Territory. At least the river had not flung her up among her enemies. If she walked east, she would come to the Old River Road—and along the road she would find people. Where was the nearest pen? Vizber? Mefis? As she tried to determine where she was in relation to the towns, distortions returned. She was not recovered; could not recover completely until she replenished her selyn reserves.

The moment she admitted her need, it became all-consuming. The battle with the river, followed by disorientation, had reduced her life energy to a degree she had not experienced since First Need at changeover.

By the time she found a Gen she would be in deeper need than she had ever known in her short life as a Sime. If she did not get a Gen soon . . . she could die!

The longer she lay there, the deeper her need. Despite dizziness and a stabbing pain behind her eyes, Risa struggled to her feet. Turning her back to the river, she forced one foot in front of the other, stumbling eastward, fighting her way through soggy underbrush and storm debris.

Need tore at her vitals. Cramps spread from the middle of her chest down her arms to convulse the small lateral tentacles, organs designed to draw selyn from a Gen's system into hers. At their roots, ronaplin glands swelled painfully with selyn-conducting fluid—the delicate organs pushed out of their sheaths, seeking, finding nothing, the rain washing away the ronaplin as fast as it bathed them.

Need was always unpleasant. If a Gen were not immediately available it could be frightening—but Risa had never known it to be so painful.

The rain-soaked sleeves of her loose shirt sogged against the sensitive organs, making her shudder, yet she was too cold to take the shirt off. She longed for her winter fur-lined cape. Her handling tentacles began to ache from holding the sleeves away from her laterals.

Everything ached. Her feet hurt. Her head throbbed. Need loomed, pulling at her. She yearned to stop fighting and let it claim her. If only it didn't hurt so much!

She couldn't give up. People were depending on her. She could feel them waiting for her, leaning on her strength. She saw them watching her with total trust—

Hallucinations!

The strange faces looming out of the rain dissolved into Kreg's face. Yes. Her brother was waiting for her. With Dad gone, he had no one else. She had to get home to him. She had to live. Where was that road?

By this time she was promising herself, *One more step and you can rest. Get to the next tree. Now another step—*

Out of the bleak night, the nager of a high-field Gen impinged on her consciousness.

Another hallucination?

Risa halted her stumbling progress, her laterals stretching in the direction of life promise. A vibrating throb of need, she moved with Sime-swift deliberateness toward the source of fulfillment.

It grew stronger as she drew closer. She operated only with her Sime senses now—hyperconscious—and as she broke out into a rutted wagon track she suddenly knew precisely where she was. Her father had brought her to this back road years ago, before they knew whether she would be Sime or Gen. Last year he had taken Kreg on this same journey.

No—she could not identify the fleeing Gen ahead with Kreg. She must have that Gen's life force to live!

Suddenly the selyn source blinked out, as if it had never been. Risa stopped in her tracks. Had she imagined—?

The shrine! That was why they had come here, years ago. Just off this little-used road was a Shrine of the Starred-cross, a shelter for newly established Gens fleeing to the safety of Gen Territory.

The shrine was carved into living rock, insulating selyn fields. The occupant would not attract passing Simes, and could rest in as much safety as was possible for a Gen until he reached the other side of the border.

The selyn field Risa had been following was suddenly there again, beckoning her with rich promise. Thought was impossible. She was a predator with her prey in reach.

Swiftly and silently, she moved toward the shrine— and she did not panic when the field disappeared again.

Sergi ambrov Keon was tired—not the healthy tiredness of a long day's effort, but the bone-deep fatigue of despair. He had failed in the worst possible way a Companion could. A channel in his care had died.

Mechanically, he lit the fire laid ready inside the shrine, and put water on for tea. He didn't unpack the food in his saddlebag; hunger was the furthest thing from his mind. He was cold, not just from the chill winds still chasing the storm, but from his own depression.

Over and over, the last few moments of the life of Erland ambrov Carre played in his mind. Sergi had been escorting Erland from Carre to Keon—the new channel Keon was so desperate for. When the storm had struck, they'd taken shelter in a cotton barn, hunching down in the center aisle between the bales—surely the safest place they could have found.

When the wind had whipped boards off the building and flung icy rain in on them, Sergi had pushed the Sime to the floor and crouched beside him, sheltering his arms from flying debris. They both knew by then that they were caught in a hurricane; there was nothing to do but hope the barn would hold through the storm.

It didn't. With a wrenching crack, the roof gave, some shakes flying, others tumbling in on them. The horses screamed and reared. Erland leaped to grasp the reins. Sergi was trying to stop the foolish Sime from exposing his vulnerable forearms when something caught him on the back of the head, dropping him to his knees.

He didn't quite black out, but his senses swam. He was aware of Erland easing him to the floor, the feel of hot, moist lateral tentacles over the throbbing point of impact, and the pain subsiding. But the channel was kneeling over him, when he should be protecting the channel.

In the wind and thunder, the mightiest shout could not be heard. He struggled to his knees, grasping Erland's flying cape to wrap the channel in it. The wind tore it from his hands as more debris fell—sticks and pebbles that cut and stung, and grit that made their eyes smart.

Sergi groped for Erland's arms, hoping the Sime had retracted his tentacles before that cloud of dust hit them—grit up the tentacle sheaths could put a channel out of commission for days.

But the Sime had moved beyond his reach. Shielding his eyes with his hands, Sergi peered through the blur, finding Erland hunched over, arms tight against his chest.

It was far worse than grit. Erland was bleeding— bleeding from a slashed lateral.

It was only then that Sergi felt his own cuts—there

was glass from a shattered barn window in that flying debris. Both men were bleeding—but only Erland fatally.

Sergi tried to force away the memory of the channel's death. He had eased the pain, and the boy had died in minutes. That was the single blessing: the wound was so severe that he died quickly, instead of lingering for days in the agony of attrition.

Sergi had known Erland only for a few days. Now he had the task of returning to Carre to give the news of the boy's death to those who had loved him all his life. If that was not enough, he must then go home to Keon without a channel, their hope of surviving for another year.

He sat staring morosely into the fire, seeing everything Keon had struggled for go up in smoke—through his failure.

Need hit him.

As powerful as Erland's death agony, the sensation aroused Sergi instantly into his Companion's mode. Perhaps it was guilt that made him think he had never responded to such depth of need before, but he knew at once that it was a physical reaction, not a psychological one.

A Sime had entered the shrine—another weary traveler taking shelter from the storm, but this one seeking more than a warm, dry place to spend the night. Sergi's overwhelming response meant that the newcomer was beyond thought, beyond stopping—a killer Sime stalking its prey, needing Sergi's life force to live!

The high field of the Gen in the shrine washed over Risa, easing her need with promise. There was no fear in it—he must not know that she was there.

Basking in his field, she became duoconscious—both her Sime senses and her other senses operating at once. She could see him silhouetted against the fire. Too large for a recently established adolescent. A full-grown Gen.

What was he doing here? Blown into Sime Territory

by the storm? It didn't matter; he was life to her. The moment he knew she was there, that tempting field would erupt with the fear she needed as much as his selyn. She would drain him, charging her aching nerves—surely that incredible field promised that for once she would be fully satisfied—

She took a step forward, just as the Gen said, "Why don't you come over to the fire and get warm?"

It was Risa who flared fear. Then she wondered what kind of fool believed only a Gen could enter the shrine.

The Gen leaned forward to poke up the fire, then stood—and she saw that he was huge. Gens were usually bigger than Simes, but this was the biggest one she'd ever seen—the absurd thought crossed her mind that his size meant he stored more selyn, although she knew the two things were unrelated.

He was turning toward her now. She moved forward, waiting for him to recognize a Sime in need, yearning for the fear that would charge his field for her kill. Her laterals dripped ronaplin in expectation. She moved forward step by step, savoring his field, waiting for the moment of recognition, of terror—the peak bliss of the kill!

Chapter Two

Sergi watched the Sime approach—a girl, covered with mud and wrung out with need. She couldn't be more than a month or two past changeover. Although he knew she intended to kill him, his heart went out to her. He held out his hands, knowing that in her state she could not resist his field. "Come here," he said gently. "I will serve your need."

To his astonishment, she stopped, actually looking at him. She expected fear, of course—any Gen but a Companion would have been terrified, seeing certain death approach.

But Sergi had no fear to give her. Instead, she woke in him an expectation of pleasure. His mind told him this little junct had nothing for him but the chance to ease his guilt by doing a kindness—but his body responded as if to a channel, more powerful than any he had ever served.

She was still staring at him, zlinning him—needing him. Unable to leave that need unfilled, he took a step toward her.

She darted back a step, stumbled, and almost fell.

No Sime was clumsy. She was hurt! As Sergi drew closer he saw blood mixed with the mud on her bare neck. "Poor child," he murmured. "Let me help you." The Sime staggered, but kept her feet and remained just out of his reach. "I'm going to kill you!" she spat, a kitten hissing at a hound.

When her threat failed to raise fear in him, she crouched, ready to spring. But instead of leaping, she shuddered, and suddenly clutched her arms to her chest.

Sergi's ache to serve her need surged—and he realized she was voiding selyn! It was attrition—if he did not give her transfer at once she could be dead in minutes.

No—no, not twice in one day!

Sergi caught her as her knees gave way, kneeling himself.

Rest on my field, he thought as Nedd had trained him, knowing his feeling communicated through his nager—the aura of life-energy that every Sime could read.

The girl struggled feebly as he held her—where did she get such strength of will?—but he balanced her against his right arm, offering her his left, sliding his hand under hers.

Her handling tentacles wrapped about his forearm like tiny ropes of steel. When the hot, moist laterals touched him, her resistance crumbled. She was already reaching for his right arm when he ceased supporting her back with it.

They knelt, face to face. Sergi bent his head, touched the girl's lips with his—and the flow began. She drew voraciously, setting every nerve in Sergi's body to singing. To give transfer was a Companion's greatest pleasure, but no channel—not even Nedd—had ever touched him so deeply.

He felt the ebb and surge as her secondary system came into play. She had no control, no smoothness, no care for him—yet she gave him satisfaction he had never known before.

But the girl was unsatisfied. Brimming with selyn, still she demanded of him, their systems clashing—

She was trying to hurt him. She needed pain, fear—a junct's need. He could not give her killbliss!

No, he thought, *you don't need to kill! Feel the pure pleasure without pain!*

They were perfectly matched in nageric strength, but Sergi had years of training and experience. He brought the transfer gently to its termination and sank back on his heels. The girl stared at him from immense dark eyes, incredulous. He smiled, touched by her innocence.

Her eyes traveled over him as he knelt patiently, knowing that immediately after transfer a Sime drank in the world through the senses denied in the days of increasing need. Sergi could smell the dampness of the girl's hair and clothing, feel the chill air coming off the stone walls. He wanted to pick her up, towel her off, and wrap her in blankets—but she was a wild thing, ready to flee into the night at the wrong move. He held still, waiting.

Risa had never been so satisfied in her life. Her whole body tingled with well-being . . . and yet she had not killed.

As her senses readjusted, she saw all that the firelight could reveal of the huge Gen, so vitally, impossibly alive.

She had seen art works of precious metal, bronze statuettes of shadow-dark beauty edged by bright highlights where handling had rubbed away the patina. So the Gen before her showed bright highlights on hair and skin, though most of his huge bulk remained in shadow. If her hands did not still rest on the living, yielding flesh of his arms, she might have thought him turned to bronze, so still he knelt, waiting.

What did he expect now? His hands remained a steady support beneath her forearms. Belatedly, she withdrew her handling tentacles, but still he did not move.

What kind of Gen—?

Wer-Gen, stirred in the back of her mind. She had heard as a child the legends of magicians who turned Simes into Gens—fearless Gens who thus produced selyn but in turn became masters over Simes, Gens who had the power to kill—

She blinked the superstitious nonsense away, and found her voice. "Who are you?"

"I am Sergi ambrov Keon," he replied in a soothing tone. The peculiar name told her what he was: a Companion, a Gen raised in a Householding. It was true, then. They could give their selyn and not die. "Let me help you," he said.

"I don't require any help," Risa replied, suddenly very conscious of his support. She tried to spring to her feet, but the world tilted, and she tottered like a child.

The Gen caught her, lifting her small weight with ease. "You're exhausted," he said. "You were disoriented."

Her response was to zlin him. His nager amazed her. She had never known anything like the warmth and concern flowing over her. "How did you know?" she asked warily.

"Juncts don't allow themselves to get that deep into need, and ... there's no use trying to explain to a Sime. Here—" He set her down on the bench before the fire and touched the side of her head so gently that she felt no pain. "—You've had a severe blow. If you were just unconscious, how did you use up so much selyn? You must have fallen into the river. Not magic," he added at her start. "Mud!"

Risa was covered in it, dry and cracking on the outside of her clothing, soggy and gritty on the inside. She felt filthy and uncomfortable, but there was no running water in the shrine, and she had lost all her clean clothes.

Sergi suggested, "It's still pouring rain outside, but it's getting warmer. Have some hot tea first, and then wash that mud off. If you sleep in that condition you'll feel miserable in the morning."

Perhaps it was his self-assurance that made her obey him. She stripped, washed herself in the rain, her clothes in the torrent from the shrine's downspout. That flow was heavy enough to penetrate to the roots of her hair; she unbraided it with difficulty, and gratefully spread it with fingers and tentacles to wash out the mud.

The Gen took her clothes inside, draping them with his over the bench before the fire. When Risa came in, he was ready with a cape to wrap her in. "Are you allergic to wool?" he asked before draping it over her shoulders.

"Allergic? Of course not." She pulled the garment about herself gratefully, for it was much cooler inside the stone shrine than outside. The Gen's cape would have easily wrapped three times around Risa; it fell to her knees, although it was probably waist-length on him.

As the garment absorbed the moisture from her body, Risa realized that it was not the Gen's traveling cape. That lay spread across the bench, steaming slightly. This cape and the dry shirt and trousers he wore had come from his saddlebags.

As she approached the fire, Risa smelled cereal cooking, and realized that she was hungry. The Gen was trimming the wick of an oil lamp with a sharp knife. Risa shuddered at the sight of such an instrument in Gen hands.

In the bright light, Risa's cape glowed red. She noticed embroidery down the front. It formed a chain—a chain of white links down the red wool.

"Why did you ask if I'm allergic to wool?" she asked.

"Sensitivity to certain foods or fabrics is a price some channels pay for their talents."

Channels? Those were the perverted Simes who drew selyn from Gens without killing them, and transferred it to other Simes, who thus lived without killing. "I'm not—"

"You are a channel," he said positively, his nager accentuating his certainty. "You do not function as a channel, but you are one. Keon needs you."

"Needs?" For a moment she thought he had misused the word, the kind of error even new Simes made if they had come from Gen Territory and were just learning Simelan. But it was obvious that Simelan was this Gen's native language. He meant exactly what he said.

"Our householding has grown so that our channels cannot keep up with the demands on their time and skills."

"Then you will have to put an end to your perverted lifestyle."

He paused, then asked in a carefully neutral tone, "Do you consider what you and I just shared to be perverted?"

"Yes," she replied at once.

"Why?" he asked, indignation flaring in his nager.

"You're alive."

His field became a neutral wall between them, as he dished out cereal and more tea. Only when Risa was dawdling over the last spoonfuls in her bowl did he speak again.

"If you will not thank me for saving your life, will you at least tell me your name?"

"Risa Tigue," she replied.

"So you know what it is to have a family."

Many Simes did not have family names, even in these civilized times, for many still did not settle, marry, found families. "Ours is an old family," Risa said proudly. "Ask anyone in Norlea about Tigue's General Store. My grandfather founded it, and my father built it into a thriving business."

At the thought of her father, the moment of his death returned. Grief welled up to overwhelm her.

"Then you can understand—" Sergi began, caught sight of her stricken look, and asked, "What's wrong?"

"My father," Risa choked out. "He's dead."

The words made it real. She would never see him again, never hear him call her by the pet name she hated, never again have him to turn to—

As the girl dissolved into tears, Sergi moved to her side, trying to remain emotionally neutral. He had seen such post-transfer reactions before. In the last days of the need cycle, Simes became numb to emotions, unable to react even to tragic loss until released from the repression of need.

"Go on—cry," said Sergi, digging in his saddlebags for a clean handkerchief. She accepted it—again without a thank you. But that was her culture—a Gen was not a person to her. "If it will help," he offered, "tell me about your father."

"He was j-just getting everything he'd worked so hard for," she said. "All he ever did was work. The st-store was thriving. We went out-Territory to trade. Best trip ever. Then the storm—the raft—"

"Today?" he asked in shock. "Oh, Risa, I am so sorry!" But she pushed him away when he tried to put a comforting arm around her. "Did he drown?" he asked.

"He was wounded when the raft broke up. Bled to death . . . voided to death . . . what's the difference?"

The image of Erland ambrov Carre rose to haunt Sergi. "It wasn't your fault," he said. "In that storm—"

"Nobody's fault," she sobbed, "but he's dead. Oh, Daddy, Daddy!"

He let her cry until she subsided into hiccupping sobs. Then he asked, "Is the rest of your family in Norlea?"

"Only my brother Kreg. We're all that's left. I have to take care of Kreg now that Dad's gone."

"Kreg is younger than you are?"

She nodded.

"Then . . . Risa, has your brother changed over yet?"

"No. He's still a child." She wiped her eyes and squared her thin shoulders. He admired the way she put aside her grief when she thought of her responsibilities—she already had one of a channel's most important disciplines.

"What will you do if he establishes as a Gen?"

"You don't think I'd sell my own brother into the pens, do you?" she snapped indignantly.

"You would break the law if you took him to the

border, and you would never see him again. Risa, you require sleep. We'll talk tomorrow—but I want you to think about something. There is one way you and your brother can remain together, even if he should turn Gen. You can join a householding."

"My brother is going to be Sime, like me," she insisted. Nonetheless, she accepted the bedroll he offered her, curled up like a child, and went off at once into exhausted slumber.

Risa woke at sunrise. She couldn't remember feeling so positively good since changeover. Except for the glowing coals of the fire, it was pitch dark inside the shrine. She zlinned the strange Gen sleeping soundly. Last night had really happened. It was not a disorientation dream.

All trace of disorientation had disappeared. It was normal for a kill to put an end to disorientation suffered in the middle of a need cycle . . . but she doubted even that could end all symptoms, including nightmares, within a day.

She went outside, and found her time sense back to normal. The sun was just up. Birds sang merrily. A few scattered clouds, last remnants of the storm, floated away to the east. The air was fresh, rain-washed, morning-cool.

Risa had wrapped herself in the red wool cape. Perhaps she could dress and leave before the Gen woke. Away from his strange nageric spell, she found the thought of last night unsettling. The fact that what he called transfer was better than any kill she had ever had was even more frightening.

There were two horses tethered a short distance away. And the Gen had had two bedrolls. Two saddles, she remembered, inside the shrine. Last night she had been too caught up in events to wonder whose the second horse was.

Inside, Risa found Sergi awake and making tea. "Good morning," he said. "Is the storm over?"

"Yes. It's a beautiful morning."

"And you're feeling well, I see." He left the shrine, then stuck his head back in to say, "Would you brew the tea, please, when the water boils?"

"Of course."

Risa's undergarments and shirt were dry, but her denim trousers were still damp. Those she carried outside and spread in the sun, using the cape as a skirt.

Her moccasins were still soggy; they joined the denims. Sergi returned as she was trying to smooth her hair with hands and tentacles. He watched her expectantly for a moment, then asked, "Risa, why won't you even ask to borrow a comb?"

"I don't want to take anything from you."

He stared, then started to laugh.

"What's so funny?" she demanded.

"The junct mentality. You take my selyn because you see any Gen's selyn as yours by right. But you won't thank me, or ask for commonplace favors, for that would be to recognize a Gen as someone to whom you owe common courtesy."

He ducked into the shrine, emerged with a small case, and handed her a comb. Annoyed at his smug attitude, Risa pointedly said, "Thank you," and began combing the tangles out of her waist-length hair.

Sergi brought two mugs of tea out into the sunshine, hung a mirror on the rough bark of a tree, pulled a razor from the case, and began to strop it.

Risa shuddered. The knife in his hands last night had been bad enough, but this—!

As if sensing her unease, he said, "If you don't zlin me, you won't feel anything if I do cut myself—which I have no intention of doing." He brought the last of the hot water outside, and lathered his face.

"You are a Gen, alone, carrying at least two lethal weapons," Risa observed.

He took a careful stroke down his jaw, then answered as he rinsed the lather, "I *am* a lethal weapon, as much as any Sime. My razor is for shaving, not fighting. My knife has a hundred purposes, but slicing up Simes isn't one of them."

"But suppose a patrol picked you up?"

"It would be a nuisance, that's all." His speech was punctuated by long pauses for even strokes of the razor. "Nedd would have to pay the fine, which Keon can't afford. I'm low-field, thanks to you, but it's still possible to be caught. I could escape easily enough—you know the dimwits in the militia—but I'm too easily identified. Keon would be assessed a double fine for my escape—I might even be confiscated. Then I'd have to leave the territory. Since Keon needs me, if I were caught I'd just have to sit in their shidoni-be-flayed pen and wait for Nedd to bail me out."

"And what happens to a Gen caught stealing horses?"

"Stealing—? Oh. The other horse belonged to the channel I was escorting to Keon. He . . . died in the storm."

The Gen's field went absolutely flat as he spoke. Risa watched in silence as he put the razor back into the case. She fastened the braid of her hair, and handed him the comb.

The Gen's hair was thick and dark blond, the top layer sun-streaked to a lighter color than his tanned skin. His eyes were a vivid dark blue, his features disturbingly alive and intelligent.

What he had said last night came back. *You could join a householding.*

If Kreg turned out Gen—

She imagined her brother like Sergi, afraid of nothing. That was not how Gens were. Gens were either stupefied animals or terrified children running for their lives. Fear was the Gen nature—fear that Simes reveled in and fed upon.

A fearless Gen was a freak of nature. *Wer-Gen.*

Sergi had gone back into the shrine, emerging with a pair of clean, dry denim trousers. "These were Erland's," he said. "I think they'll fit you well enough for riding . . . if we can make an agreement."

"An agreement?"

"We're both going to Norlea. If we go separately, you walk, and I take the woods and back roads, each taking twice as long to get there as if we travel together. Pose as my escort, and you may ride Erland's horse."

"I could just take the horse . . . or both of them."

She zlinned an interesting clash of responses in his nager. For a moment she thought he would say she *could* not take the horses. What he did say was, "But you would not. You are no thief."

"It wouldn't be stealing. They're not yours. A Gen cannot own property. You *are* property."

"No, I am not. The householding charters with the government provide that our Gens are *members* of the householdings, not owned by them. The wording makes little difference to the politicians, who tax us just the same, but it makes a great deal of difference to *us*." He added, "My horse is mine. I will return Erland's to Carre."

It was a sensible arrangement. The journey would be much more comfortable on horseback than walking. While Risa knew little of the technical matters governing householdings, she did know what everyone knew: their Gens were not allowed outside the walls of the householdings without Sime escorts.

"Very well. I will escort you."

The trousers Sergi offered fit well enough once she belted the waist in and rolled up the cuffs. She was ready.

Inside the shrine, Sergi was checking into the corners with the lamp, to be sure nothing was forgotten. Risa was about to pick up the smaller saddle when he said, "I must do one more thing before we leave."

He was shining the lamp on a design carved into the stone wall: a five-pointed star superimposed on an even-armed cross. Over the symbol were carved the words, "Have faith in the starred-cross, and do not fear the Sime in need."

Sergi had replenished the firewood. Now he chose a

weathered piece of pine, and took out his knife. His hands moved deftly; he did not measure or mark on the wood, but in moments carved a small replica of the design on the wall.

Risa had seen starred-crosses before, usually wood, often just the design burned crudely into a medallion. Even when made by Simes they were usually lopsided—hurried creations made in a desperate attempt to protect a fleeing child.

In bare minutes, Sergi ambrov Keon created a thing of beauty. The star stood out from the cross, and he whittled out the points to form a filigree. Then he rubbed it, the oil from his hands smoothing the finish, and threaded it on a thong. "There," he said, hanging it on a peg under the design on the wall. "Someone may want that before long."

"Do you really believe in that superstition?" Risa asked.

"It isn't superstition," Sergi replied. "The symbol represents the true union of Sime and Gen. And you have experienced what happens when a Gen does not fear."

"It doesn't work for most Gens," said Risa. She had seen starred-crosses on the corpses of selyn-drained Gens.

"It works for those who believe," he replied.

They saddled the horses. Risa was shortening her stirrups before mounting when Sergi came up to her. "Risa," he said, "you fear your own need. Every junct does."

He drew something from under his shirt, lifted it over his head, and held it out to her on the palm of his hand: another starred cross, this one made of precious metals, white on yellow gold. It was beautifully crafted, exquisite in balance—and Risa suddenly remembered that she had heard this Gen's name before. The jewelry made by Sergi ambrov Keon was fast gaining a reputation in Gulf Territory in spite of its creator's being a householder. But it had never occurred to anyone of her acquaintance that such an artist could be Gen!

Sergi spread the chain and dropped the charm over

Risa's head. "Simes don't wear the starred-cross," she protested.

"They should," he replied. "You should. I will wait for you at Carre, Risa. When need stalks you, do not fear. Come to me."

"I can't—"

"You can. You will. We will share transfer, and then we will go home to Keon, where you belong. You and your brother—come and live where you can always be together."

At that moment it seemed plausible—but when they were working their way through woods and swamps to the eyeway, Risa shook of Sergi's hypnotic spell. What nonsense! She had a business to run. How badly had the storm hit Norlea? Was Kreg all right? She wanted to gallop the moment they reached the eyeway, but they had a long, hard day's journey ahead.

At midmorning, Sergi suddenly pulled his horse up and started down a side road toward an inn.

"Where are you going?" Risa asked.

"To get breakfast. Come on."

"We can't go in there!" she exclaimed. "That place caters to—"

"Perverts?" He laughed at her, then added, "This is the only place between here and Norlea where you and I can be served a meal at one table. Since I'm buying, I refuse to be fed slop in a holding room."

"*You're* buying? I can't let you—" She remembered that she had no money. "Well, I don't have to eat today."

"You certainly do!" he insisted. "If it will ease your conscience, you can pay me back when we get to Norlea."

"I will do that," she promised, then realized that she had acknowledged herself in debt to a Gen. She had never met anyone who could confuse her as much as Sergi ambrov Keon.

The inn was situated a day's journey from Norlea, but Risa's father had always passed it by, refusing to enter a place with such a terrible reputation. She didn't know what she expected—certainly not a clean, light place with the smells of stew and freshly baked bread permeating the air.

The decor was simple—wooden tables and benches—and one window was boarded up, aftermath of the storm. But nothing about the place suggested the unnamed acts of dark perversion that Morgan Tigue's attitude had hinted at.

A man came out of the kitchen, wiping hands and tentacles on a clean apron. "Sergi! I zlinned you the moment you left the eyeway. Welcome, Naztehr—and you, too, Hajene," he added to Risa with a little bow.

Risa saw Sergi smother a knowing grin. "Risa, this is Prather Heydon. His kitchen produces the best food between Keon and Norlea. Prather, Risa Tigue."

At her name, the man frowned, and his nager swirled with curiosity—but Sergi's field plainly said, *Don't ask questions.* Aloud Sergi said, "We'll have some of your stew, fruit, bread, and tea."

"Just bread and honey for me," said Risa.

"Oh, no you don't," said Sergi as if to a recalcitrant child. "Stew for both of us, Prather—a double order for me. I've had nothing but some cereal since yesterday."

When the man had gone, Risa said furiously, "How dare you—!"

"Do you want to have any teeth left five years from now?" Sergi interrupted. "Risa—juncts eat all wrong, if they eat at all. Half the month they have no appetite, and the other half they eat sweets instead of good body-building food. Most Sime diseases aren't diseases at all—they're deficiencies."

"What makes you such an expert?"

He laughed. "That's my *job.* Companions keep channels healthy, so channels can keep everyone else healthy. Ah—there comes our meal. Eat up."

Prather Heydon was even taller than Sergi, but thin in the Sime manner. His skin was a deep mahogany, his hair black and tightly curled. He smiled when Sergi praised the food, and Risa noticed his strong, even, white teeth—at variance with the sprinkle of white in his hair that said he was many years past changeover. Much as she hated to admit it, the Gen was right—most Simes did have missing teeth by the time their children were old enough for changeover.

The thick vegetable stew smelled delicious. Once she started, Risa found it easy to eat the portion she had been served, along with a dish of orange and grapefruit slices. She hadn't had such an appetite since before changeover!

Then she realized that the appetite was Sergi's, broadcast on his nager. He finished his double servings, along with a slice of nut bread, and said, "Now you may have bread and honey if you wish."

"Now I don't want it," she replied, sipping tea. "I never eat like that."

"But you should. Not just today, when you are healing an injury, but every day."

"If you hadn't been so hungry, I wouldn't have thought about food."

"Exactly," he said. "That's why householding Simes are much healthier than juncts. Not only do they not abuse their systems by killing, but they live side by side with Gens, as nature intended. They eat right, suffer no need tension—"

"What do you mean, abuse their systems?" Risa interrupted. "The kill is normal. Your way is unnatural."

His blue eyes studied her. "Do you know mathematics?"

"I'm probably the best bookkeeper in Norlea, now that Dad's gone. Why?"

"Have you ever heard of the Numbers of Zelerod?"

"Who?"

"A Sime from Nivet Territory—a junct, but a mathematician. He did a study of Sime longevity and population growth . . . and discovered that in a few generations the world would reach a point at which there would be an equal number of Simes and Gens. Do you realize what would happen in the month in which precise balance occurred?"

"Theoretically, the Simes would kill all the Gens."

"And the next month?" he pursued.

"The Simes would all die of attrition. Theoretically," Risa repeated. "Life doesn't proceed according to theory."

"No. It wouldn't happen that neatly. As soon as the Gen shortage became acute—maybe fifty years from now—Simes would start violating the border treaties in masses, not occasional raids. Civilization would collapse, Sime fighting Sime over the remaining Gens. Do you want to live in such a world?"

"Fifty years from now I'll be dead."

"Not if you come to Keon. But never mind that. Do you want your children or grandchildren to live in such a world?"

"I don't believe it will happen," she replied. "There are far more Gens than Simes. Show me the proof."

"I can show you at Keon—or Carre. We have copies of Zelerod's Numbers."

"Suppose—hypothetically—this Zelerod were right. What can be done about it? What did he do?"

"Disjunct," Sergi replied. "Zelerod died trying to disjunct, but he was too old. You are not."

"Dis-junct? You keep calling me junct."

"Joined to the kill," he explained. "It is an unnatural state, Risa, but an addictive one."

"How can it be unnatural? It's how every Sime lives."

"No," he said firmly. "Not every Sime. Most of the Simes at Keon have never killed. Risa, you just said you expect to be dead fifty years from now. If you remain junct you may live fifteen, perhaps twenty years past changeover. You are a channel, though—so make that seven to ten years, even less because you are female. If you have no training in control of your dual selyn system, you are likely to die in childbirth."

"You are trying to frighten me into doing what you want."

"No. Fear is not adequate incentive. Disjunction requires positive commitment. Forgive me—I should not dwell on negatives. Come observe our way of life at Carre or Keon. Both householdings have healthy Simes forty or fifty years past changeover. The *really* old Simes live sixty or seventy years past changeover. One channel at Carre is seventy-three years past. There is no one that old at Keon only because the house was founded thirty years ago, with young people."

"I don't believe you."

"Come and see for yourself. The householdings are the answer to Zelerod's Doom. All those Simes living long, healthy lives—and *never* killing. Gens living without fear, providing new selyn each month without dying—it is what nature intended for Simes and Gens. It can be yours, Risa. All you have to do is come inside the walls."

All the way to Norlea, Sergi watched Risa, wondering how effective his words had been. They rode in silence most of the way, Risa deep in thought.

Storm damage was worse farther south; even though it was late in the day, some causeways were under water, and no detours had been marked. Risa zlinned the way through the swamps, and took the lead back on the eyeway as darkness fell. Neither suggested stopping so close to their goal.

Closer to the city there were marked detours—deliberate frustrations, it seemed, to keep them from getting where they were going. The city gates were a heap of rubble, blocking the direct route into town. Sergi could see nothing but wreckage beyond where the gates had stood—the storm had demolished this whole section of Norlea.

"We'll have to go around to Rivergate," said Risa. "That will bring us to my place first. You can sleep there for the rest of the night, and I'll take you to Carre in the morning."

Although Sergi was concerned about the householding—a short distance inside the main gate—he was glad to spend more time persuading Risa. He would meet her brother Kreg, too—a boy who was not yet certain he would be Sime might be more receptive to new possibilities.

The road around the town had been cleared, the debris piled up on either side. Their tired horses plodded between banks of broken trees, pieces of houses and furnishings—even boats thrown far inland on the hurricane winds.

Rivergate was open—was, as a matter of fact, gone altogether. Only the stone arch that had weathered many a storm stood gaping a welcome to the weary travelers.

Sergi had never been in this part of Norlea before, but no Sime city was ever so quiet, even in the hours after midnight. Simes normally slept only part of the night—but in the last two days the people of Norlea had spent their strength against the storm. Probably no one had slept last night. Sergi and Risa rode through a silent city.

Jagged mounds of collapsed buildings added to the effect. Risa urged her horse to a faster pace. Sergi knew she feared to find her own home a pile of rubble.

Not all the buildings had fallen. They rode through a narrow passage between solid walls, echoing the muddy plopping of their horses' hooves. As they came out, there was a rustle and skitter. Something fled at their approach.

"Looters!" Risa exclaimed in a sharp whisper, and kicked her horse into a trot.

Her goal seemed to be a building farther up the street, where shadowy figures were stealthily moving objects Sergi could not make out from the porch to a cart.

Before he could even think to stop her, Risa kicked her horse viciously and rode straight at the looters, shouting, "Stop, thief! Off my property you shedoni-doomed lorshes!"

She was unarmed, galloping into the midst of a swarm

of Sime looters, kicking at them as she slid off her horse and sprang to the porch. "Get out of here, you scum!" she threatened, picking up an ax and clanging the head loudly against more loot they had piled up.

Two of the thieves took off at the noise, but the others quickly saw they were five against one small girl. They rushed Risa, who disappeared in a tangle of bodies.

Sergi forced his horse to a gallop, hoping to pick Risa out of the heap and go for help—but he could not even see her in the mass of writhing Simes. He saw the glint of a dagger—and without another thought dove into the fray.

Chapter Three

Risa squirmed, kicked, bit—tried to slash with the ax, but there were too many people on top of her.

Augmenting, she bent her knees and drove her feet into one man's solar plexus. He staggered back, but someone wrenched the ax from her hand while another raised a knife—

A giant hand closed over the upraised forearm—closed and squeezed—the knife fell as the man let out a howl of agony at the pressure on his laterals.

Sergi tossed the man aside and picked up a woman by belt and collar, throwing her off the porch into the street. She sprang back, as did the man Risa had kicked, augmenting as they grabbed at Sergi.

From inside the building rose a mad caterwauling. Risa was only half aware of it as she scrabbled for the knife.

She zlinned Sergi's incredible nager charge with fury as he flung off Simes. One of them wrapped tentacles and both hands about his left arm, and hung on tenaciously.

Fighting with a tall man who breathed foulness in her face, Risa had only a fragment of her attention on Sergi when his field flared with a jolt of searing energy. The woman clinging to him screamed and dropped, radiating pain.

A beam of lamplight sprang from the back of the building, and a mass of fur, claws, and teeth leaped screeching onto the man struggling with Risa.

Risa grabbed his knife and sprang to her feet, backing against Sergi. Back to back, they faced a circle of four Simes. The woman Sergi had burned sagged, half-fainting, on the steps. But the others were ignited to madness.

A blur of gray-and-black stripes, and Risa's cat, Guest, was at her feet, arching and spitting at the attackers.

"Get out!" Risa panted. "Leave, and you won't be hurt!"

The man whose arm Sergi had squeezed rasped, "Gimme that Gen! You don't need no kill."

Neither did he, but in his pain he was raising intil—the state in which he would kill, need or no. He circled, trying to face Sergi. Risa could zlin the Gen's efforts to control his emotions, but anger charged his field enticingly.

"Get outa my way, bitch!" the Sime said, trying to come in under Risa's knife.

"You let my sister be!"

A whip slashed out of the doorway, stinging the buttocks of the man facing Risa—only irritating him more.

"Kreg!" It was her brother who had lit the lamp, his child's nager hardly affecting the highly charged scene on the porch.

The man turned in fury, and jerked Kreg onto the porch. He threw him at Risa, who dropped the knife to catch him.

Kreg's weight knocked Risa against Sergi. Risa and Kreg went down, and Sergi whirled to face the angry Sime—who had the knife again. He got in a glancing blow to Kreg's shoulder—at her brother's pain Risa crouched to charge—the Sime raised the knife—

Sergi stepped over Risa, his field pure enticement, his hands outstretched.

Helpless before that nager, the Sime dropped the

knife and reached for Sergi in killmode. The Gen let him make contact, allowed one instant of selyn flow—and shenned the Sime to a screech of abused nerves.

The shock ricocheted through all the Simes. Even Risa, full to brimming with selyn, doubled over with the pain of denial.

The agony cut off as abruptly as the selyn flow. The Sime fell dead at Sergi's feet.

The other looters stared, zlinned, their fields wavering with shock and fear to equal any Gen's. Then, as one, they fled into the night.

Sergi knelt beside the fallen Sime, feeling for a pulse. "I only meant to shen him, not kill him!"

There was no excuse under the law for a Gen murdering a Sime. Risa picked up the knife one last time, and plunged it into the dead man's heart. "I am responsible," she said.

Kreg was kneeling, staring wide-eyed at Risa and Sergi. "Risa," he said at last. "Risa, you're alive! They found Dad's body in the river, and everyone thought—" He leaped into her arms, hugging her as if he would never let go. How much he looked like their father, especially the gray eyes.

Risa held her brother close, and felt a trickle of blood. "You're hurt, Kreg. Come inside. Where's Jobob?"

"He helped me board up the windows this morning, then went to help his ma clean up her house. They asked me to stay with them, but what if you came home and I wasn't here? And you *did* come back! Oh, Risa, everybody said you were dead!"

"Well, I'm not." They walked through the store. Sergi picked up the lamp and followed. One corner of the roof was gone—the looters' entry. The windows were boarded up, and the front door showed no sign of being forced. "Jobob may wish *he* was dead by the time I get through with him," Risa muttered, "leaving you with that open invitation to thieves!"

"We were gonna fix it in the morning," said Kreg.

"Besides—I was locked in the back, with Guest to protect me."

The cat walked between Risa's feet as they entered the living quarters. The big main room was kitchen and sitting room in one. Risa sat Kreg at the table and turned on a water tap. "Hot water. Good."

"I stoked it," said Kreg.

"Good boy. Now take your robe and shirt off."

The wound was little more than a scratch—but she shuddered to think what that looter's knife might have been used for. Sergi said, "If he shows any sign of infection, bring him to Carre."

Kreg looked up, studied Sergi's bare forearms, and asked, "Risa, what are you doing with a householding Gen?"

"He saved my life—twice now. I think we owe him a bed for the night, don't you?"

It was of Risa that the boy asked, "Did something happen to Carre? I know that part of town got hit bad."

"I don't know. We came around by Rivergate. Now back to bed. And you," she added, bending to pick up the cat, who had been rubbing her ankles all this time, "You dumb animal! I always thought you were good for nothing but keeping mice out of the storage bins. You sure proved yourself tonight."

She hugged Guest, burying her face in his soft fur. He stood it for a moment, even rewarding her with the rumble of a purr, then squirmed to be let go.

"I'll see to the horses," Sergi offered.

"The stable's gone," Kreg said. "One of our horses was hurt—ol' Brink had to destroy him. But the rest're all right. Me and Jobob fixed 'em up with hay out back."

"Then I'll put our horses behind the building," said Sergi—but as he got up there came a shout out front.

Risa took the lamp from Sergi, and opened the door. There stood the local constable with two other officers. "Well now, what's been going on here?" He gestured with two tentacles toward the corpse on the porch. One of the officers bent over the body, laterals extended, zlinning it.

"And where were *you* twenty minutes ago?" Risa resorted. "Looters broke into my store—look, their cart's still in the street with my goods on it. I got home just in time to run 'em off. My little brother could've been murdered in his bed. Where were the police my tax money pays for?"

"We been runnin' in circles keepin' order."

"Sergeant, come and zlin this," said the officer examining the body. "This man didn't die of—"

Kreg padded quietly up behind Risa and slipped something into her hand. "I'm sorry," she said quickly. "I was caught in the storm, too. It must've been terrible here in Norlea. There's no harm done. I dispatched that lorsh when he attacked my little brother. Here—zlin Kreg's shoulder." She pushed the boy forward.

The three police officers zlinned them, then the body again. "You're Risa Tigue, ain'cha?" the constable asked.

"That's right. We were fortunate. This is for the fund for those left homeless." She proffered the purse Kreg had put in her hand. The weight was just right—not too much, but enough to remind the constable that Tigues had money . . . and knew which tentacles to warm with it.

"But Sergeant," the officer protested, "the wound—"

"Shut up, Neski," he said as he took the purse from Risa. "Any fool can see he died from bein' stabbed through the heart—in self-defense." He wrote it down in his report book. "If you'll just put the body in your disposal area, I'll have the pickup crew get it in the morning. Now," zlinning Sergi, "what about this Gen?"

"Salvage," Risa replied, staking her claim.

"Eh?"

"It belongs to a householding. I'll take it to Carre in the morning. Likely they'll pay me a nice salvage fee, rather than have to bail it out of custody. They set store by their tame Gens. Can't understand why—no good for the kill."

The constable laughed. "If you think you can hold that one till morning, good luck! I've known 'em to disappear out of a locked holding room. It'll be inside Carre's walls afore you wake up tomorrow. Come on, boys—we got patrolling to do. Miz Tigue, if I uz you I'd get this stuff outa the street."

When they were gone, Sergi said, "Thank you," rather stiffly.

"We're even," said Risa—for if the police had realized that Sergi had killed the looter they would have dispatched him on the spot.

Would he have fought for his life to the extent of killing a police officer? She didn't want to know—almost hoped that the Gen would indeed be gone in the morning. She understood why he called himself a lethal weapon . . . and yet, after they had taken care of the horses and stowed the looted goods back in their proper places, Sergi sat drinking tea at the kitchen table, Guest purring in his lap, looking and zlinning as harmless as Kreg.

"Why do you call your cat Guest?" he asked.

"Because he acts like one, expecting to be waited on. But after tonight, he's family."

"Then you must bring him to Keon," the Gen said with a contented smile.

"I'm not going to Keon, and neither is Kreg. Tomorrow you go to Carre, and that's the last I will ever see of you."

Kreg stared from Risa to Sergi and back. "What really happened, Sis? You had a kill a month ago, and you're not in need now. There's something funny between you and this Gen."

Sergi took a breath as if to speak, then let it out and waited. Finally he said, "You must tell your brother, Risa."

"Later," she said. "Kreg, you're a growing boy. Back to bed—and I *mean* it this time!"

She got up, took her brother's hand, and pulled him to his feet. Suddenly she realized she was looking *up* into his gray eyes. He had grown again in the month she'd been away—almost as tall as their father. What if he *did* turn Gen? He was all she had left! Did she have to lose Kreg, too?

When Risa returned Sergi to Carre the next morning—and did not ask for a reward—he walked into so much work that he had no more time to think of the young junct channel. The householding had opened its gates to the hurricane victims.

Carre was in the oldest section of Norlea. Its stone buildings had suffered only superficial damage. The renSimes—Simes who were not channels—had roofs replaced and windows glazed in three days' time. The grounds were quickly cleared of debris, and except for the sick and injured, everything appeared normal.

As First Companion in Keon, Sergi was qualified to work with Yorn, Sectuib in Carre. Often after an eight-hour shift with Yorn Sergi would work with one of the other channels until he was so exhausted he fell asleep at his work.

Left homeless by the storm, many children ate and drank whatever they could find. When they became ill, they had not yet the pride of adult Simes to keep them from Carre's gates—but often there was little the channels could do for them. Cholera claimed dozens—and the householders ached with the double knowledge of young lives lost and the rumors that would surely follow that the householders had murdered them.

But Carre turned away no one. They were able to save some children with medication. They were close to one hundred percent successful in saving adult Simes . . . except for those with lateral injuries.

Whirling winds through a thriving city had turned windowpanes, shingles—any sharp object—into instant death. Reaching out hands to secure a rope, rescue a child, stuff wadding under a door where water poured in, meant exposing a Sime's vulnerable forearms—and hundreds were critically injured. Some died quickly, like Erland. Some sustained only bruising, and would recover after days or weeks of pain.

But many were injured just badly enough to use up selyn in healing the delicate laterals, to descend then into need—and die of attrition because the healing was not advanced enough to allow them to draw selyn.

Sometimes it seemed punishment for allowing Erland to die that Sergi was assigned to sit for hours with dying Simes, his field easing their death agony. On one level his instinct to ease pain made him glad to accept the task—but as nights passed with too little sleep, and days with no answer to the message he had sent to Keon and no word from Risa Tigue, he felt trapped in a nightmare of endless death.

Eventually the Simes in the lateral-injury ward either recovered or died—all but one.

Verla was her name, her story the same as all the others. Her arms had been around her eight-year-old son, her infant daughter protected between them. She never even knew what hit her, badly bruising both her inner laterals.

Her right inner lateral was so badly crushed that the channels had no hope—yet day by day she had healed, soon alert enough to ask about her children.

Disorientation and healing plunged her into need by her seventh day at Carre. Both Yorn and Sergi expected a repetition of previous deaths.

She had never had channel's transfer before; her body rebelled. Sergi saw the injured lateral—an ugly purple instead of the normal pinkish gray—spasm and retract despite the promise of life Yorn offered.

Sergi put his hands over Verla's right hand, adding true Gen enticement to Yorn's projection. When the recalcitrant tentacle licked toward him, Yorn captured it with his.

Verla screamed with the pain of contact. Sergi's stomach knotted in empathy, but he controlled at once, then relaxed his own system to allow Yorn control of the fields.

The hardest lesson Sergi had had to learn as a Companion was to let go totally, to give up his will and become for a moment a channel's instrument rather than fellow physician. Situations requiring it were rare—but always critical.

Using Sergi's field to control Verla's pain, Yorn completed the contact by touching his lips to Verla's. Selyn burning through her injured nerves made her shen out twice before Yorn managed to hold on and drive enough life force into her to support her for a few more days—precious days in which that lateral would heal.

When Yorn lifted his lips from Verla's, his face was strained but triumphant. "You'll be all right now," he told her, and sagged against Sergi.

The woman's face was contorted with pain—for a moment it resembled the face of a Gen killed for selyn, the rictus of agony from having one's nervous system burnt out.

Then she relaxed as her body adjusted to the new life flowing through it—and she managed a weary smile. "Thank you," she whispered. "Now my babies. . . ." She was asleep before she could finish her sentence.

Yorn, his strength returning, grinned at Sergi. "That's what we do it for."

"You think I don't know that?"

The channel laughed. "Of course you do." Then he sobered. "You know, Sergi, you were not my choice of Companion tonight, but Lorina and Quis are both completely exhausted. You've always had that incredible strength—but I was afraid you wouldn't be able to give it over to me."

"It's not easy," Sergi admitted.

"Nedd would be proud of you. Which reminds me, if you want to leave tomorrow I'll arrange an escort. I'm sorry I can't spare another channel for Keon, but—"

"No, I'm not leaving," said Sergi. "I will take a channel to Keon, but I must wait for her to come to me."

"Her? What are you talking about?"

Sergi had told Yorn about Erland's death, but they had had no time to talk further about anything but work.

"I met a girl in the storm," said Sergi. "A woman, technically, since she's Sime, but obviously just past changeover. She was disoriented, into attrition . . . and the transfer she gave me—"

The channel studied him, zlinning. "You didn't overmatch me a month ago," he said. "Now I suspect you do. You met a channel all right, Sergi—but if she didn't come from Keon or Carre, where—?"

"She's junct," Sergi said flatly.

"A junct channel? You can't think—"

"She'll have to disjunct, Yorn. Once a channel has had one good transfer—"

"Oh, she'll crave it again," Yorn assured him, "but she'll deny it. Juncts don't disjunct because we think they ought to. And junct channels—" He shook his head. "You're Gen. You'll never truly understand need— the devastation in every nerve, the emptiness yawning to claim you. Be glad you'll never know it, Sergi—but try to understand that in a junct need is not just for selyn—it is for the kill."

"I know. She tried to kill me, but . . . the pain turned to pleasure."

"No, you *don't* know," Yorn insisted. "Even I don't *know*. I've never killed."

"I have," Sergi said softly.

". . . what?"

"I killed a Sime who tried to kill me. I shenned him, and he dropped dead." He managed a grim smile. "I don't think it's addictive for Gens—it was disgusting."

"You're back in last century, up there at Keon," said Yorn, assuming Sergi was speaking of an incident long past. "Killmode attacks." He grimaced. "We're harassed aplenty, but never with juncts trying to kill our Gens. I suppose we've been here so long, they know better."

Sergi really didn't want to talk about the incident—it

was the first time he had thought about it since it had happened, and he realized that he felt no guilt at all. Was this the way a junct felt about the Gens he killed?

Yorn continued, "You have no idea what you're getting involved with, Sergi. But never mind—you won't be involved because you'll never see that girl again."

That was after midnight. Sergi slept until just before noon the next day. He showered, ate lunch, checked the schedule board, and found that his name no longer appeared. He was now a guest in Carre. A polite way to drive a working Companion home was to give him nothing to do.

Sergi, however, had his own plans. He strode across the square lawn that formed the center of the householding grounds, but as he passed the central statue of a man on horseback—supposed to be Rimon Farris, the very first channel, although no one knew what he had looked like or how much that was told of him was legend—he came upon a sight he could not resist stopping to watch.

Verla was sitting in a lawn chair, her baby on her lap, while her eight-year-old son demonstrated cartwheels. He tumbled to the side as often as he completed one, but his enthusiastic audience cheered just the same.

Sergi waited until Verla noticed his field and smiled an invitation. Then he went to her, and examined her arms. The left appeared completely healed; the swelling was gone from the right, and only a slight discoloration of the inner lateral showed through the sheath.

"You're going to be just fine," he told her.

"Oh, I know I am. I can raise my babies, thanks to you and all the others who cared for me." Her little boy started chasing a butterfly, and she called, "Dinny!"

"Let him run," said Sergi. "He can't get off the grounds, and he's safe anywhere on them."

"Safe," she pondered. Then, "Sergi, do you have to work, or can you spare me a few minutes?"

He sat down on the warm grass. "What can I do for you?"

"I . . . don't have anything left but my children. I never saved much money—"

"Verla, you are not expected to pay for the help Carre gave you," he assured her.

"But I want to!" she protested. "I'll save it up, and then . . . Sergi, what does it cost to join a householding?"

"To join—? Verla, you can't."

"Yes I can. I can work hard. I've got good reason—I want my children to grow up here, where it's clean and safe and people care about each other. I don't want them dragged up in the streets, like I was. Look—I know it means I've got to stop killing, and let the channels . . . like last night." She shuddered. "But I'll do it! It's for my kids."

Sergi fought back tears. How little juncts understood!

"Verla, it's not that Carre would not want to have you—and I assure you, money has nothing to do with it. But . . . you're too old to disjunct."

"Disjunct?"

"Stop killing. You're what—ten, twelve years past changeover?"

"Nine. I got pregnant with Dinny practically right away. But I'm not old. I'm strong. I can work hard."

"But your body cannot adjust," Sergi explained, trying to hide his disquiet at the thought of Verla pregnant during First Year. Even juncts should know better than that.

"Disjunction can only happen in First Year," he continued, "when a Sime's system is very flexible. Disjunction crisis comes six or seven months after the last kill. A Sime must start disjunction in the *first half* of First Year, or the crisis comes after flexibility has ended. The body cannot adjust. It's not the Sime's fault—it is a physical condition. You cannot disjunct now, Verla. You could only die trying."

Sergi left Verla pondering, and went to the stable. Soon one of Carre's renSimes, a young woman named Etta, came to saddle a horse. "Are you going into town?" Sergi asked her. "I'd appreciate an escort if you don't have to come right back. I want to go down to the docks."

"Sure, Sergi. You're a pleasure to be around any time."

They stopped at a pharmacy, where Etta paid twice the going rate for a supply of fosebine—Carre had used up huge amounts of the analgesic since the storm. Sergi was accustomed to householders being cheated . . . but he wondered how Risa might handle the situation. He didn't know how much she had given the constable as a bribe. When he had tried to pay her back, she insisted that she had done it only to avoid an incident on *her* property.

Sergi and Etta rode on through town. Stares of annoyance and anger followed the householders.

The resentment rode on a wave of need—unnatural need, it seemed to Sergi. Many Simes would have taken kills since the storm, thrown off schedule by injury or augmentation. There should be *fewer* Simes in need than on an average day.

Near the center of town they came upon a queue—Simes in need lined up almost two blocks from the entrance to the city's central pen. Sergi looked ahead to where the green pennants flew—and saw only one, atop a makeshift pole. The pen, source of life force to the Simes of Norlea, had been a casualty of the storm!

"Come on!" said Etta, turning into a side street. "Shen! I'm sorry, Sergi—we heard that the storm wiped out more than half the pen Gens, but it never crossed my mind that they wouldn't be restocked yet. It's over a week!"

Sergi noticed posters—new ones, not faded from the weather. Headed "EMERGENCY," they listed priorities for receiving Gens: changeover victims, the injured, pregnant women, and those within twenty hours of critical need. Even as they were reading, a police officer came along, protecting a boy pasting "twelve" over the "twenty."

"This means trouble," said Etta. "Come on, Sergi—your errand can wait until the pen is resupplied!"

"It's only a few more blocks," he protested.

Another boy came down the street in the opposite direction, also putting up posters. Sergi recognized Kreg Tigue. His posters read, "STORM SALE. BEST BARGAINS EVER AT TIGUE'S. DON'T MISS IT!"

She's liquidating her property! Sergi thought with a surge of hope.

The police officer and his charge were well up the street, out of hearing, when Kreg stopped to post a notice nearby. Sergi said, "Hello, Kreg. How is your sister?"

The boy looked around furtively before replying, "She's fine, but don't you go near her!" He came closer. "The Gen shipment didn't come. They're talkin' 'bout raiding Carre!"

"Kreg," said Sergi, "if they didn't threaten—if they would just come and *ask*—the channels could satisfy everyone in desperate need until the shipment arrives."

The boy turned astonished gray eyes on Sergi. "You're crazy!" he whispered fiercely, and ran on down the street.

"You *are* crazy," Etta agreed, turning her horse.

"Because I suggest preventing a need crisis? You know I'm right, Etta—it's those juncts who are crazy. I know; they'd never consider approaching the channels, even to save their lives."

"That's not what I mean," she said as she led the way through back streets. "All Companions are soft in the head over Simes in need. What I mean is what your field did when you asked that boy about his sister—your little castaway? You really *have* lost your mind, Sergi. The First Companion in Keon is in love with a junct!"

Risa had the storm-damaged goods priced and set up at the front of the store by the time Kreg got back. Most would be perfectly usable after a good washing—

but it was cheaper to sell at reduced prices than hire people to clean them up.

Back in the storeroom was her secret treasure: nearly half the cargo she and her father had brought from Nivet Territory had been carried on the violent currents of the river to the mud flats near Norlea ... along with Morgan Tigue's body. Kreg, despite grief and fear, had laid claim to the property in Risa's name—and she had arrived home before the authorities could declare her dead, confiscate the goods, and hand Kreg over to a foster home.

Her little brother was growing more like their father daily; she was so proud of him she could have burst.

Jobob and his younger sister Alis—Kreg's age and also still a child—finished the last display. By morning most of Norlea should have seen Kreg's signs. Maybe she shouldn't have lowered prices quite so much ... no—it was good business to provide bargains this week. Next week, when she unveiled the rare metal goods at high prices, those same people would flock in and fill her coffers.

Kreg looked around. "Hey—it looks really good, Sis."

"Did you put all the signs?"

"Every one. I stopped by the newspaper office. They expect to have an issue out by the end of the week, so I placed an ad."

"Kreg, you're a wonder. Are you tired?"

"Naw—just hungry. Risa—come on in back with me, okay?"

"Jobob—Alis—call us if you get busy," Risa instructed, and followed Kreg back into the living quarters. As he made himself a sandwich, he told her what he had seen in town.

"People are really bad off. No one can have a Gen till they're twelve hours to critical need. The Gendealer's tryin' to get people to keep 'em in the pen and come kill 'em there, but people don't trust that they'll *be* there in twelve hours."

Risa knew the paranoia that came with need. Zlinning

the nager of a Gen in his holding room enabled a Sime to think of something other than his slow descent toward death.

What would it be like to live side by side with a Gen like Sergi ambrov Keon, knowing he would always be there—?

She shook off the thought. That shidoni-be-shenned arrogant Gen wanted to run her life. His way was unnatural.

Kreg, not noticing her lapse of attention, continued, "The storm flooded the big Genfarm near Lanta. Over a thousand Gens drowned. The government says not to panic, there'll be a Gen for everyone—they're just having problems transporting them. They're s'posed to bring Norlea's shipment over to the river to ship 'em down."

Kreg fell silent as he ate. Then he added, the ring of curiosity in his childish nager belying the casual tone he attempted, "It's a good thing you don't need another kill soon. You're not coming up short this month, are you, Risa?"

"No, I'm not," she replied before she realized that his sharp mind was calculating even as those innocent gray eyes studied her. She had been home six days and had sidestepped Kreg's questions about when and where she had killed. By now she thought he had forgotten.

"You're not at turnover yet," he observed, "and you must've augmented a lot with the storm and all."

His attitude invited comment, but Risa remained silent, calculating to herself. Eight days since Sergi had given her his selyn—and she *had* augmented since. Yet she had not reached turnover, the point at which she would use up half the selyn in her system and begin the slow descent into need.

In most Simes that point came two weeks after a kill. In women it generally coincided with menstruation. Risa, though, might feel the first tentative tickle of need anywhere from ten to twelve days after a kill— and once it had been only eight. Considering the way she had used extra selyn in the past few days, no wonder Kreg was already watching for the crankiness that marked her turnover day.

But she was definitely pre-turnover ... and feeling more relaxed and confident than any month since her changeover. *Maybe my cycle is stabilizing at last. Dad hoped it would before the end of First Year.*

Then she realized that Kreg had something else to tell her. "I saw that Gen in town," he said tightly. "You know—from the householding."

"Sergi."

"Yeah. He had the nerve to ask about you."

"What did you tell him?" she asked, hiding her amusement at her little brother's protectiveness.

"I told him to stay away from here!" Then, toying with the remains of his sandwich, "Risa ... I also told him what I heard in town. Some of the people who can't get Gens are talkin' 'bout attacking Carre." The gray eyes suddenly looked up defiantly. "Well, you said he saved your life!"

"You did the right thing, Kreg."

"Yeah, but— People're sayin' Carre rounded up kids left orphans—and murdered the ones that refused to take a blood oath to join 'em!"

"Oh, Kreg, don't you remember what Dad always said about rumors? Nobody saying those things ever set foot in Carre."

"Well, who'd want to?" he demanded self-righteously, and began clearing the table.

Risa knew her brother was worried about her association with Sergi. There was no reason, for she would never see the big Gen again—at the end of the month he would go back to Keon, out of her life forever.

Yet ... she somehow couldn't bring herself to tell Kreg that Sergi had given her transfer.

The next day, business at Tigue's General Store was brisk—yet not as brisk as Risa would have liked. The Gen shipment was still delayed, and edgy Simes were concentrating on need, not yard goods, wagon wheels, or tea glasses.

Alis and Jobob's mother, Treesh, was clerking, along with her two children. Her husband worked on a riverboat—Risa sensed her worry, for she had heard nothing from him since the storm. The boat had been due back two days ago.

Risa had known Treesh for years; hers was a hardworking family exactly like the Tigues, and Morgan Tigue had been happy to hire any of them. Jobob and Risa had a strange relationship; she was nearly four natal years older than he was, and she had classed him with the "kids," Alis and Kreg, until he changed over two years ago and was suddenly an adult while she was still a child. Since her changeover their positions had reversed again; as her father's partner, she was Jobob's employer. The final adjustment seemed to be working smoothly; Jobob did his job without resentment.

Kreg and Alis were the same age; they had gone to the same school—Treesh as determined as the Tigues that her children should have a good education—and had the happy rivalry/friendship that often happened when a boy and a girl grew up together. Risa and her father had always expected that the two would change over at about the same time, and eventually marry.

Alis had put her blond hair up like her mother's, and both children tried to act like adults in the tense atmosphere. Both Treesh, a few days past turnover, and Risa, who was still feeling satisfied, seemed to provoke Simes close to need near them, either by reminding them of their condition or by causing envy. Risa tried to let the children, with their unprovoking nager, wait on as many customers as possible.

Risa was renewing supplies from the stockroom when Treesh came back to her. "Risa—word is spreading that the pen will be completely out of Gens by midnight! What will we do?" Her laterals licked out of their sheaths, a sheen of ronaplin bathing them despite the fact that she had at least a week's supply of selyn still in her system.

"Shush," said Risa. "You'll be all right. The shipment left Mefis two days ago. And Jobob's still pre-turnover." She put her arm around the woman, and Treesh buried her head against Risa's shoulder. Risa wanted to ease her need—and found that somehow she could.

Treesh looked up. "How did you do that?"

"What?"

"Feel so . . . I don't know. I've stopped feeling need. Thank you. I'm sorry I got upset. I've been so worried about Rang, and Alis was crying all last night with nightmares—it's not at all like her. I'm so afraid it's a premonition—all she could say was 'Dead!' over and over—and I was so afraid it was her father—"

"Now Treesh, don't get upset all over again. Rang will be home any time now—why, maybe his boat will bring the Gen shipment. Come on—help me bring out this cotton."

The two women restocked the yard goods. Alis was bending over a tablet, chewing on a pencil as she tried to add a column of figures. "Oh, dear!" she said in frustration, "that's the third different answer I've gotten!"

"Children shouldn't be waiting on customers," said the woman waiting impatiently to pay for her order. Risa started over to help, but Kreg got there first.

"I'll have it for you in a moment, Miz Carder," he said, plucking the pencil from Alis's hands. Risa watched him run the point down one column, then another, and jot down the answer. "There you are—quite a bargain today."

Risa approached, trying to exude good will. "I'm so pleased that we had all these things you were looking for, Miz Carder. Jobob, come carry these packages—"

Risa's voice faltered, and she fought every instinct to suppress the dagger of fear stabbing her in the chest.

The Sime woman gave her an odd glance, but Jobob was picking up the packages, and she had to follow, saying, "Now you be careful with that!"

Selyn production! Faint, but sure, Gen cells were beginning their task of producing life force—selyn to be torn from them by a Sime in need—Kreg!

No, not Kreg, Risa realized in painful relief as she let her laterals creep out of their sheaths so that she could zlin more accurately. Alis.

"Alis," she said as gently as she could, "you've worked very hard today. Come into the back and rest. Kreg, you and Jobob can handle things. Treesh, please come with me."

The girl and her mother followed, Treesh saying, "I told you she didn't sleep last night. I'm sorry, Risa."

Risa shooed them into the living quarters, closed the door, and leaned against it. "Treesh—zlin Alis."

"What?" But the woman did so. No reaction. "Is she sick? I can't zlin anything—"

"Do a lateral contact."

The girl knew, then. Risa could feel her fear—it charged even the faint field she had, illuminating the growing promise of life—

Treesh took her daughter's arms, extending her laterals. In her shock, she squeezed, and Alis cried out in pain.

"Stop!" said Risa. "Treesh—you've got to get her out of here!"

"Yes," said Treesh, gathering Alis against her. "Alis, it's going to be all right, baby. I'm going to get you away."

"Where?" Alis asked, eyes wide with fear.

"The border. I'll take you, darling. Don't be afraid—oh, Alis, don't be afraid or they'll catch us—"

How could Alis help being afraid, Risa wondered. Fear was the Gen nature.

Sergi's fearless nager warmed her memory. "Treesh—you can take her to Carre!"

"You know I can't! I've got to sneak her out of town. Risa, please—oh, please—"

"I won't report it," Risa assured her. "Better take her out the back way. I'll check that it's clear."

No, Treesh could not take Alis across town to Carre—the law prohibited taking a Gen child to a householding to save its life. Only *before* the child established or changed over could a parent give it to the householders—and who would ever do that?

She zlinned through the back door without opening it. Shen! A wagon was pulled up to the loading dock, three Simes sitting around waiting, all in varying states of need. She opened the door a crack and peeked out—oh, yes, Dran Muller's crew, come to pick up his order. They were taking a break, drinking porstan—but any minute they'd be at the back door, wanting the order.

"You'll have to go out through the front," Risa said. "Hurry. Alis, your field is hardly noticeable yet. Just pretend nothing is wrong, and you can walk right out. Your mother will take care of you. Trust her."

Treesh was holding her daughter, stroking her hair. It was a good thing she was past turnover, Risa thought; she would not burst into tears and give everything away.

"Jobob—" Treesh began.

"No," Risa said firmly. "Just go. When I know you're safely away, I'll tell him what happened."

Risa led the way into the storefront. Kreg and Jobob were each waiting on a customer, and two women and a man were waiting. Risa asked, "Who's next, please?" and turned toward the woman who raised a tentacle. Treesh and Alis walked through the middle aisle, as far from the customers as possible—and froze facing the front door.

Two Simes entered, a man and a woman, both in hard need. These were ordinary people, neatly dressed, regular customers who occasionally asked for credit and always paid their bills. Good people, just exactly like Risa's family, like Treesh and Alis and Jobob.

"It's only a two-hour wait," the woman, Sairi, was saying. "Our Gens will be ready when we go back,

Brovan. Come on—it's better to *do* something than sit around worrying—"

"Shuven!" Brovan gasped, his hands reaching out toward Alis. "Gen!"

Jobob turned, saw, understood—and leaped!

"She's mine!" Brovan growled, throwing the boy aside and lunging for Treesh's throat as she tried to thrust her daughter behind her. The girl's field shrieked with terror as the Sime choked her mother.

Sairi came after her husband. "She's *mine!*" she shouted. "I'm on the roll half an hour ahead of you!" She tried to pull him off the pile. Alis cringed between her mother and the attacking Simes. The woman grasped one of Alis's arms, Brovan the other. The girl screamed with pain as they almost tore her apart. Treesh grabbed her about the waist, trying hopelessly to drag her free.

Risa shouted, "Stop!" but the Simes could not hear her.

Jobob flung himself on the nearest attacker, Sairi, pulling her off Alis—allowing Brovan to swing the screaming girl into kill position. His tentacles wrapped around her arms, laterals setting hotly into place, splashing ronaplin as he thrust his face against hers. He missed her mouth, took the fifth transfer point off her cheek—and the ambient nager shrieked with the kill.

Treesh stared, immobile. Alis dropped from Brovan's tentacles, limp, empty, dead. Brovan's field rang with momentary satisfaction, then settled into a weak pattern—Alis had not yet produced enough selyn to satisfy him. Kreg buried his face against Risa's shoulder. Jobob began to sob.

And the Sime woman knelt and began to beat on her husband, gasping, "It's not fair! It's not fair! She was mine, I tell you—*mine!*"

Chapter Four

At dawn on Risa's killday, she went into Kreg's room and shook him awake. "Come on, Kreg. Get up. We're leaving."

He woke slowly from the deep sleep of childhood. When his eyes focused on Risa's traveling clothes, a cold stab of fear made Risa wince. "Has it happened?" His gray eyes grew enormous in the dim light. "Am I . . . Gen?"

"No," she assured him quickly, knowing that the fear had plagued him ever since Alis's death. "You're going to be Sime," she said positively.

Kreg pulled his arms from under the covers and stared at them. "Changeover? I don't feel anything—" His fear was just as great. Risa knew she had made the right decision; having seen a close friend killed, Kreg was a likely candidate for the emotional trauma that made children die in changeover.

"No, Kreg, it's neither. You're still a child—but we're going where it won't matter if you do turn Gen, and you won't have to kill if you're Sime."

"What? Why?" Risa was in need, sensitive to every ebb and flow of selyn. Kreg's field whirled with confusion—but it could not mesh with hers.

"I don't want you to be like Brovan. *I* don't want to

be like that. Think how you'd feel if you were the one who killed Alis."

"I'd never—!"

"Yes, Kreg, you would if you were desperate, in hard need. And any situation like the storm, delaying Gen shipments, can make that happen again."

"There's plenty of Gens now," Kreg protested. "You've got yours waiting."

"I'm not going to kill it," she replied.

"Then . . . what *are* you going to do?"

"We're going to Carre."

"No! They're perverts!"

"Oh, Kreg. Do you even know what that word means?"

"They're dirty. They do unnatural things."

"Am I dirty, Kreg. Unnatural? I know you guessed it—but I couldn't tell you before. Last month I didn't kill."

"No." Kreg shook his head, closing his eyes. She waited. Finally he looked at her again and said tightly, "It was that Sergi, wasn't it?"

"Yes. Sergi is a Companion. He gave his selyn freely—and he will again. Kreg, it's so much better than killing—"

"No! Gens are s'posed to be killed! That's what they're raised for!"

"Was Alis raised to be killed?"

"She wasn't s'posed to be Gen," he said sullenly.

"But she shouldn't have died," Risa insisted. "If Brovan hadn't been walking around in hard need, she wouldn't have. After the hurricane, Gen supplies will be short for months."

"They'll bring in more Gens!" Kreg protested.

"From where? Raiders will make a fortune—but what if the Gen Territory army decides we've broken the border treaties? Think, Kreg. Stop letting your prejudices think for you. Looters. Nice people crazy with denied need. It can happen again so easily—a storm, a flood, poor crops on the Genfarms. Remember the panic a few years ago, when there was an epidemic in the government pens?"

She watched his face settle into respectful attention before she brought out her most logical, yet most radical argument. "Kreg—it doesn't make economic sense to use a Gen only once. If you take his selyn without killing him, he produces a new supply the next month. A Sime could use the same Gen for years! That's the secret of the householdings—and I'm going to learn it."

"Well . . . it makes sense, kinda. But that Sergi—he doesn't act like a Gen. How come he let you take his selyn?"

Memories of the Shrine of the Starred-cross stirred through Risa's need-sensitized nerves, but she could not explain it to Kreg. "What else can he do with it? In the householdings the Gens supply selyn, and the Simes take care of the Gens. I want to learn how the householders live, and the only way to do that is to go live with them."

"What about the store?"

"I've sold off the bulk of the inventory—and Treesh and Rang are buying the rest. We have plenty of money for now. I'll invest it when we get to the north part of the Territory, so it will start growing again."

Kreg pushed his dark hair back—a gesture that reminded Risa painfully of their father. "You had it all thought out, all planned. What if I said I wouldn't go?"

She would not force him. "I'm sure Treesh and Rang would be happy to adopt you. You know they love you."

He threw his arms around her, oblivious to what even his child's emotion did to her. "Oh, Risa, I can't let you go alone! I don't want to be like Brovan, either! I'll come with you. I love you, Sis!"

Within the hour they were on their way in the quiet of early morning. They skirted the edge of the produce market, where fruit and vegetables were brought in fresh each day.

Laughter and music drifted from the taverns nearby. Women in gaudy dresses smiled invitingly at men going in. Their business must be poor now; three-quarters of the town was between turnover and hard need, with no interest in sex. That included the women flaunting themselves—if they found customers, they would pretend a desire they didn't feel. Risa wondered what a man could get from that—but maybe if he was in condition to hire a partner, he didn't care.

Kreg had seen these women every day, known their occupation for at least a year or two. He knew the facts of the Sime cycle, even if he had never experienced it . . . and he thought the householders unnatural?

"Psst! Psst—Risa!"

One of the gaudily dressed women came out into the street. Risa knew her: Verla, a customer at the store. Sometimes she would come in late in the morning, still in her wilted finery. At other times she might be with her children, looking every bit the respectable matron.

Verla had occasionally tried jobs around the docks, but as she could neither read nor write her opportunities were limited. Risa had once heard her tell Morgan Tigue, "I enjoy my work. It's easy, it makes people happy—and it gives me days with my kids."

Now Verla looked up at Risa, a big grin on her painted face. "You're goin' to Keon! Oh, I'm so glad. Sergi will be so happy. You tell him hello for me, you hear?"

Her voice was pitched low, so no one else could hear, but the combination of Verla's glee and Risa's astonishment caused several people to zlin them curiously.

"You know Sergi?" Risa managed.

Verla laughed. "He's not a *customer*," she assured Risa, "though I'd take him free if he wanted it." Obviously the thought had never crossed her mind before. "Shen! I wonder what it'd be like with a Gen?"

"Verla, my brother is—"

"Still a child. I know. Sorry, kid," she said with a wink at Kreg. "No, no—Sergi saved my life, him and the channels at Carre. If it hadn't been for them, my babies wouldn't have a mama. The householders are good people, no matter what folks say.

"You tell 'em all I'm thinkin' of 'em. And I'm making plans. I'm too old to disjunct, but I got kids. We're gonna work *something* out."

"I hope . . . your plans work out," Risa faltered.

"Hey—I'm sorry. I'm delaying you when you need Sergi. You go on now. He'll be waiting for you!"

Risa rode on in the gloom of hard need. She had made Kreg take the pen Gen, while she carried Guest. Now she said, "Put the pack horses between us, Kreg." That put some distance between her and the unappealing but provoking Gen field. The world was dissolving into shifting selyn fields, and it became more of an effort to use her other senses.

Verla stayed on her mind, though. Why would men pay women like Verla for what was readily available free? "Supply and demand runs the world," her father had always said.

And her father had lived while her mother had died when Kreg was three years old. Risa had been eight, and had not then understood the whispered words not meant for her ears: "miscarriage," "selyn drain," "hemorrhage," "attrition."

What Sergi had told her was fact: women died in childbearing. Not just her own mother. Three school friends had lost their mothers as they were growing up.

All the other factors—accident, disease, raids—caused equal numbers of men and women to die . . . but within a few years after changeover there was an imbalance in the sexes. Supply and demand; hence Verla.

But when she reached the gates of Carre, Sergi was waiting, and her morbid meditations ceased. Her need receded to a distant echo. When he placed his giant hands around her waist, she let him lift her down from her horse without protest, although it was absurd for a Gen to help a Sime.

She became duoconscious without effort, her Sime senses and her other senses operating simultaneously. The urgency of her need was distanced; she had no desire to attack Sergi on the spot, as she had half-feared she might, to her disgrace.

Someone lifted the pen Gen down. It was a male, pale, expressionless as all such Gens were. The boy was as clean as Kreg had been able to scrub him, but there was a grayness of ground-in dirt on his hands, feet, knees, and elbows. His nose was running. Not an attractive specimen—but Risa had had to take what she was assigned.

The man who took charge of the Gen was Sime . . . and yet Risa had the disturbing sense that he zlinned like another Gen. She stared, lifting her hands toward him so her laterals could sense his field.

"This is Yorn, Sectuib in Carre," said Sergi. "He is a channel, like you, Risa. You'll learn to do what he's doing."

Yorn was projecting a pleasantly Genlike field that soothed without competing with Sergi's. "I'm pleased to meet you, Risa," he said, his smile extending to his nager. "And you, too, Kreg," he said to the boy who still sat on his horse. "Come in, both of you. I'll get someone to take care of this boy." He unfastened the collar from the pen Gen's neck, broke the tags off and pocketed them, and tossed collar and chain into a barrel near the wall.

"You're throwing away good money," Risa said automatically—and was immediately sorry. If the house-holders wanted to waste precious metal, that was their business.

Yorn laughed heartily. "Oh, you are a Tigue all right! Many's the hard bargain your father has driven with me! Don't worry—we recycle the metal." He urged the pen Gen along.

"Um . . . I didn't know if I should bring the Gen here," Risa said. "If you can't use it—"

"You did the right thing," Sergi quickly assured her. "He will be safe here. If nothing else, his selyn will give a Sime life every month—but chances are that he will become self-aware and useful both to Carre and to himself."

Risa seemed to be enclosed in a nageric sphere beyond which nothing captured her attention. At one point she realized that they had left the horses behind, but she didn't care. Then they were in a building. The pen Gen was gone. Kreg took Guest from Risa's arms. Yorn turned to her, saying, "I think you and Sergi had better—" He broke off as he zlinned her deeply. "You rode across town in this condition? And didn't attack that Gen? Sergi, she is in hard need."

"I know. I have it under control."

"But she's junct," said Yorn. "She should have had transfer hours ago. You're treating her like a working channel. Take her off and give her transfer—immediately!"

Although she felt none of the urgency Yorn seemed to expect, Risa followed Sergi without protest. They were alone in a small room, walls and windows draped with heavy fabric. He had her lie down on a couch, and sat facing her, sliding his hands under her forearms, his field beckoning—

There was no violence this time. When his lips met hers selyn flowed as fast as she could take it, warming her, filling her emptiness, casting out the fear of death. It was breathtakingly beautiful, singing-sweet . . . and when she sought some sharper satisfaction, she was rewarded not with killbliss but with his peaking pleasure through depths no one else reached—the wrung-out bliss of Gen satisfaction. It was not what she had reached for, but it fulfilled her need.

As her body adjusted to life renewed, Risa's other senses returned, intensified. The couch she lay on was covered in soft pile fabric, and contoured to support her comfortably. She could smell Sergi—soap, a medicinal tang in his clothing, and his own individual scent beneath, tingling along her memory from a month ago. She dismantled her grip on his arms, and Sergi sat back. A part of the couch moved with him—it was designed to support the person giving transfer so his muscles would not cramp. Now he smiled at her. "Thank you."

" . . . what?"

"No one else satisfies me the way you do," he explained. "You waited the full twenty-eight days. I've been expecting you for the past week."

"How did you know I'd come?"

"You're too intelligent not to."

"And *you* are too smart for a Gen!" she replied. "Yes, I see that it makes sense not to kill Gens, to let them produce more selyn every month. There'd have been no panic in Norlea if everybody had his own tame Gen."

Sergi laughed, deep masculine laughter. "I'll teach you about tame Gens, little channel! Now stay put while I make us some tea. It's right here—I'm not leaving you—"

Risa sat up. "Why are you hovering over me? I've *got* your selyn now. I don't need you again for four weeks."

He frowned, then resumed a bland expression. "I forget that you're used to having nothing but a corpse to dispose of at this point. That's another reason juncts are unhealthy; the kill is a shock to the nervous system, and afterward there is no Gen or channel to aid in recovery."

"You don't have to lecture me about my health. I've already made up my mind to disjunct."

"That is the first step," he replied. "The hard part is making up your heart."

Sergi felt so good after his transfer with Risa that it was easy to forget the difficulties ahead. As they rode northward, he controlled his urge to tell Risa everything at once, to paint a glowing picture of his home in the rugged foothills of the Misty Mountains.

Instead he tried to draw Kreg out, sensing that the boy was uneasy about his sister's decision. Once out of the swampy lowlands, the eyeway stretched broad and straight. "Do you know why it's called an eyeway, Kreg?"

"Sure. Everybody knows that. The Ancients laid out their roads straight ahead, as far as the eye could see—put them straight through mountains."

"Not quite," said Sergi. "We'll go over a mountain where the road curves quite a lot. But you will see places where the Ancients cut the road through solid rock."

"I know. I've been this way before." Then he challenged, "I suppose you think the Ancients were Gens?"

"No, indeed," Sergi responded positively.

"Why not?" Kreg asked. "All their pictures and statues look like Gens."

"The Ancients were neither Sime nor Gen," said Sergi. "Nature doesn't make mistakes like that—only people do."

Risa joined in the conversation. "If you're right that Simes could kill off all the Gens and die of attrition, then the division into Sime and Gen was a mistake of nature."

"No, Risa—fear was the mistake, not the Sime/Gen mutation. We are supposed to be a symbiosis, not a threat to one another. Any Gen without fear is safe among Simes."

"Maybe you're a new mutation," Risa suggested.

Sergi laughed. "You seem to think I'm unique. I should have introduced you to some of the Companions in Carre—but my Sectuib wanted me to come home at once." He didn't add that the message had arrived over a week ago.

"You haven't said why you think the Ancients weren't Gens," Kreg persisted.

"What would they have done with their selyn?" he replied.

"Build eyeways?" Risa suggested.

"No—they used machinery for heavy work. If they produced selyn, they couldn't utilize it as a Sime does."

"That doesn't prove they weren't Gens," Kreg said.

"Kreg, if you turn out to be Gen, and you ever once give transfer, you will know why Gens need—yes, *need*—Simes. The Ancients could not have been Gens. There would have been no way for them to complete their existence without Simes."

"But out-Territory Gens live without Simes," Kreg protested.

"And they're not much healthier than junct Simes. They live in terror of each other—of their own children. Juncts live in terror of need—of themselves. Separately, what have we achieved? Where are either Simes or Gens building eyeways today? Where are wagons that run without horses? Where are the flying machines?"

"Flying machines?" Kreg asked, wide-eyed.

"Sergi, don't confuse Kreg with fairy tales," said Risa.

"They're not fairy tales. This is history, Risa." He told them of the models he had built as a boy, from diagrams in Ancient books.

"If the Ancients invented such things," asked Risa, "why can't we?"

"We can. It's happening in the householdings. Have you seen pictures in Ancient books—pictures so real that no one could possibly draw or paint them?"

"Yes," both Risa and Kreg responded.

"They *weren't* drawn or painted," Sergi explained. "They're called photographs—writing with light. Householding Zeor has revived the process—I've seen some of the pictures.

"Such things are happening in the householdings because there people are not constantly occupied with fear or need. And we are together, Sime and Gen, two halves of one whole."

Maybe Simes and Gens were meant to live together, but not this close together, Risa thought as she surveyed the room they were assigned at Prather Heydon's inn. There was one double bed, and a short, narrow bed by the window.

"No, this won't do," she told the Sime who showed

them upstairs. "If the Gen cannot have a separate room, then at least—"

Sergi stepped between her and the Sime's shocked surprise. "This will be just fine." He dropped a coin into the outstretched palm, and the man hurried out.

"Sergi, I was thinking of you!" Risa said. "You can't sleep on that thing!" She gestured toward the narrow bed.

"I," he said, tossing saddlebags on a chair and sitting down on the double bed, "intend to sleep here. You two can argue over the rest of the accommodations."

"Why you arrogant—!"

"We are traveling as channel and Companion. We are expected to share a bed."

"How *dare* you!" she flared.

He grinned, putting his feet up and leaning back against the pillows with his hands behind his head. "What are you afraid of? Kreg is here to chaperone."

"Well, then, Kreg can sleep with you! The other bed is plenty big enough for me."

"I will, Sis," said Kreg, very much her protector.

At the boy's tone, Sergi stopped laughing. "Risa, you will have to get used to it. When householders travel, they stick together, Sime and Gen—a public declaration of unity. Prather gave us a room with an extra bed for Kreg, not you."

"Who is this Prather Heydon, that he can decide our sleeping arrangements?"

"Prather ambrov Carre. He's nonjunct—has never killed. He grew up in Carre, changed over there . . . but as a renSime he didn't have a channel's duties, or a Companion's. He likes taking care of people. You may have noticed."

"Does Carre own this inn?"

"No—Prather does. It's a kind of experiment, nonjuncts living outside a householding."

"More than one?" Risa asked.

"Prather's wife and son. Their daughter established and has to live at Carre because of the law that they can't keep their own Gen child—but they see her each month when they go to Carre for transfer."

"Now *this* is interesting," Risa told him. "The experiment is obviously working. The place seems prosperous. Dad would never stop here because it caters to . . . householders. I wonder if he knew the whole story?"

"I doubt it. There have been enough incidents without that—in fact, vandals burnt the whole place down five or six years ago, when there was a Gen shortage. But Prather insisted on rebuilding, and he seems to be doing fine."

"Fine indeed," said Risa. "An inspiration."

Despite Sergi's protests, Risa slept on the single bed. The next morning they started out at dawn, and camped that night in the rolling hills west of Lanta.

By the fourth day on the road they were wending their way up Eagle Mountain, where they came upon a caravan of Gendealers urging their teams of horses up the steady incline.

The wagons were laden with pen Gens, sitting in their usual stupor, staring blankly at the passing scene. Standing out from the dull fields of the pen Gens, though, was a vibrant nager, alive and growing.

In the last wagon, a young girl sat pressed against the bars, her legs dangling out the back. The pen Gens all wore gray knee-length smocks; this girl wore denim trousers and sturdy boots, a faded checked shirt, and a heavy wool sweater draped loosely over her shoulders in the day's warmth.

As they came closer, Risa felt a shock from Sergi. Did he know the girl? Then she realized what had caught his attention: on the girl's chest dangled the starred-cross he had carved and left in the shrine. *She had faith in it*, thought Risa, *and look where it got her!*

Nonetheless, Risa's hand went to the starred-cross Sergi had given her, lying warm against her skin beneath her shirt.

I should have given it to Alis, she thought for the

thousandth time. But it had never crossed her mind in those panicked moments of trying to help the girl escape—and truly, would it have protected against Brovan's ravenous need?

She had reasoned that it would not—but nevertheless her need nightmares had taken the form of Alis, accusing her, "You wanted the starred-cross for Kreg, and you don't even know he'll be Gen!" The dream continued with Risa helplessly attacking Alis—killing—but the corpse that fell afterward would be Kreg. And once, the last time she allowed herelf to sleep before going to Carre . . . it had been Sergi.

Now, still a week or more from turnover, the dreams were distant echoes, ludicrous. But whan need ruled a Sime's existence such nightmares were horrifyingly real.

The girl in the wagon was blond, like Alis, but paler. Her hair was almost white, her eyes so pale a blue that they seemed unnatural, as did her nager.

For she did not fear. She was angry. She was frustrated. She was stiff and sore from the Gendealer's treatment—but her field rang with defiance.

As Risa, Sergi, and Kreg approached, the girl looked them over—and hope soared through her field.

"Householders! Hey—come over here!" she called.

Risa felt pain flare in Sergi's nager as he rode close to the wagon. What was the matter with him? Here was a chance to rescue a self-aware Gen from the kill.

"Yes, we are householders," Sergi told the girl.

Before he could continue, she interrupted, "Buy me! I was running to Carre when they caught me. Honest!"

"She's telling the truth," Risa assured Sergi. "Of course we'll—"

"We can't," Sergi interrupted. "Risa, it's not allowed."

"Not allowed? Not *allowed*?! What kind of lorshes are you? You think *I'm* junct? What are you?"

"Frustrated. The law prevents the householdings from taking all the choice kills—as if we could afford it. Go ahead. Try to buy this girl and see what happens."

Risa rode to the front of the wagon. "You the dealer?" she asked the driver.

"Yup. And the choice kill ain't for sale," the woman replied. "You perverts want her, you git over to the Nashul Choice Auction an' bid like everybody else."

"I'm not a householder," said Risa.

The woman laughed. "I suppose that fancy Gen just got neglected for years, while he got that big? You freaks make me laugh—too good t'kill like the rest of us, treatin' Gens like people, usin' Simes t'—" She shuddered, unable even to speak of . . . Risa found her own mind rejecting the idea. A Sime giving selyn to another Sime? It *was* perverted!

Risa forced the thought away, as the Gendealer zlinned her curiously. She wanted to say she wasn't with Sergi, but then they could confiscate him as an unescorted Gen.

Defeated and upset, she rejoined Sergi and Kreg, who had ridden forward to where the girl they were discussing couldn't hear. "Can we buy her at the auction?" she asked.

"I'll ask Nedd—but it's seldom we can afford the price of the kind of Gen who would make a great Companion."

Zlinning the girl, then Sergi, Risa observed, "You're *not* unique, are you?"

"No. I told you, any Gen who doesn't fear—"

"Then why channels? Why not a Gen for very Sime in the householding?"

As they picked their way around the heavily loaded wagons, Sergi explained, "Not all Gens can learn not to fear—and most require time after establishment to learn to behave safely around Simes. Otherwise a Gen might provoke a Sime he's not equal to, and be stripped even if he doesn't fear."

"Stripped?"

"Gens *do* require small amounts of selyn to live. It is possible to kill a Gen not by burning out his system, as in the junct kill, but by taking every bit of his selyn.

Unlikely, as the Gen will resist and be burned, but theoretically possible. I believe there is a documented case among the Farrises. There's a documented case of almost any hypothetical situation you care to name among the Farrises."

"I've never heard of them," said Risa.

"You will," Sergi promised, then returned to his explanation. "In such a situation, one or both parties will be badly hurt—the Gen burned, the Sime shenned—if they can be stopped in time. If it goes to termination, the Gen dies—and chances are the Sime is *still* shenned at the Gen's death because there wasn't enough selyn for him. And while any Gen has the potential for selyn development to handle any renSime, not every Gen is able to realize that potential. You get the standard cycle: a startling situation, a provoked Sime, a frightened Gen, an attack . . . a dead Gen and a junct Sime."

"Do you segregate Simes and Gens in the householding, so incidents like that can't happen?"

"That would negate the value of our lifestyle. No, only at hard need do our renSimes avoid the Gens who are not Companions, and that is just a precaution. All our Simes are nonjunct or disjunct. Their systems are so accustomed to channel's transfer that they will not be attracted to Gens."

"Is that . . . what you plan to do to me?" Risa asked warily.

"We can't. You *are* a channel, and we desperately need the skills you can develop. Risa—no one will tell you that disjunction is easy. It's the hardest thing you will ever do in your life. But I will be with you through every moment."

And then what? Risa wondered. She looked at Kreg, so much like their father. She clung to that thought: Kreg was depending on her. She couldn't let him down.

Sergi was glad to be home, even if his homecoming was a scolding from Nedd Varnst, Sectuib in Keon. Nedd had now missed two transfers with him—but that had been planned anyway, as Sergi was supposed to train Erland, and Gevron was certainly as much Companion as Nedd required.

Besides, Nedd was right. "A junct channel! Sergi, have you lost your mind? I told you to forget this nonsense and come home. Why didn't you?"

"Because I knew Risa would decide to disjunct. I was right, Nedd—and she has the capacity—"

The older man zlinned him, then sat down at his desk, rubbing his eyes with his hands and running handling tentacles through his hair; he had none left on top, and what little was left on the sides seemed to have turned whiter while Sergi was away. "Shen that woman!" he said. "Yes, I can zlin what she's done to you."

"*For* me."

"As you perceive it. She's probably juncted you."

"Nedd, I'm Gen." He carefully controlled a stab of shock as he recalled killing the Sime looter—and noticed that Nedd missed his reaction. Risa sensed every nuance of his field.

"What I mean is that she probably forced a kind of simulated kill out of you, and—"

"No! It wasn't like that at all. Either time. Nedd, she was half-drowned, injured, disoriented—on the edge of attrition the first time. I was completely in control. And the second time she had made her commitment to disjunct, so she let me deny her killbliss. There's a toughness about her, though she looks as if one touch would break her."

"She zlins like a stone wall—all strength, no subtlety. There's no match here for her but you, Sergi. I can't disjunct her. Shen and shid! I hoped you could bring Erland up to your strength—"

"He never would have matched me," said Sergi. "Risa does. Nedd, she *wants* to disjunct. Will you turn her away?"

"No, of course not. I can't even refuse to use her as a channel. We had three more changeovers while you were gone. It reduces the Gen tax, but it threw the schedule into chaos and it's not back to normal yet. Why couldn't you have obeyed my order to return? Then if this Risa had decided to disjunct she would have been Yorn's problem, not mine!"

"She'll be a blessing, not a problem, once she disjuncts," Sergi insisted stubbornly.

"Well, let's find out what she knows. Bring her in."

When Risa entered Nedd's office, Sergi said, "I hope you're ready to start lessons right away."

"Let's find out how much control you have over your secondary system," suggested Nedd.

On occasions like this, Sergi wished he had the Sime ability to zlin fields. It was frustrating to watch the two channels, Nedd saying, "Try this," and, "That's right, but not so strongly," and not be able to perceive a thing happening. Only at one point, when his own body's natural response to Nedd's presence diminished, did he know that Nedd was demonstrating transfer mode—his channel's secondary system masking his own primary system, projecting as a Gen.

Sergi felt a surge of sympathy toward Nedd, and knew he was projecting a feigned need, to give Risa a target.

Sergi had had little response to Risa's field since their transfer. She was still pre-turnover, and lacked a householder's habit of seeking comfort in Gen fields. Still, he had a growing awareness of her presence, and it was a shock when that awareness cut off. He had no more nageric response to her than to another Gen!

Nedd said, "Yes—that's it, Risa. But you would provoke an attack that way. You'll learn control in your training."

Sergi felt Risa's presence again. "Sectuib—" she began.

"I am not your Sectuib, Risa," Nedd told her. "I hope I will be one day—but for now call me Nedd."

"Nedd, then. I think you should know my misgivings

immediately. I assume these exercises have to do with functioning as a channel?"

"Yes. You have a natural talent, Risa. With practice and development, you'll make a fine channel."

"I don't really want to be a channel," Risa explained. "Sergi tells me you need one—and I want to disjunct. I know I will be a burden to you until I do—and for that I will owe you. Tigues always pay their debts. I will work for Keon until you can find a channel to take my place. Or, if you find one soon I will pay you whatever you consider reasonable. Sergi tells me Keon is short of funds as well as channels."

Nedd stared from Risa to Sergi and back. "You are very young, and you do not understand. You will feel different once you disjunct. But let me reassure you, Risa: you owe Keon nothing. The virtue of our house-holding is freedom. No one is bound to Keon except by his or her own choice."

He gestured toward the Keon crest, woven into the tapestry behind his desk. "Our color is red, the color of love—passion, if you will. The interlocking links of white chain have many meanings, which you will come to understand as you live among us. We say, 'The only true freedom is the freedom to choose one's chains.' You have chosen to break your bondage to the kill."

Risa nodded serenely. "Yes. I understand the symbolism: the white chain which binds Gens destined for the kill. I want to disjunct because being bound to the kill is as true for Simes as for Gens."

For the first time, Nedd smiled. "Good. In the days ahead, when you find yourself weakening, think of yourself as a link in Keon's chain—never alone, always with others to support you. A chain is as strong as its weakest link—and we will lend you strength when you require it, when you need it. And you will freely share your strength with us."

"I told you: Tigues pay their debts."

Nedd sighed. "Not debts. A householding is a family, not a business."

"So was Tigue's General Store," said Risa. "We were family first, but we always turned a profit."

"Well, there is no sense arguing," said Nedd. "You'll find out what Keon is by living here. We can't afford to waste your First Year learning capacity. Tomorrow I will teach you to move selyn within your dual system. I want you to learn as much as possible before you get too close to disjunction to concentrate."

"All right," said Risa, but Sergi sensed a faint reluctance in her tone.

He was sure Nedd must have zlinned it in her nager, but the channel continued smoothly, "I'm a few days past turnover. I want to check your health as thoroughly as possible, Risa—about six days from now I will be at my most sensitive, so I will fit you into my schedule for an examination then. Meanwhile, you'll follow the regimen for all Simes in the householding, which includes showing up for breakfast and dinner every day—no excuses."

"Sergi already insists on that schedule."

"Very well, then. Just one more thing today." He pulled a blank card from a file, and filled in Risa's name. "How old are you—natal years?"

"Seventeen."

Both Nedd and Sergi stared in astonishment. "But you're still in First Year!" Sergi protested.

"Mine may be the latest changeover on record," Risa said cheerfully. Then she added more seriously, "Dad was terribly worried when I passed sixteen, and nothing happened. But when it did happen—it was easy. I mean, it wasn't fun, but everybody predicted that at that age I'd die of horrible complications. Instead, I had a perfectly normal changeover, even quicker than most. Less than a day."

"That's typical of channels," Nedd told her. "Lateness isn't. You were fortunate. I can tell that you are still very young as a Sime, but I must have your exact age. How long ago was your changeover?"

"Nine months."

Though Sergi felt sudden panic, he refused to let it affect his field, clamping down tighter control than ever before in his life.

Nedd must have exercised the same control, for when he asked, "Then you were eight months past change-over when Sergi first gave you transfer?" Risa agreed calmly, apparently noticing nothing amiss.

"You killed at your changeover, and seven times there-after?" the channel pursued.

"Yes. Oh—I see," said Risa. "Eight kills, but it wasn't eight full months because I was always came up short." She gave the date of her changeover. "So it's actually only a little over eight months *now*."

"Yes," the channel nodded, taking notes. "Very well, Risa. Go and rest now, until dinner time. I want to talk to Sergi alone."

When the insulated door closed behind Risa, Sergi let go of his control. Nedd winced, then said angrily, "How could you *do* that to her? Why didn't you ask her age?"

"Nedd—I'm sorry. It never *occurred* to me that she could be so long past changeover! She looks twelve—I thought she was thirteen or fourteen only because *Kreg* is twelve. She still moves like a child half the time—you saw it. And whatever you zlinned in her field—"

"She has so little subtlety, I thought as you did. But *I* had the sense to ask." Nedd sat back, resting his elbows on the arms of his chair and pressing his hands together, handling tentacles stretched to touch his fingertips. It was a gesture intended to enforce calm. "Shen it, I *like* her, Sergi, junct as her ideas are. What do we do now? She *could* reach crisis right at the end of First Year. *Maybe* she would have the flexibility left to survive it." He cocked his head to one side, watching Sergi and waiting.

So Sergi was forced to say it: "Maybe she will survive. But chances are she will have to kill . . . or die."

Chapter Five

It was a tossup as to which of the newcomers was less satisfied with Keon. After dinner, Kreg went off with some other boys his age while Sergi showed Risa the grounds.

The earth was brown, not the blood-red found farther south, the buildings an ugly patchwork of tan and gray stone. Outbuildings were weathered gray wood. Except for a large oak shading the front of the main building, only a few bushes broke the monotony of brown and gray.

Guest trailed Risa, as it was the time she usually fed him. She asked Sergi about it. "He'll hunt rats and mice for his keep, but he's also a pet."

"Of course," said Sergi, changing course toward the dining hall. "All the animals get scraps after dinner. But you'd better—"

Sergi's voice was suddenly drowned by a loud "Woof!" and two enormous red-gold dogs came running down the path to leap on him, wagging huge plumes of tails as they nearly knocked him over in their ardor.

He buried his fingers in their thick fur and hugged them as they licked his face. Then he ordered, "Down, Leader! That's enough, Feathers!" and squatted down to pet them.

Guest decided to challenge. He shot past Risa, halted

with back arched and fur standing on end, and spat defiance.

The dogs barreled over Sergi, dumping him onto his back, and took off after the cat with a happy bugling.

Sergi called, "Leader! Feathers! Come back here!"

Reluctantly, the male dog loped back to his master. The female, though, sailed after the fleeing cat until Guest swarmed up a tree on the far side of the kitchen garden, yowling and spitting abuse at the barking dog below.

Sergi said apologetically to Risa, "I gave Feathers her name because her fur looks like feathers on her legs and tail—but she sometimes acts as if the feathers are in her head! I'll get a rope and—"

"Guest can take care of himself," said Risa.

Sure enough, as soon as Feathers abandoned her frantic barking and began sniffing around the base of the tree, Guest leaped, landing on Feather's back. The dog yipped in surprise, rose straight up in the air, and landed running. Guest jumped off and ambled back toward Risa, but Feathers kept going as if pursued by mountain cats.

"I don't think he hurt your dog," said Risa, "but I'm afraid he's going to fight every animal here."

Sergi watched Leader studiously ignore the approaching cat. "I doubt he'll face too many challenges!"

But Risa did, not the least trying to encourage Kreg while her own enthusiasm rapidly drained away.

Kreg complained at being made to go to classes when he had already finished school. "Changeover class, that's all right," he told Risa. "Doesn't hurt to brush up. But *art* class—ick! Why would I ever paint silly flowers? And Genlan—English, they call it. Why learn the Gen language?"

"For the same reason Dad made me learn it," Risa told him. "If you can't understand your enemies, how can you learn their secrets?"

"But in First Year I can learn it in no time," Kreg protested.

"If you turn out not to have a First Year, when will you learn?"

"You used to be sure I'd be Sime," the boy complained.

"Remember what Dad said: goods and money can be lost or stolen, but nobody can take away knowledge."

"Yeah. At least I get to learn metalworking. That could be worth something."

Risa's misgivings were not so easily overcome. She hated being closed behind walls. She knew she could walk out . . . but then she would ally herself with those people the walls protected Keon from. But she began paying the price of admission to Keon her second day there.

After putting her through the same exercises as before, Nedd told her, "First you will learn to shunt selyn between your own primary and secondary systems." He demonstrated with his Companion, Gevron, while Risa zlinned. Then she took Sergi in transfer grip, leaning her head against his chest instead of making lip contact, and found that she could indeed control the selyn within her body.

As the energy surged, Nedd said, "Not so fast! Risa, you always try too hard!"

It was a very weird sensation. She could fill her own primary system to repleteness without satisfaction, then empty it into her secondary system and know need without urgency.

"Now," said Nedd, "return your systems to normal."

She tried to find the configuration, the balance her fields had had before the lesson had begun. She overbalanced one way, then the other—

"Relax," Sergi murmured in her ear. "Rest on my field and let your systems find their own levels. Relax your hands—you're hurting me. That's it—"

He talked her through until she finally stopped trying to control, and her fields adjusted themselves.

"Good job, Sergi," Nedd approved. "Risa, you should have learned relaxation exercises in changeover training."

She nodded. "I never thought I'd require them again."

"Sergi will work with you later. While you're still pre-turnover, I want to start you on channelling. You overmatch me—there's no one here who can handle you except Sergi, and this he cannot teach you."

"What are you going to do?" Risa asked warily.

"Draw a little selyn from your secondary system, then return it. That will let you see for yourself that it does not affect your personal supply and how it feels to let someone else manipulate your fields. A channel must be able to control completely, often under tremendous stress, but relax completely when necessary. Since we have no channel here who matches your strength, you must learn not to use that strength against someone trying to help you."

As Nedd was explaining, Sergi massaged Risa's neck and shoulders, easing away her tension. As if reading her mind, he said, "Nedd may not have your nageric power, but he has discipline you cannot master until you disjunct, and many years of experience. Trust him, Risa. He's brought many Simes safely through disjunction."

Risa was placed on one of the strange contoured couches, Sergi standing behind her, Nedd in the seat from which transfer was given. Gevron moved to the precise point behind Nedd at which all four fields blended into a bubble of nageric privacy. *How do Gens do that?* Risa wondered, knowing they had no organs for perceiving selyn fields. Gevron's field was a pale echo of Sergi's and in appearance he was a portly middle-aged male, hair fading from sandy brown, skin weatherbeaten into creases, eyes overhung by bushy eyebrows flecked with white. Yet he had the same fearless ease of manner Sergi had, the same ability to make a group of Simes and Gens totally comfortable.

Risa relaxed as she concentrated on the Gens. It already seemed normal for their fields to mesh with hers. But this was different. Now a Sime was placing his hands under her forearms, saying, "Extend your laterals, Risa."

She couldn't.

The lateral reflexes were both voluntary and involuntary, like blinking or breathing. A Sime in need could not prevent his laterals from extending when he grasped a high-field Gen. But Gens were what they were supposed to touch, not Simes.

Nerve-rich organs, as sensitive to selyn as eyes to light, the laterals might touch a child, zlinning for illness, or for signs of changeover or establishment. Otherwise they were private organs, no more to be touched than one's eyes.

Sergi placed his hands on her shoulders. "It's all right," he murmured. "Nedd's a channel. He won't hurt you."

Swallowing hard, Risa forced the recalcitrant tentacles from their sheaths on either side of each forearm. Weak and vulnerable, they depended on her handling tentacles to hold contact during the kill—or transfer.

"Very good," Nedd murmured. "Now mesh handling tentacles. Develop a secure grip, Risa. Bring your ventrals over my lateral extensor nodes—now your dorsals around and over them." He twined his handling tentacles with hers. "Your patient cannot slip away, and you can force his laterals out if necessary. Retract and reverse, your hands under mine—"

They practiced until her handling tentacles assumed the correct position even when he resisted. "Good work. You didn't hurt me, even though you had your tentacles on my extensor nodes. Let me take channel's grip now, Risa."

She let his tentacles entwine with hers. Simes often entwined one or two handling tentacles as a gesture of friendship. But then he said, "Extend your laterals again."

When Nedd's laterals licked out of their sheaths, Risa's instinctively shied away.

This was it. This was the perversion of the householders, Sime to Sime, lateral to lateral.

Risa's gorge rose. Her laterals retreated. "I can't!"

"You can," Nedd said soothingly. "You can do anything you want to do. You want to disjunct. You want
to be of use to Keon—"

Tigues pay their debts.

I have to learn it.

Once more she forced her small, vulnerable laterals
out of their sheaths toward Nedd's laterals, lying still
against her arms. They touched—creating a sensation
weirdly resembling transfer without selyn movement.

Nedd allowed her time to become accustomed before
he continued. "Activate your secondary system. Stay in
channel's mode and I cannot touch your primary system. I'll just withdraw some selyn, then return it."

Risa tensed as Nedd touched his lips to hers. The
Sime heat of his skin, his tentacles entwined with hers,
were alien. She shuddered, but endured, resting on
Sergi's calm.

When Nedd completed the circuit, a small but steady
flow began. Risa fought down the suffocating sense
that he was stealing her life away, reminding herself
firmly that only her secondary system was open. It was
painless, but frightening. When it ended, Risa wilted in
relief.

Nedd lifted his head and smiled reassuringly. "You're
doing fine, Risa. The worst is over. Stay in channel's
mode. I'll put the selyn back, and that will end today's
lesson."

Risa's trust in Nedd had grown all through the lesson, so she was caught off guard when the sensation of
Sime selyn grated along her nerves—

Involuntarily, she squirmed. Nedd's field flared imitation Gen, only making things worse with the deception.

She fought, her system refusing to accept the wrong-
flavored energy—pain skittered along Nedd's nerves as
he took the backflow.

Distantly, she perceived Gevron supporting Nedd,
but immediately her awareness was enveloped in Sergi's
field, radiating a firm, benevolent, but very strong
negative.

From somewhere, she found the strength to stop fighting, to lie there with some distant part of her soul whimpering as Nedd's selyn entered her.

Nedd dismantled his grip and leaned back against Gevron.

Risa pulled her arms across her chest, tentacles tightly retracted, curling up against the violation.

"Risa," said Nedd, "why did you fight me? I didn't mean to hurt you—"

"It didn't hurt," she said, hating the way her voice sounded like a frightened child's. "It was . . . wrong, that's all!"

"Wrong?" Genuine puzzlement in his voice and nager.

"Sime selyn," she said, the words a bad taste on her tongue. "How can you *do* that to people? Expect me to—"

Her whole body trembled. Sergi moved to sit on the edge of the couch, wrapping her in his arms and his field.

"Risa, that was *not* transfer!" Nedd explained. "I made no attempt to satisfy you—just return your selyn. Channels often have to exchange selyn. It should have been meaningless, not disagreeable."

"Are you so perverse that you can't see that meaningless *is* disagreeable? Disgusting?" She shook Sergi off and jumped down from the couch. "I can't do that. It's— it's—" When she couldn't find a word ugly enough, she ran.

She couldn't learn to give Simes such a sad substitute for satisfaction! Around her, the people of Keon were working, Simes and Gens together, but separated by the channels. They didn't even know what they were missing!

She had to take Kreg and—

What if he established?

She had already dragged him away from one life. What would she take him to now if they left Keon?

It was time to look for an answer. She went back to her room for the things she required, and met Sergi.

"Where are you going?" he asked.

"I have business in town."

"Risa, you don't know Laveen. It's a rough border town—"

"Am I a prisoner here?" she demanded.

"Of course not. But I'm on the work schedule—I won't be free to escort you until sometime tomorrow."

"*I* don't require an escort! I certainly don't want a Gen tagging along, marking me as a pervert!"

"Risa—" His field rang with concern, regret, hurt.

"I'll be back. Shen it, Sergi, you don't think I'd desert Kreg, do you? I'll be back for your shidoni-be-flayed dinner. Now get out of my way!"

The town of Laveen was indeed rough—a border community of misfits. There was a small pen, foul-smelling, green banners tattered. Risa was glad to claim no Gens from there.

There were three saloons, with horses tethered outside, although it was early afternoon. Laughter and shouts from inside told her there was gambling going on.

The livery stable was also none too clean or prosperous. The general store, however, was well-stocked and scrupulously kept. Risa lingered for almost an hour, nursing a lemonade. There were farms around somewhere; several men and women came to town on plow horses or in wagons, and two girls and a boy ranging in age from perhaps eight to eleven came in to pick up an order and get a special treat of licorice sticks.

Risa did not approach the customers, but pumped the proprietor for information. The store required no outside investor's money. Risa would have to look elsewhere.

At least the town had a bank. Risa flashed her letter of credit, and was escorted into the president's office.

Tannen Darley wore a suit that had surely been tailored in Norlea, boots that shone like glass, and a diamond ring of the exquisite work Risa recognized as

Sergi's. The man clearly knew quality—Risa saw him appraise the fine tailoring of her otherwise plain outfit.

"Tigue," he said. "You're Morgan Tigue's girl? What brings you to this part of the territory?"

"My father died in the hurricane last month."

"I'm sorry. He was a good man—and one shendi-fleckin' horse trader! Obviously—" he flicked the letter of credit with a ventral tentacle "—you don't require financial help. What can I do for you?"

"I'm looking for advice. After the storm, I sold out the store and brought my brother here for a fresh start. I'll open an account, and later make some investments."

"I'll be glad to help you, Risa. You just get to town? The hotel's not exactly a proper place for a young lady—"

"Kreg and I have a place to stay, thank you," Risa said hastily—but then had to lie a few minutes later, not wanting to put Keon as her address on the account. "As soon as I have a permanent address I'll let you know. Meanwhile, surely I can withdraw on my signature."

"Of course, of course. It's your money. And I'll be on the lookout for investments. Old Skif's been wanting to fix up the livery stable—"

"Old Skif doesn't know *how* to fix up a stable," said Risa. "There's no secret to soap, water, and hard work. I said I want to *invest* my money, Mr. Darley, not throw it away." She studied his nager, then asked, "How much does old Skif owe you, anyhow?"

He laughed. "Shrewd, Miz Tigue. Your father's daughter, all right. We're going to get along just fine!"

Sergi didn't see Risa again until dinner. Kreg joined them, plate piled high. *He certainly eats like a Gen,* Sergi thought, then suppressed the idea. Her brother's establishment would be the wrong reason for Risa to commit herself to Keon.

Kreg rattled on excitedly about his day. Risa answered in monosyllables, and Sergi remained silent.

He focused on the boy, looking for signs of Gen growth. Kreg was taller than his sister, but then so was almost everybody. Simes often grew tall, especially with proper nutrition. What Sergi looked to was the muscle development that sometimes preceded establishment of selyn production.

If anyone should know there's no predicting, I should, he reminded himself.

Still he studied Kreg, weighing the options. With two Sime parents, chances were two in three he'd be Sime. If he changed over while Risa thought channel's transfer was cold and unfeeling, would she let a channel touch him? But if he established, might she not remain at Keon for her brother instead of discovering her own reasons? Her personal need to live without killing was crucial to disjunction.

Stay a child, Kreg, Sergi thought. *Don't go either way until your sister makes her commitment.*

Sergi accompanied Risa from the dining hall. "You didn't get your assignment for tomorrow," he told her. "Nedd wants you to read some Householding history. The story of Rimon Farris, the first channel—what little is known of it."

"Farris," she said. "You told me I'd learn about Farrises."

"They originated the idea of householdings centuries ago, over in Nivet Territory. Nedd wants you to read how Simes and Gens first learned to live together. Then tomorrow you'll witness him giving transfer—see that it's no less satisfying than the kill."

She looked up at him, her large dark eyes studying his face. "I don't think the kill is satisfying, Sergi—not after transfer with you."

He resisted the impulse to withhold the truth. "Unfortunately you *will* crave killbliss in a few months. By far the worst is yet to come. We will not lie to you, Risa."

"I've survived late changeover, a hurricane, and psycho-spatial disorientation. I'll survive disjunction . . . with you there to help me through."

"I know you will. But you have to survive it *now*; there is never a second chance at disjunction. If you kill—"

"I won't!"

"Your body will betray you," he replied. "You're approaching turnover. Between turnover and transfer, you must avoid Gens unless you have a channel or a Companion with you. Keon is not a junct world, with the Gens locked up in pens or holding rooms, out of your reach."

"Sergi, I'd never touch a Gen who—" She faltered to a halt, then amended firmly, "I would never kill another Gen."

"Risa, you are being naïve," he told her. "You will discover how much more enticing householding Gens are than pen Gens could ever be. We will not have you—and one of Keon's Gen members—become victims of a cascade."

"What's a cascade?" Risa asked curiously.

"Something triggers fear or startlement in Gens who are not Companions. Simes in need nearby attack. It is possible to provoke even a nonjunct renSime to kill if he is deep into need, sick, injured, stressed beyond his limits."

"Or a channel?" she asked. "Sergi, are you saying that I could go through all this only to—?"

"No!" He calmed himself and continued. "No, in your channel's training you will learn to deal with such situations. But you must disjunct first, and that means avoiding the danger in the most innocuous situations."

"I can take care of myself," she insisted. "Besides, why would I want to kill? I'm getting wonderful transfers from you. That's what Simes need, Sergi—Gens that can give them transfer. If someone like Gevron can do it—"

"Not all Gens *can*," he insisted. "At least not as the

world is now. We'll talk again tomorrow, after you've witnessed real channel's transfer."

But the next day Risa seemed little more convinced, and didn't want to talk. "I'm going into town," she announced.

"Again?" Sergi asked.

"I asked about having my horse shod this morning—she's about to throw a shoe. I don't understand you people. Keon specializes in metalwork, but doesn't have a blacksmith!"

"Not *that* kind of metalwork," Sergi protested. "We make jewelry. Our pieces have won the Arensti competition five years running."

"Which gives you nice ribbons to hang on the wall, and an empty moneybox! Why can't you design something *practical*? There's no reason the holders for tea-glasses can't be beautiful, is there? If you would lower yourself to producing plowshares or nails or fence wire you might not always be on the verge of being confiscated by the tax collector!"

He recognized her flare of temperament as a symptom of disjunction—a very early symptom, this fault-finding with the people she must depend on. Good. The sooner the process began, the more likely she would reach crisis in First Year.

"I'll think about your suggestions," he said, trying not to project condescension. "Ask at the stable if any other horses should be taken to the blacksmith. No sense someone else having to make the trip in a day or two."

"Uh . . . yeah . . . maybe," Risa fumbled. "I'll see you at dinner, Sergi." And she turned and practically ran.

Now, what was going on in her strange junct mind? She was still pre-turnover. Had she met someone in town—?

He refused to entertain the thought. As a Gen, he now had free time for lunch and a brief rest. He took a sandwich and a glass of tea from the dining hall and returned to his room. His sketchpad was covered with designs for a new householding ring, suited to the small, slender hands of Simes. The one Sergi wore openly now that he was safe at home was massive, perfectly suited to his large hands. On Nedd and some of the other men the design was acceptable—but on the hands of most Sime women it appeared unwieldy, heavy.

He toyed with the sketches while he ate, without much interest. His glance went to the tea glass in its plain metal holder. Turning to a clean leaf in his sketchpad, he began to draw—tentacled arms hugging the glass, drawing comfort from trin tea. He drew a trinrose in one hand and surveyed the effect. No, it should have a lighter touch, less obvious—

At the blacksmith's, Risa again encountered Tannen Darley, and was immediately glad she had not brought any of Keon's horses. "Fine animal," the banker appraised her mare. "Care to sell her?"

"No, thank you." She kept her tone and her field pleasant, as she zlinned that the banker was within two or three days of hard need.

"I'm riding over to the Nashul Choice Auction," said Darley. "Care to come along?"

"No, thank you," she replied. "My taxes pay for pen Gens."

"After you zlin the local pen, you may reconsider," he said. "There's an investment for an ambitious young person. A little pressure on the inspector, and Nikka would lose her license. You could do some breeding, bring in choice kills—"

The man's voice turned to a buzzing in Risa's ears. In her mind, poor Alis fell limp from Darley's tentacles.

Sergi says I'll crave it again. How could I? Simes don't have to kill. Gens don't have to be raised to die.

She didn't know what she said to Tannen Darley, except that she had no intention of becoming a Gen-dealer. He had no patience for conversation either, and mounted his horse as soon as the smith was finished.

"In a few days, Risa," he promised, "we'll find you exactly the right investment."

Risa explored the town further while her horse was being shod, ending back at the general store. A beekeeper was delivering honey. She could not think of any business suited to a community this size that Laveen did not already have. She wandered over to the livery stable, pondering how much it would cost to clean the place up, repair the rickety building, get in the proper feed—

But was the stable so run down because the owner was lazy—or because there wasn't much call for boarding horses here? Supply and demand. She would investigate further.

On the way back to Keon, she considered what she had learned that morning. She had zlinned Nedd giving transfer to two Simes who had obviously been quite satisfied with his Gen imitation. It was not cold and unfeeling—his caring flowed with the selyn just as when Sergi gave transfer. Nonetheless, it lacked something.

"Something *you* need," Nedd tried to explain, "but that renSimes do not. Channel's transfer provides everything a renSime needs. Tomorrow you will begin to learn it."

Determined more with every day she ate Keon food, knew Kreg was in Keon classes, slept in a Keon bed, Risa tried her best to do the one thing Keon asked of her in return. The mechanics she mastered; the emotions were beyond her.

With her turnover, she began to feel edgy whenever Sergi was not nearby—most of the day, since there were only seven Companions for Keon's three channels. She felt isolated by the proscription against her approaching any group with Gens in it.

Life was routine; no crises interrupted the flow of daily life, but if Sergi was right, that flow could be interrupted easily and fatally.

The schedule board showed where every channel and every Companion was at any time each day. Rikki, one of the channels, had the duty of arranging the schedule. "A channel has to do it," he explained to Risa when, looking for permitted company, she watched him one morning. "You have to know where each channel is in his cycle, how long he has been working on what—and the Companions' strengths, who's good under pressure—and who falls asleep. The Gens coming to donate aren't much problem at the moment; they're all long-time donors except Lewsiel, who established last month. Nedd hopes she'll be able to train as a Companion."

"Why aren't all the Gens Companions?" Risa asked.

"In theory they could be, but it's very hard to overcome fear traumas. Two years ago the local Pen had a shaking plague scare; the juncts were afraid to take pen Gens, so they raided Keon and broke into a Gen dormitory. Eight young Gens were in the building that night; one managed to give transfer, one was badly burned—and the others couldn't help being frightened. Six deaths. The boy who was burned, Jori, is barely able to donate. Only Dreela managed to become a Companion—and three kids who weren't in the dorm that night were so shaken by what had happened to their friends that only one of *them* could overcome it."

Rikki went back to working on the schedule board. Risa said, "Tell me about everyone on today's schedule. I'll observe them all eventually. If I can't channel until I disjunct, maybe I can help with scheduling."

Before she knew enough for that chore, though, Risa found another job she could do for Keon.

On her way to observe donations one day, Risa passed Nedd's office. He should have come out at that moment; instead, the insulated door remained closed as she walked past and continued a few steps down the hall. She had never known anyone at Keon, Sime or Gen, to be late. She went back to the office. Despite the insulation, she could zlin faintly that he was in there, alone. And upset.

"Nedd?" She tried the door, which opened to her touch. "Nedd, is something wrong?"

He looked up from a mass of papers, deep frown lines etched in his face even when he relaxed so as not to disturb Risa in her approaching need. "Just book-keeping."

"Can I help?" Risa asked. "I'm good at bookkeeping."

"It's taxes," said the Sectuib. "According to this state-ment, we owe twice as much as I had figured—and I don't know where we're going to get it."

Risa had never seen such a shambles. "Who's your bookkeeper?"

"It's my responsibility. Technically, I own Keon's land, and all the Gens here. It's not really that way, but by territory law—"

"I know the law," said Risa. "Look what you're doing here—the tax assessor won't allow you farm credit be-cause you don't sell your produce. But you use it for Gen food—put it in *that* column, and you receive full credit. Where are your receipts?"

He handed her a box overflowing with slips of paper.

"But they're not in order! Here—leave this stuff with me and go take your donations. I'll straighten this out."

It took until dinner time, when Sergi came to get her, but Risa matched the receipts to the credit catego-ries on the tax form, reducing land and Gen taxes dramatically.

The next day she attacked the householding account book. With the receipts already sorted, it took only a few hours to bring all up to date. In doing so, she found out precisely how precarious Keon's financial state was. "Sergi, you don't have any choice," she told the Gen that evening. "If Keon does not start produc-ing a salable product, you will bankrupt yourselves and be turned off your land."

"I'm working on it," he replied, and took her to the metal shop. There he showed her six beautifully crafted teaglass holders in base metal. "I'm going to reproduce these in silver—" he began.

"No, no—at least not now. *These* people can afford. Let me take them into town tomorrow, to the general store. I'm sure they'll buy them—or at least take them on consignment. Start making more, in this metal and in brass. There's only one person in Laveen I know of who can afford silver—and if I work it right, he'll order them on commission, and pay twice what he would if I walked in with them ready made."

Risa spent a restless night, for she refused to allow Sergi to sleep in her room as Nedd insisted she ought to when she was approaching need. She had never been so sensitive to need before, nor had such nightmares. Over and over Alis died in her dreams, or Kreg, or Sergi; over and over she relived her father's death, selyn pluming away to nothingness—

She woke in a cold sweat, and realized she had slept less than an hour. It had seemed like hours on end while she was enduring it. She got up and paced. Kreg slept soundly in the next room; she would not disturb him.

It was cold tonight—autumn came early in the northern hills of Gulf Territory. Risa flung a cape over her shoulders and left the guest quarters.

The Gen dormitory lay over to her left, a small building similar to the guest quarters. There lived all the young people who had established but were not yet capable of handling themselves among Simes without supervision. Even those who did not become Companions soon learned to gauge Sime need, keeping out of the way of Simes past turnover unless they had recently donated. In the daytime, with all the Gens awake and active, Keon was a ballet of shifting fields, choreographed so as never to place a Gen in jeopardy or a Sime in discomfort.

And all that could be interrupted so quickly by juncts barreling through the gates or over the walls, to kill—

Risa walked over to the walls. They were high enough to keep one Sime from vaulting them, but a group of

Simes would be over in no time, climbing on one another's shoulders. Was that how the juncts from Laveen had come in? There was a lookout, who zlinned Risa as she passed but did not challenge. The gates were closed—constantly closed, only a small door opened to let a person leading a horse in or out.

There had to be a way to make Keon so acceptable to the local Sime community that those gates could stand safely open.

Despite the protests of both Nedd and Sergi, Risa took the teaglass holders into town the next afternoon. She stopped at the bank, and displayed them to Tannen Darley. He was now in an expansive mood, having recently killed. "Fine work," he said. "Where'd you get 'em?"

"What do you care? They're for sale."

"Hmmm. Nice design, but cheap metal. Can you get more—maybe in silver?"

"I can commission some for you in silver," she replied.

"Ahah! Now I know where I've seen work like that! Keon," he said, comparing his ring to the work before him. "What're you doing trading with householders?"

"When did *you* trade with them?" Risa countered, placing the tip of one handling tentacle on his ring.

"I didn't—I don't want anything to do with them. But . . . they do make fine jewelry, and now this— All right, you want to trade with the perverts, you'll make a profit. I'll take a dozen, in silver."

Risa collected a deposit from Darley, gave him a receipt, and started out of his office in ill-concealed glee. Making money, even when it was not for herself, made her forget the discomfort of need.

Darley moved around as if to open the door, but instead barred her way. "Risa—you'll have to kill in the next couple of days. Let me show you something."

"Uh—"

"Right this way." He led her out another door, and down a back street to a house that faced out onto the next street. He unlocked the back door, and Risa entered warily. He knew she was in need, couldn't want—

"Daddy? Daddy, you're home early!"

A little girl of ten or eleven came running to meet them, dark curls bouncing. She wore an apron, and there was flour on the end of her turned-up nose. A smell of baking warmed the air, but in Risa's condition it elicited no appetite.

"Mmm," said Darley, picking up the child, "what smells so good?"

"I baked you a cake, Daddy—it's s'posed to be a surprise. You'll be hungry tonight."

"That I will, sweetheart. Risa, this is my daughter Susi. Susi, Risa Tigue," he finished the introduction as he set the girl on her feet.

"How do you do, Miz Tigue?" the girl said in practiced tones, dropping a curtsey.

"I'm very well, thank you," Risa replied, charmed by the beautiful child. With her huge blue eyes, dark hair, and delicate complexion, she would grow up to be a striking beauty. "I'm pleased to meet you."

Susi's father was clearly schooling the girl not to rely on looks or charm, for he said, "You'd better get back to the kitchen, Susi. You wouldn't want that cake to burn," and the girl left without protest.

"What a lovely child," said Risa. "You must be very proud of her."

"She's everything I have to live for, since my wife died," he replied. "Now, let me show you what I brought you here for." He led her through an elegantly furnished parlor and down a hall.

"I bought two Gens at the choice auction," Darley said. "I was going to keep this one for next month, but if you'd like to make a whole day of it tomorrow— maybe the next day if you want to be really keen—"

He went to his holding room. Anxiety permeated the ambient nager the moment the insulated door was opened.

Without thought, Risa was drawn a step into the small room, toward that tempting field. With a shock, she brought herself hypoconscious, denying her Sime senses.

No! I don't want fear!

But she did when it was offered. Horrified, she faced the knowledge that since her first transfer with Sergi she had not been near a frightened Gen when she was in need. The Gen she had taken to Carre—the ones they had passed in the caravan—all had been stupefied, not frightened.

All but one, the girl who had been all defiance—and who now sat staring at her from the depths of Tannen Darley's holding room. It was the same girl with the almost-white hair and pale blue eyes. She was now dressed in the culottes and shirt put on choice kills for transportation, but Sergi's starred-cross still hung on her breast. She clutched it as the two Simes looked in at her.

"Do you want it?" Darley was asking. "I thought tomorrow, Risa, but if you need it right now—"

Risa's Sime senses took over as the girl's anxiety sparked to real fear at Darley's words. Risa had never had a choice kill, a Gen who understood, delicious terror ringing in sweet thrills along her nerves.

Risa's laterals slipped from their sheaths, drinking in the luscious emotion. This was what she needed! This was the true Sime nature—not what they were trying to do to her at Keon!

Alive in every cell of her being, she stalked toward the trembling Gen.

Chapter Six

The Gen became less fearful—still anxious yet hopeful.

The shift brought Risa duoconscious, and she saw recognition in the pale blue eyes. The girl clutched the starred-cross so tightly that Risa could feel its points digging into the palm of her hand.

The girl took Risa for a householder come to rescue her, a miracle unquestioned in her desperation.

I want to kill her, Risa realized. *I want the pleasure of shattering that pale hope into shrieking terror.*

I am no better than Brovan—worse, as I am still a day away from hard need.

Never in her life had Risa been so out of control at this point in her cycle. *Must get away from here!*

Fighting intil, grasping the shreds of her dignity, she squared her shoulders and sheathed her laterals by force of will. "No, thank you, Mr. Darley," she said with a calm she did not feel. "I will not become addicted to choice kills."

"Have you seen what's in the pen?" he asked. "My wife caught shaking plague from a Gen from that pest hole! I've never touched one of them since, nor will Susi."

His mixed anger and grief cleansed the ambient, and Risa regained control. "Surely the health inspector—"

"They closed the pen, destroyed the Gens, and

fumigated—and Nikka went right back to her old habits. So if you want this Gen—"

"Not now," said Risa. *I can control!*

Fate had thrown this girl in her path twice now. If she could talk Darley out of her, how would she get her back to the householding without killing her along the way?

"Mr. Darley, your generosity overwhelms me," she said as she looked around the holding room for what had changed the girl's attitude from defiance to fear. There were half-healed cuts and bruises on the Gen's arms and neck, and a dark contusion on her left cheek. None of the marks were fresh, though; no whip hung in the room, nor did Darley carry one.

Risa judged that the dealers at the choice auction, not Tannen Darley, had beaten the defiance out of the girl. She was still staring at Risa with those strange pale eyes.

"Let's . . . move out of this nager and discuss it," she said, although her nerves screamed, *Stay, terrorize, kill!* The Gen's nager lit with pleading at Risa's words.

When the insulated door was closed, Risa released control and almost collapsed. "Mr. Darley—"

"Tan."

"*Mr. Darley*, I cannot accept such an expensive gift—"

"It wasn't that expensive—they had to knock it senseless to bring it to auction. No good for a prime kill then—but I meant to kill it next month. It's already recovered nicely."

"Then let me buy . . . it."

"Risa, call it business if you prefer—a gift to a depositor likely to bring in a great deal of money. No more arguments. Stay the night, and enjoy your kill tomorrow."

"No, I—my brother—" she fumbled, then, drawing on all the acting ability she could muster, she said, "I told you I refuse to become addicted to choice kills—you know I haven't that kind of money. I will not accept the Gen as a gift because I would sell it—at a profit. If you will sell it to me, I know a buyer."

He burst into laughter. "Well, I've heard it said, for the right price a Tigue will sell you his boots in snake country! Now I've seen it, and I still don't believe it."

His laughter died to a smile. "At least you're honest. And you've saved me a trip to Nashul next month. I wish you the best of Nikka's pen . . . but do come back after your kill, Risa. Surely even a Tigue has some relationships that are not purely business?"

So Risa escaped with her secret and her dignity—but the Gen girl was still in Tannen Darley's holding room. She avoided thinking about it while bargaining with the proprietor of the general store over the teaglass holders, but as soon as she was on the road to Keon her guilt rose again.

She wasn't superstitious. Her father had taught her to disregard tales of ghosts and wer-Gens and gypsy magic. Yet she could not shake the feeling that it was more than coincidence that she should twice have opportunity to rescue that same Gen girl . . . and twice fail.

She allowed Sergi to sleep in her room that night. All the guest rooms had two beds, and the Companion was very much attuned to her, not questioning her agitated state.

Risa presented Nedd with the money from the store and Darley's deposit. "There's plenty more where that came from," she told him. "Make pots and kettles and—"

"Risa, slow down," said the Sectuib with a sad smile. "You've done us a favor, for which we thank you. We can and will make more teaglass holders, and other small items that can be made of base metal—but no food or drink containers."

"Why not?" she asked blankly.

Sergi replied, "The lead in the base metal is poisonous. Pots and pans must be made of iron and tin."

"Well, *make* them of iron and tin, then!"

"Where do we get them?" asked Nedd. "And if we could, how would we pay? We make small, artistic objects because we cannot obtain the raw materials to open an ironmongery."

Risa had no more answers. After bludgeoning down intil she had no energy to think, so she let Sergi take her back to her room, her need distanced by the promise of his selyn.

That night she slept, as Sergi assured her that she would not have nightmares. He was half right.

Risa dreamed that she was a berserker—a child born in Gen Territory to Gen parents, but turning Sime at adolescence. In terror, she left her bed in a comfortable farmhouse and hid in the barn. There, among the horses restless in their stalls, changeover progressed through pain, blackouts, near-suffocation—and then the breakout of hideous tentacles on her arms, and the yawning vacuum of First Need.

The sun was up—she was supposed to have finished her chores and be in at breakfast, but she couldn't see or hear—only perceive in some strange new way that said she was dying, and life was clustered somewhere nearby—

Life moved toward her!

She sprang up the ladder to the loft with new agility, and crouched as a man entered the barn. He wore a faded plaid shirt and denims, his face tan and weathered, his dark eyes concerned . . . and he carried a shotgun.

She saw and heard again—the man calling, "Fight the demon, son—go to God's glory with your father's blessing. Lest you kill, come out of the shadows—"

Need outweighed his words. She leaped!

The man struggled, but her strength was greater now—the gun dropped as she shook him. His energy field was charged with utter surprise, then soaring terror as she gripped his arms, forced her face to his—

Fed by fear, life seared through her nerves, untold relief, bliss greater than any she had ever known—

Sensing of energy was gone. She saw, heard, felt the limp body fall. "Father!" she screamed in agony at the twisted, dead face. The eyes were open, accusing—not the familiar dark eyes but very pale blue eyes—

Risa woke, unfrightened, but very confused. The dream was clear in her memory—a nightmare without the terror of a nightmare, yet she had seen, heard, zlinned everything. Such odd things. Go to God's glory? She had never heard anyone say such a thing. And now she realized that although she had experienced the dream from inside the berserker's head, she had been a boy, not a girl.

How very strange! Was it her anxiety for Kreg? He would never be a berserker. Although she had had a few terrifying need nightmares in her time, she had never before been anyone but herself in them. The man identified as "Father" in the dream bore no resemblance to Morgan Tigue, either.

Only the transformation of the man's eyes to the pale blue of the Gen girl's made sense. Guilt could certainly cause nightmares.

Now that she was awake, Risa was disturbed as much by her lack of emotion as by the strangeness of the dream. Sergi stirred and woke. "Risa—are you all right?"

"I'm fine. It's just a dream. Go back to sleep."

But the dream would not leave her. She dreamed it again, identical in every detail. When she woke it was only an hour till dawn, so she got up and read more of the history Nedd had assigned her until Sergi woke with the sun.

She had gone a full twenty-eight days again, and with Sergi by her side it was easy to wait out the two hours to her transfer. Then she felt ready for anything.

As they were drinking tea after transfer, Sergi asked, "Can you tell me what disturbed you during the night? Even asleep, I should have kept dreams from bothering you."

"That's probably why I didn't feel the dream as a nightmare," she said. Remembering that telling a dream was supposed to make it stop recurring, she told Sergi—except the part about the father's eyes. For some reason, she was reluctant to tell Sergi she had met the Gen girl again.

"It was the strangest dream I ever had—being someone else. A boy. And living out-Territory, on a farm. I've never lived on a farm—never even stayed on one. I've certainly never lived out-Territory."

"And you're certainly not a boy," he said with a grin.

"Yet it only seemed strange afterward, not while I was dreaming. That man *was* my father—but it *wasn't* my father—my real father, you know? It doesn't make sense."

"The gypsies say everybody lives many lives, as man and woman, Sime and Gen. Maybe you were once a berserker."

"That's just superstition. I don't believe in anything that can't be proved."

The dream haunted Risa's rare moments of solitude. For the next few days, Nedd had her taking donations from the most experienced of the householding Gens, and transferring selyn to himself, Rikki, or the third channel, Loid.

Risa learned quickly. When she completed the first day's task under the channel's supervision, he told her, "You can handle donations without me—which will ease my schedule. Sergi will be with you. After you disjunct, you won't have to have a Companion for this kind of donation—only for the skittish donors, to protect you more than to protect them."

"Why aren't these donors Companions? No one was frightened today. Most were more concerned about putting *me* at ease than about letting a ... junct ... touch them."

"But how much selyn did they give?" asked Sergi.

"More than a renSime needs for a month."

"But not enough for a channel," Nedd explained. "These people have years of experience. If they had had the attitude in adolescence that they have now, they could have become Companions. But they didn't. They donated with courage, out of duty ... but not joyfully and without fear. Attitude is as important as physical ability. A Gen's selyn production levels off soon after his body reaches full growth, if he does not experience selyur nager."

The need to give. Risa understood the term well; she felt that Gen need in Sergi, Gevron, the other Companions.

"There are exceptions," Sergi pointed out. "We call them Natural Donors—adults who are able to train as Companions."

"Like Sintha," Nedd agreed. "Have you worked with her yet, Risa?"

"No, I don't think so."

"You'd know," said Sergi. "She speaks Simelan with a Gen accent—she was captured out-Territory by raiders. Nedd and I were at the choice auction that month, thank goodness."

"Despite what she'd been through, she was able to develop a Companion's abilities," Nedd added. "Now—no more history lessons. It's time to practice transfer. Instead of my drawing the selyn, I want you to transfer it into my secondary system—as if I were a renSime in need."

In channel's mode, Nedd's secondary system masked his primary. He projected the restless need of a renSime. Risa found transfer grip and completed the circuit, letting her own secondary system take precedence. Nedd accepted about as much selyn as a renSime would, then broke contact. "Do you really think that would satisfy anyone?" he asked.

"What?"

"You gave me *nothing*, Risa—nothing but selyn. Come on, now—give me some feeling along with it."

She tried again, projecting pleasure and fulfillment. "That's better," said Nedd, "but it's not egobliss."

"Egobliss?"

"Not killbliss—a Sime accustomed to that might seek it in the kill. But you must give a renSime the same quality of peak experience that your Companion gives you."

Again Risa tried—and went on trying day by day until her turnover, when she went back into semi-seclusion.

Her turnover was two days early; she didn't understand why, for Sergi had provided her with plenty of selyn at their last transfer, and she had done no augmenting.

Sergi explained, "You are not consciously augmenting, but you are on edge, expending selyn in tension."

"But if I reach hard need early, what about you?" she asked in panic, remembering what he had said about draining a Gen to death. "You won't have replenished your selyn!"

"Risa," he said calmly, "zlin my selyn production."

She could sense his very cells at work, pulsing in rhythm with hers, preparing to serve her need however great it might be. His field enveloped her, making her feel safe, secure.

She spent as much time as she could within Sergi's nager. She accompanied him to the metal shop, watching him create and burnish the teaglass holders for Tannen Darley. Searching for other small objects that could be cast in metal, she had thought of fancy pencils or pens, belt buckles, harness ornaments—things the local people would do without or carve from wood. Sergi designed some, and the general store took a few, but only the teaglass holders sold well.

Staring at the holders one day, though, Risa remembered another beverage served in glasses in holders: porstan. *They probably serve it in thick mugs out here!* she thought, and wondered if Laveen was ready for the refinement of delicate glasses in metal holders. "Let's try it," she told Sergi. "Make some, and I'll approach the saloon owners."

"Porstan glass holders? I've never been in a Sime saloon. I don't know what design would be appropriate."

"You have at least drunk porstan?"

"Of course I have!" he replied. "It's available in the dining hall. But ... juncts don't use it just as a thirst-quencher after a hard day's work. They get drunk, maybe even have shiltpron music."

Porstan alone could not inebriate a Sime, but in combination with the music of the Sime instrument, played in a nageric as well as an audible range, it could produce one roaring drunk—and a mind-splitting hangover the next day. Risa had seen her father in that condition twice within three months after her mother's death, and then never again as he adjusted to his loss and focused his caring on his children.

"Design a shiltpron into the holster," Risa suggested.

"That's obscene!"

"Exactly!"

When Risa took samples into town two days later, she came away from the first two saloons with orders that would keep the metal shop busy for the next two months. In the third saloon, as she approached the bar she was suddenly stopped by a cheerful, "Risa! Risa Tigue! How are you?"

It was Verla, the young woman from Norlea, wearing her gaudy working clothes. The men in the saloon studied the two women, zlinned Risa's state of need, and lost interest.

"Come over here where we can talk," said Verla, leading Risa to a corner table. People were at the bar, and several were gambling with dice around a table, shouting loudly at every throw. No one paid attention to the two women.

"I'm making a better life for my kids," Verla informed Risa. "There're even more men for each woman here than there were in Norlea, so I have plenty of work—but I'm not gonna do this forever. I'm gonna open my own business."

"That's very good, Verla," said Risa, afraid to ask what kind of business the woman planned.

"Does Keon have a school?" Verla asked abruptly.

"A school? Well, not exactly. They have classes for their own children—"

Verla's voice dropped to a whisper. "Can I get my kids in? Can I visit them if they live there? Risa, my Dinny stole candy from the store a coupla days ago. I've raised my kids honest—I whaled the tar outa him for stealing, but the boys here in town are a bunch of ruffians. I can't make him stay in all day—we got nothing but one room in the hotel. He minds his sister; I can't afford someone to keep the kids.

"Look, Risa," she added, very serious, "my Dinny, he knows what his mama does—but I don't want my little girl to have to do the same. In Norlea we had a house. Here we got no privacy except a screen in front of their bed. I don't like it—but I can't see anything different for a long time. Unless Keon will take them in."

"Verla, if it were up to me, of course I'd say yes—but I'm not even a member of Keon. I'm just a guest, paying my way by keeping the books, doing some trading for them—" She showed Verla the glass holders.

"Ooh, aren't they pretty? Shiltprons on porstan glasses!" She giggled. "That's really clever." Then her eyes took on a faraway look. "Laveen doesn't have a shiltpron parlor! If I can save enough money, I got a friend plays so great— My kids'd have a future! What do you think, Risa?"

"Well, you'd probably make a lot of money," Risa said dubiously. It was not Risa's kind of business—but for Verla it would be a step up. So she tried to be encouraging. "I will ask the Sectuib in Keon about taking in your children. You understand that they would learn householding ways—?"

"I want them to!" Verla said in a fierce whisper. "Risa, I wanted to disjunct at Carre, but they said I'm too old. Please—you tell the Sectuib I don't want my kids to kill. I don't want to give them away—I want to be their mama—but I want them to live the way I saw at Carre. Please, Risa—if you can get the Sectuib to talk to me—"

"I'll do my best," Risa promised, so astonished at the woman's desire that her own approaching need subsided.

Nedd was both surprised and delighted at the money Risa brought back that day. "And that's only the deposit," she told him. "Zabrina, who owns the biggest saloon, wants to know if you can make these out of steel—she says this base metal breaks when people throw it."

"Throw it?"

"Apparently they frequently have fights. Can you make steel?"

"No, Risa, we can't. If we could, we would be trading in knives—even I have that much business sense."

"Don't you know how, or is it too expensive?"

The channel explained, "The best steel comes from out-Territory. Sergi's got some pieces of Ancient work—I've often scolded him for spending Keon's money on such things, but he is fascinated by different types of metal. He more than earns what he spends—but we're always so short of cash."

Keon's books had told Risa more than just that Nedd was a poor bookkeeper. The householding was run as a family. Everything belonged to everyone, and consequently to no one. If someone went into town, he took money from the petty cash supervised by Nedd's wife, Litith, who acted as householding secretary. Large purchases had to be approved by Nedd.

Money brought in went into the community coffers. It set Risa's teeth on edge to think of wasters bankrupting hard workers under such a system, although she had seen neither waste nor laziness here. She bit back comment, reminding herself that she was a guest here—but she could not live permanently under these conditions. She had to know what was hers, control her own property, as her father had taught her. She kept up his principles with Kreg, giving him an allowance every week. But the boy had no place to spend it here, and simply locked it into his "treasure box."

Kreg showed no impulse to leave the householding,

nor did Verla's children after they saw that their mother did indeed visit them often. Nedd was perfectly willing to take them in; "How could we possibly refuse?"

He would take no money for room and board—and Verla later told Risa, "When I open my shiltpron parlor, Keon is gonna have a share in it—you mark my words."

Risa tried to smile tolerantly, but in her last days of need the woman's impossible dreams irritated her. She bit her tongue to keep from telling Verla that she would never be anything but a pitiful whore, selling her body for barely enough to live on.

The day before Risa was scheduled for transfer, Sergi finished the first batch of porstan glass holders. Risa was with him, but he could feel her restlessness. "I'll take them into town," she said.

"Tomorrow," he replied, "after our transfer."

She bridled, and he knew he had mishandled her again. Keon had never before tried to disjunct a channel, so Sergi had never before dealt with a disjuncting Sime who did not yield easily to his efforts and his nager. "What if I wanted to go today?" Risa challenged.

"But you really don't want to, do you?" he asked calmly, deliberately projecting a seductive lethargy. It wasn't hard—she had kept him up all night.

Her dream had returned in nightmare form. Her terror wakened him, and they spent the rest of the night talking.

"You should take a nap," Risa told him. "Let's go back to my room. You sleep and I'll read."

"I'll be all right if I eat something," he replied. "I've gone on less sleep in other emergencies."

"But there is no emergency now," she began, then suddenly broke out, "You don't trust me! You think if you fall asleep I'll run away to town—maybe kill somebody! You lorsh!" she exclaimed, dark eyes flashing anger. "I'd be safer in town than here. Only Simes in town. *You're* the one who kills *Simes*, you wer-Gen!"

Risa jumped down from her stool and ran. Sergi followed, but despite his long legs she outdistanced him by augmenting.

She started for the stable, then veered toward the main gate instead. "Get out of the way!" Sergi shouted at some Gens in her path, and Simes darted in to pull them from Risa's way. When she ignored them, he recognized in relief a common mood for a disjuncting Sime, not seeking a kill, just running from Companion or channel who seemed to stifle her. Still, she had to be stopped and calmed down, or she would augment herself into genuine need, possibly miles from a Companion.

The door in the gate was closed. The guard jumped down from his platform to bar Risa's way. She charged him. He took a stance to ward her off as other Simes ran to help.

At the very last moment, Risa spun away from the crouching guard, swarmed up the ladder to the lookout platform, and flung herself over the wall.

Sergi pounded up to the door, tearing at the latch. A Sime was immediately beside him, pulling the heavy bolt. "Get a channel!" Sergi told her. "And get my horse! We may have to chase her down!"

He charged through the door just as Risa disappeared into a road at the end of a tree-lined lane.

She had turned away from town. She sought solitude, not a kill. Then, as he was about halfway down the lane, Risa reappeared, trotting cautiously across his field of vision, arms outstretched in the direction of the road to town. She was zlinning something—

Sergi's hope disappeared in a rush of adrenalin. He put on speed as Risa broke into a run.

Keon's gate was well back off the road; by the time Sergi reached the end of the lane he could hear horses galloping from town, and turned the corner to face disaster.

Risa was a good fifty paces down the road. A horse bore down on her, a child's pony with two riders. Far down the road a second horse pursued, the distant rider Sime and male. The two riders on the pony were female, one of them only a child, the other a Gen in traveling clothes, collar about her neck, tags jingling—

The pony shied as it approached Risa. She reached for the reins, frightening it further. It reared, tumbling both riders onto the road.

The child scrambled to her feet, trying to shield the Gen girl. "Let her go!" she pleaded. "She's going to Keon!"

Sergi saw Risa back off, fighting her instinct to react to Gen pain as the girl climbed to her feet, limping— but she must not be flaring fear. No. Sergi recognized her: the pale blond girl they had seen on their way here. She had a Companion's spirit—

"It's all right, Susi," the Gen girl said. "She's a householder. She won't hurt us."

But the Sime bearing down on them certainly would!

"Run!" Sergi shouted, as close to the three now as the rider on the other side—but a horse was faster than a man!

The Gen girl grasped Susi's hand and started to run toward Sergi. The little girl, though, held her ground, shouting to the rider, "No, Daddy, no!"

The man pulled his horse to a stop and jumped down, thrusting the child out of the way. Sergi recognized him: Tannen Darley, the banker.

The Gen girl backed away, limping, eyes widening—

Sergi felt intil surge in Darley, who was closer to need than Risa—but disjunction had made Risa ultra-sensitive.

They were two Simes in need, faced off over a frightened Gen!

Desperately repressing his fear for Risa, Sergi dashed between them—but how could he handle both? Risa needed his selyn; he would give her transfer right here in the road if necessary—but how could he let Darley kill the Gen girl who had escaped and come to them?

Edging between the two Simes, Sergi felt drawn to Darley. The man was truly in hard need, Risa only raising intil. With Sergi's field intervening, she came out of it, and he turned to Darley. Behind him, he heard people coming from Keon. He had to keep Darley from killing only for moments—then the channels would take over. If only Risa understood that he was not going to give him transfer—

Darley turned eagerly toward the tempting field Sergi projected, laterals extended and dripping ronaplin as he reached for the Gen's arms—

"No!" Risa screamed, leaping on Sergi with augmented strength, knocking him all the way across the road and into the ditch. "No!" she cried again. "I won't let you kill him!"

Chapter Seven

Tannen Darley leaped for her throat—a killer Sime trying to choke the life out of her for stealing his kill.

She was small enough to get a grasp on his arms and swing up to kick him in the solar plexus. Darley staggered back with a "Whuff!" and his hold relaxed.

His need deepened as he augmented to fight her, triggering Risa's need again—

The scene in her store, Alis's death, replayed before her eyes. *No! I must control myself!*

She would not be an animal, brawling over a kill! The long days of practice at controlling her selyn fields suddenly paid off—she flipped over into channel's mode.

Her need was distanced—but Darley's was an aching cry for life. Risa's sympathy surged. He was further into need than any Sime normally allowed himself to get. A trip back to town in that condition would be agony—yet she could not allow him to kill the Gen girl!

I cannot fail again!

Practice had become instinct. Risa projected a Gen field and grabbed the hands again reaching for her throat. They came willingly now, grasping her arms urgently. He did not know how to entwine tentacles, but she did—the grip was secured, their laterals met, and Risa balanced on her toes to touch her lips to Darley's.

He drew with junct demand. Risa gave him all he needed—so little selyn! He sought something she could not give, but finally accepted a flare of pleasure and allowed termination.

Darley retracted his tentacles as if to let a dead Gen body fall. Risa, though, retracted only her laterals, leaning against him. The world spun giddily. Then Sergi was behind her, his hands on her shoulders, and she leaned gratefully back against him. Her vertigo subsided, but not her glee.

Susi was staring, eyes huge and round. Other people had arrived—one of the channels, Rikki, suddenly spun the frozen Gen girl away from the scene. "Run!" he said. "Get inside the gates, girl—then he can't claim you!" The girl came out of her startled trance and hobbled toward the lane. She had to get to the gates on her own; if someone from Keon supported her, he would be stealing Darley's Gen. Keon personnel, Sime and Gen, formed a line to block Darley's path.

The banker, though, had lost interest in the Gen. He was staring at Risa, astonishment turning to rage. Then his daughter moved, running to him, crying to Risa, "What did you do to my Daddy?"

The child's concern interrupted her father's anger as he reassured her, "I'm all right. She didn't hurt me. She—" His hand went to his mouth. "You're one of *them*! You lied to me! Pervert!"

Risa was able to remain calm with Sergi's support. "Even your own daughter could see that it was you who attacked me."

"You stole my Gen!"

"No—your Gen escaped, and now is salvage. I don't think Householding Keon will have much trouble keeping her."

"Thieves! I'll have your filthy householding torn down stone by stone—"

Susi cried, "Daddy, *I* let Triffin go! Please, Daddy—!" Huge tears rolled down the child's face. "She told me stories and played with me. I didn't want her to be dead, like Mama!"

Darley stared down at the child. "Susi, it wasn't like your Mama. It was a Gen—"

"I don't care!" She sobbed harder. "I'm not sorry—I'm not! I couldn't let Triffin be dead!"

With a soft moan, Darley hugged the child tightly. "Who told you such things?" Then suddenly he looked over Susi's head to Risa, angry again. "You! How could you use a child's grief over her dead mother—!"

"Mr. Darley," said Risa, "I have met your daughter only once before, the day you introduced us. No one from Keon has talked with her. Ask her."

"Triffin told me," Susi said. "She said you'd kill her—make her dead, like Mama. But if you were just gonna do like you did with Miz Tigue—why did you lock Triffin in? Why did you chain her up, Daddy?"

"I . . . will explain it all to you when we get home, Susi," Darley said, climbing to his feet, lifting the child. "I was going to tell you soon. You're old enough—"

How had he protected the child? Risa remained silent, seeing that Darley's basic honesty and his love for his daughter were mitigating his anger. Then Rikki spoke. "Mr. Darley, may we offer you a place to rest, some trin tea?"

"I'm not taking Susi in there!" Darley replied quickly. He mounted his horse, set his daughter before him and, leading her tired pony, rode back toward Laveen.

Rikki said, "Please move aside, Sergi, and let me zlin Risa." She steeled herself as the young channel examined her. Then he said, "No harm done—except that we'll have to schedule your transfer a little earlier. Sergi, have Nedd examine Risa, just in case."

"I'm all right," she protested.

"I want to talk to Nedd about what happened," Sergi insisted. "I wish he'd been here!"

Rikki hurried back to his work. As Risa and Sergi walked up the lane, the Gen asked, "What made you think Darley could kill me? Surely you know I can handle a renSime."

"I was afraid you'd kill *him*. He's not some nameless looter, Sergi."

Sensitive as she was at that moment, Risa was overwhelmed with his guilt. Then his field went flat as he said, "That looter should not have died. I should have known he could not stand being shenned with my strength. A Companion should have better judgment. He was trying to murder you . . . but I shall regret my hasty action for the rest of my life." He shuddered. "Today it put your life in danger."

"Nonsense!" she said. "I could handle Darley."

"I don't mean the transfer. If it hadn't been for his daughter, he probably would have strangled you *afterward*."

Risa and Sergi found Triffin in Nedd's office. The Sectuib was healing her ankle with Gevron's help. "Just a sprain," he said. "She'll be fine in a day or two."

The girl looked up at Risa. "I knew you wanted me. You tried so hard to buy me, twice—and they kept refusing—"

"Twice?" asked Sergi.

"I offered to buy her from Darley last month," Risa explained. "I tried to think of a way—"

"She had to do it herself," Nedd said softly. "She must choose her place of her own free will." Then he turned to Risa. "Let me zlin you."

"Rikki already—"

"Sit!"

More obedient than Sergi's dogs, Risa endured another examination. "Much better than I would have expected," said the Sectuib. "How did you manage not to turn to Sergi for immediate transfer? If Triffin understood correctly—"

"All I did was give transfer," Risa said. "You've certainly put me through enough drills—"

"But you are junct and in need, Risa," he said, shaking his head. "How you kept from attacking this girl—"

"Sergi was there. Forgive me, Triffin, but your field is nothing to his."

"It may be, eventually," Nedd suggested. "After everything she's been through, zlin her."

The girl's field was steady now, relaxed, pleasant. It was increasing quietly, pulse by pulse, like a Companion's. She asked, "What do I have to do to stay here?"

"You've already done it," Nedd told her. "When you have rested and had a good meal, we will talk. You must decide whether you want to stay at Keon—"

"What choice do I have?" she asked.

"Keon, Carre, or Gen Territory," he replied.

"You said you were going to Carre when we first met," Sergi remembered.

"Yeah—but only because it was closest and I'd been there before. Don't you live the same way here?"

"Essentially," Nedd replied. "But why were you at Carre before? As a child?"

"Yeah. I came from a Genfarm. They sold some of us preGens to fruit pickers a few years ago. I been all over the Territory, pickin' citrus, peaches, nuts. When we worked at Carre, the people were nice to us kids. They told me about the householdings and the starred-cross." She put her hand to the symbol she still wore. "I found this in a shrine. The next day I was caught, but I knew if I had faith—"

Nedd peered at the starred-cross. "Sergi, that looks like your work."

"It is," said Risa.

"See?" said Triffin. "I *knew* I belonged with you! You're not gonna make me leave, are you?"

"No, child, of course not," Nedd reassured her, but it was Risa the pale blue eyes were fixed on.

The eyes in her dream—come to life, as if she had made up for killing her dream father by saving the girl's life. But it was not merely one Gen life; she had stood between the Sime and the kill, expiation for her kills before she met Sergi. She knew her nightmare would not return.

"Risa," Nedd asked, "are you up to a little more practice at channel's functions?"

"I thought you didn't want me channeling while I'm in need."

"Zlin Triffin's state of health, then let me show you how to heal. Being in need is an advantage when healing Gens."

Risa found the girl unexpectedly healthy. The effects of the beating she had received at the auction were gone. She was somewhat undernourished, nothing serious. Her left arm had been broken at some time in the past, but had healed cleanly. Otherwise she was in good condition except for her ankle. Risa zlinned in amazement the way selyn production, and hence cell replacement, increased when she extended her laterals over the injury and allowed herself to feel need.

Nedd smiled sadly at her delight. "Winter is coming. You'll soon get plenty of practice at healing."

Gevron brought a tray heaped with food. The three Gens ate voraciously, Nedd managed some fruit, and Risa sipped tea while Triffin told of her escape from Tannen Darley's house. "Once I got Susi to open that door, the rest was easy. Till today. She'd come in and let me tell her stories—but she was really scared about stealing her father's keys to loosen the chain. The only way I could get her to do it was to tell her he was going to kill me. She didn't even know what it *meant!* But she knew what dead meant, because of her mother—"

Tears rolled down Triffin's face. "I didn't want to hurt that little girl! But what could I do?"

Sergi said gently, "She had to learn the truth—and her father loves her. Don't worry, Triffin—he won't punish her."

It was Risa that Tannen Darley punished, letting the whole town know that she was a channel of Keon. The day after a less than ecstatic transfer with Sergi, she was treated with hostility. The storekeeper accepted the teaglass holders, but there was no more conversation. People shied away from her in the street. Only in the saloons was she welcome—but not as a friend. Whispers and nudges followed her, and she was zlinned openly as she passed. She might as well be wearing one of Keon's bright red capes—or be accompanied by a Companion.

Defiantly, she pulled Sergi's starred-cross from under her shirt, to lie sparkling against the plain fabric. It gave her courage, just as the symbol had done for Triffin.

Finally she braved the bank, for she had money to deposit into Keon's account. Her own money was still lying fallow—would she ever find an investment now?

Tannen Darley would not see her. The bank clerk was rude and abrupt. Messages told her that land she had considered buying was no longer for sale. Even Skif, at the stable, was short with her.

She was walking back toward where she had left her horse when she met Verla, dressed now in a plain wool shirt and pants, with a cape against the drizzling rain.

"Risa—I'm going out to Keon to visit my kids. I'll ride with you. You look cold—come up to my room for tea first."

"Are you sure they won't run you out of Laveen if you're seen with me?" Risa asked.

"Nah—I don't matter. Risa—you do know I wasn't the one told people about you?"

"It was Tannen Darley," Risa replied. "Does everybody know what happened?"

"His daughter turned his Gen loose, and the Gen tried to run to Keon. Tan chased them down—his little girl has been kept in the house ever since, or maybe she doesn't want to come out. I guess that's the first time she ever saw a kill—hard on the poor kid since she'd made friends with the Gen."

By this time they were in Verla's hotel room. Risa said, "Susi didn't see a kill. She saw a transfer. I couldn't let Darley kill the Gen girl."

"Bloody shen!" Verla said in an awed whisper. Then, "I won't tell—don't you worry. But ... it sure does make me respect Tan even more, that he didn't tell what you did. You'd've had your throat slit by now if the locals knew."

"I wonder why he didn't tell?"

"Surely you knew he was sweet on you? I guess he still likes you, 'cause you're all he talked about to me."

"Darley talked to you?"

Verla nodded. "He spent the last two nights here. He's a nice man—I wish all my customers were like him. He kept saying you lied to him—and I told him I didn't think you lied, just didn't tell him everything. I think if you explained that when you first came to town you didn't know if you could stay at Keon—he'd understand."

Risa shook her head. "I can't do that."

"Well, you're just lucky he didn't organize a raid, that's all. But then, you're always lucky, aren't you?"

"I don't think so."

"You found Keon while you were still young enough to disjunct. Now Darley's not telling what you did to him. I call that luck—so how about rubbing a little off on me?"

"Hmmm?"

"Look." Verla took a small box from a dresser drawer, and pressed her handling tentacles in a precise pattern onto the design on top. It popped open, and Verla took out a gold coin, a heavy copper ring, and a brand-new bankbook. There was a single entry, for a hefty sum, bearing the date of the day before.

"Tan was gambling two nights ago," she said. "He was post and still mad as shen. He can afford to lose money, but he was just *throwing* it away, betting bad odds—

"Well, I tried to get him away from the table, thinking maybe he could throw some money my way, and suddenly he said, 'Here—you play for me!' and stuffed his money into my hands. Risa, I'd never touched so much money all at once in my life!"

"And you talked him out of gambling it?"

"No—I had to do what he asked. But I bet good odds, and I started winning— Now I know how gamblers get addicted—it's like a good kill to win so much!" She blushed. "Sorry. Anyway, I cleaned out everyone at the table. They were betting lucky pieces and jewelry by the time it was over. Tan insisted on splitting the winnings with me, even though I started with his money. He still got more than he came with—and look! Risa— I'm on my way to my shiltpron parlor!"

"Not if you try to raise more by gambling," said Risa.

"No—oh, no, never. But look—there's enough here to make a down payment on Laster's saloon."

"Laster's?" It was the smallest saloon in town, and the least attractive, but it still pulled plenty of customers.

"Laster's tired of staying in one place," Verla explained. "It needs a lot of fixing up, but there're some men in town who'll pay me with carpentry instead of money—and Dinny and I can do the painting. I'll send for my friend Ambru, the shiltpron player—and if you'll give us some backing, we can be open in two or three months."

"Give you backing?"

"Risa—you're looking for an investment. Now there's nobody who'll go into business with you . . . but I will. Unless—does your money belong to Keon now?"

"No, it's still mine," she replied, her head spinning. A shiltpron parlor? What would her father say? Supply and demand. Her money was sitting in the bank, doing nothing. But to risk it on Verla—?

"I will have to be a silent partner," she said before she even realized she had made the decision. "We'll split expenses and profits—"

"Half of mine belongs to Keon," Verla said firmly. "I won't tell them till it's successful—but then half my share every month goes to the householding, for my kids."

"You do what you please with your half, Verla—and I'll take care of mine. I'm going to look at Laster's.

Don't you come—if he knew we were partners, the price would double."

In half an hour Risa was back, having carefully inspected Laster's. The building was sound, its shabbiness superficial. It was a good investment for what Laster was asking.

She went back to the hotel, twined handling tentacles with Verla, and they toasted their agreement with trin tea.

While Risa was in town, Sergi met with Nedd to discuss her progress. "I really thought that incident with Darley would precipitate her crisis," he told the Sectuib.

"No—it's too soon. Only four months since her last kill. But if the crisis doesn't come next month, she will be technically out of First Year, although in actual time—"

"Which is it?" Sergi asked. "Twelve months, or twelve need cycles?"

"That's usually the same length of time," Nedd replied. "But it's the time—I once heard about a Freeband Raider disjuncting who'd probably had a dozen kills in his first three or four months as a Sime."

"Nedd, that's part of the oral tradition of the founding of Zeor. Are you sure it's true? Zeor's always making exaggerated claims—"

"And living up to them," replied the channel. "Still, you're right—that is where I heard the story. And channels never follow the rules anyway. Stick close to Risa—she'll resent you more and more, but don't you let her out of your sight. No more trips into town, unless you go with her."

"It's Risa who has to make that promise."

"The promise of a junct Sime in need? You care too much for that young woman—and not just as her Companion. Don't trust her! If she fails disjunction . . . you have to let her go forever. Sergi, you must be the

ultimate Companion. Only then will she have the slight-
est chance of disjuncting."

But Sergi's determination melted when Risa returned
from Laveen. She was wearing his starred-cross openly!
He wanted to hug her, but resisted the impulse, telling
Verla, who had ridden out from town with Risa, where
to find her children.

The cold drizzling rain had the children inside during their afternoon activities. While the youngest children played, the older children, Dinny and Kreg among
them, were bagging cornmeal for winter storage.

Risa's brother was the tallest child there, and Sergi
noticed that his face was maturing. The huge gray eyes
with their fringe of dark lashes were as startling as
ever, but the boyish softness of his face was giving way
to the firmness of expression he would have as a man.
One way or the other, Sergi thought, *you'll grow up soon
now, Kreg.*

"Risa, I've hardly seen you," Kreg accused. "You
don't look so good." Then he turned to Sergi. "You're
supposed to take better care of my sister."

"She is approaching disjunction, Kreg. As soon as
she passes the crisis, she'll be healthier than ever."

But as the days passed, Risa's health deteriorated.

Not that she complained. She took the donations
Nedd assigned her, practiced diligently at channel's
functions—and on her turnover day, at the very moment her system had used up half its selyn and started
the downward plunge toward need, she fainted dead
away.

Released from work for the day, Risa and Sergi and
Kreg had bundled up in heavy sweaters and gone up to
the high hill overlooking the household complex to fly
airship models. All about them, the hills burned with
autumn coloring. Sergi's dogs ran about, as red-gold as
the maple leaves.

"It's so beautiful here!" Risa exclaimed. "We never
had anything like this down south."

Kreg laughed as the brisk wind carried the models to

the treetops before dropping them down the hill. Feathers ran after them, barking madly, while Leader chased Kreg. Sergi remembered being that age, feeling the same delight—

Then an updraft caught one of the models, and Kreg began chasing it, shouting, "Look! It's flying away! Maybe all the way to town!"

The boy was looking up at the airship as he ran. Risa cried, "Look out!" as he neared the edge of an outcropping—too late. Kreg tumbled over—Risa gasped with the boy's pain.

Before she could get away from Sergi, Kreg reappeared, only his dignity hurt. Leader ran to sniff at him, but he laughed and called, "I'm all right," pushing the dog away—and that was when Risa collapsed.

Sergi barely caught her, but lowered her to the ground without injury. Kreg came running. "What happened? Risa!"

"She fainted," said Sergi, feeling the cause in his increased response to her. "Turnover. I'll carry her, Kreg. You run ahead and get a channel."

Risa was already coming to. "What happened?"

"You fainted."

"I've never fainted in my life," she insisted, shaking her head and immediately wincing. "Let me up!"

"No, I'm going to carry you down the hill—and no arguments. Kreg's gone for a channel."

"Don't be such a—Companion! It's nothing but turnover."

"And after turnover, you must defer to your Companion, remember?"

Loid met them at the bottom of the hill, a very anxious Kreg hovering as he examined Risa. "I don't zlin anything seriously wrong," the channel reported. "Rest this afternoon, Risa. Nedd will check in on you later."

But despite Risa's insistence that she was perfectly all right, she grew steadily worse. From that day, she could not keep food down, although she dutifully swallowed the soup Sergi brought. Finally he and Nedd decided that what little nourishment she might get from it was wasted in vomiting it up, and they stopped giving her anything but tea and fosebine.

She was too jittery to rest, too weak to walk far, and totally miserable. The weather didn't help; brisk winds brought freezing rain. The leaves fell, turning to a slippery mess underfoot. Sleet turned back to cold, dismal rain.

Verla came daily, and Risa would insist Sergi take a break, not knowing that every moment he was not with her was spent in fear of some crisis that only he could handle. And in the midst of it all, Kreg established as a Gen.

The boy was ambivalent at first, then angry when he was kept from Risa's side. "You wouldn't keep me away from her if I'd turned Sime."

"No, we wouldn't," Nedd explained, "because if you were Sime you would not have the power to hurt her. Sergi, this boy feels as you did when you first established. You're going to have a rival."

"Then teach me how to handle Risa!" Kreg insisted. "Please, Nedd, Sergi—let me help her!"

"You can't learn it that quickly," Sergi explained. "No—don't let the Simes give you any nonsense about Gens not having First Year learning powers. A Companion can get all his training in a few months, just as a channel can. But a few *months*, Kreg, not a few days."

"I want to see her. Let me donate—then I won't be able to hurt her."

"If your field is anything like mine," Sergi replied, "you are a walking menace to Simes until you learn to control it. Even low-field, Kreg. Nedd can tell you how I went around disrupting the ambient when I established—"

"Yes," Nedd agreed. "I was ready to carry him to the border myself, and pitch him over."

"Why?" Kreg asked. "Didn't you want to be a Companion?"

"No," Sergi replied, "I wanted to be a channel."

"You?" Kreg's adolescent voice squeaked in amazement.

"Oh, I was a skinny little kid when I established—I did all my growing afterward. Kreg, my whole family were channels. Both my parents, my brother—and my sister would have been, but she died in changeover. I expected to be a channel, too.

"Then my brother went to Householding Imil, over in Nivet Territory. I see him at the Arensti. My parents—" he swallowed hard, forced himself to go on, "were coming back from trading with Carre, about eleven years ago. They were ambushed by Freeband Raiders where the eyeway winds around Eagle Mountain. Everybody in the party was murdered."

"Well, I've got nobody but Risa," Kreg said defensively. "My mom and dad are dead, too."

"That isn't the point," Sergi told him. "Keon lost my parents and another channel. From having had so many channels the year before that we could trade Georg to Imil, we suddenly had too few—and that situation has obtained ever since.

"I was old enough to change over at the time of the ambush. I thought I was supposed to take my parents' place as a channel . . . and then I established."

Kreg said, "I know how you felt. Like you were . . . rejected. The way I can't help Risa—not even talk to her."

"Yes," Sergi agreed. "When Nedd told me I'd established—I ran. You know that cave up on the hillside? I hid there for two days, until I realized that no one had come after me because everyone—all the Simes, anyway—knew where I was. They let me come back of my own accord. After a while, in an adolescent boy, hunger wins out."

"Yeah," said Kreg, sharing the faint humiliation of Sime taunts about hungry Gens. "But you became a Companion."

"If I hadn't been able to serve a channel's need—I

don't know what I'd have done. But Nedd is not always subtle."

The channel grinned. "Neither were you, with that field. And you had to find out what you could do." He sobered. "It was a decision made in need, and to my advantage."

"But you were right," said Sergi, locking eyes with his mentor in a moment of shared memory.

"What happened?" Kreg asked.

"Nedd ignored me, and everyone else acted as if I'd never been away. The tragedy of my life—and no one cared!"

Kreg nodded in sympathy. "I know."

"Come on, Kreg—I was wallowing in self-pity. I realized that Nedd was going to make me ask for Companion's training—at least that's what I thought. But when I went to his office— Have you felt it yet, Kreg? The need that wakens all your hope, your desire, your pride that you can serve—?"

"No," the boy replied.

"You will. And the moment you do, you will stop feeling sorry to be Gen. When I went to Nedd's office that day, he was alone . . . and in need."

"It didn't frighten you?" Kreg asked, eyes wide.

"All I wanted was to ease his need. The fact that I *could* was the greatest joy I had ever known. Nedd just said, 'Don't you think it's time we qualified you?' And he did."

"And you think I can—?" Kreg looked from Sergi to Nedd.

"I know you can," the channel replied. "Let me watch you, and choose the right time. I must ask for your trust."

Kreg nodded. "You have it. But if I give transfer—then can I see Risa?"

"Although the answer is yes, you cannot give transfer for that reason." Sergi knew Nedd was deeply worried about Risa—yet after he had sent Kreg off in Gevron's

care to move his things into the Gen dormitory, he
began to talk as if Risa's disjunction were assured.

"Once she is past crisis, she'll recover in a day or two.
She's tough and smart, Sergi; all she'll really have to do
is hone her skills, learn some subtlety." He rubbed his
hands over his eyes, handling tentacles through the
hair at the sides of his head. "I'm tired, and so are
Rikki and Loid. Another channel—especially one of
Risa's capacity—will mean a more normal life for all of
us. But the responsibility rests with you. None of Keon's
channels can handle an uncooperative Risa."

"I will disjunct her," Sergi replied.

Nedd dropped his hands abruptly. "I didn't expect a
Gen reaction at this late date. She has to disjunct herself, Sergi. You cannot do it to her."

"I meant that I can serve her need, even at disjunction crisis."

"That I know. What concerns me is how to force a
choice on her. There is no reason for her to choose
anyone but you."

Risa was in her own room, having refused to go to
the infirmary. Triffin and Dreela sat on either side of
the bed where Risa lay listlessly, Guest curled up at
her side.

The Companions moved carefully, allowing no abrupt
shifts in the ambient. Traffin, who had insisted on
helping as best she could, lost control as soon as Sergi
was between her and Risa. Drella put an arm around
her to lead her out.

Controlling his own feelings, Sergi sat down next to
Risa, between her and the wall her room shared with
Kreg's. She tried to smile, her eyes huge in her drawn
face.

"Think you can drink a little tea?" Sergi asked.

"Yes," Risa whispered obediently. Dehydration was
complicating her condition. She managed only a couple
of swallows, though, before pushing Sergi's hand away.

Guest awoke and stretched, then put his paws up on

Risa's chest and licked her chin. She allowed it for a moment, then murmured, "Your tongue's scratchy," and pulled the cat down. He curled up on her other side and began to purr.

Sergi said, "I've got something to show you," and brought out a ring, the new design he was working on: a Keon pledge ring with the brilliant ruby already in place, but small, designed for slender Sime hands.

Risa looked at it politely, murmuring, "Pretty."

"It's only roughed out," Sergi explained. "The crest will be carved in the stone, and the chain will be carved and enameled around it."

"You could make enameled pots and pans," Risa said out of the blue. "No poison."

He smiled at her. "Always business. We'll try it as soon as you're back on your feet. But here, try the ring on. I want to see if it's right for Sime hands."

It slid too easily over her shrunken finger, but Sergi judged that it would fit right when she was back to normal. Her pledge party would have to wait a day or two after her disjunction. He would have time to finish the ring, and carve her name inside

Risa studied the ring with real interest. Her hand went to the starred-cross at her breast. "Why isn't the starred-cross on the ring?"

"There isn't room for everything—not even on a big ring like mine," he replied, holding out his hand for comparison.

Risa focused on the design, touched it with a tentacle-tip, and suddenly shuddered. "I hate that chain!"

"You told Nedd you understood, remember? The only true freedom is the freedom to choose one's chains."

"I don't want to be chained." She pulled the ring from her finger viciously, and threw it at Sergi. It stung when it hit his shoulder, but he caught it. Risa held the starred-cross in both her hands. "This is freedom," she said. "No killing. No owning. No chains." She looked up at him, hollow-eyed. "How can you make something this beautiful, and also make symbols of bondage?"

"Risa, that's need talking—you did understand, and you will again. Concentrate on the starred-cross. Have faith, Risa—do not fear your need. Trust me. I will always be here when you need me."

He managed to soothe her to sleep, let Guest out when the cat jumped down from the bed and went to the door, then felt his own weariness overtake him and lay down on the other bed.

Risa woke screaming.

She was augmenting wildly, and Sergi could not calm her. She hit at him, and his best projection of calm only left her gasping for breath as she writhed on the bed.

Nedd came with his wife, Litith, who sprayed something into Risa's face. She passed out. Litith zlinned her, and said, "It will be safe to move her in about half an hour—Sergi, you stay with me." She assured him, "You did everything right—but now she must be moved to the infirmary. It's *good*, Sergi—she's progressing through stages, just as in changeover. She has to reach her crisis before she runs out of selyn, exactly the way a changeover victim has to reach the breakout of tentacles. The sooner Risa reaches crisis, the more reserves she will have. Understand?"

"Yes," whispered Sergi, who had attended many changeovers. It was always good when the stages went quickly. "How long?"

"A day or two. You'll stay with her. I'll give her medication to keep her from augmenting away her reserves until she becomes coherent again—but when she does, she will have to make her choice. And you must be there."

"I'll be there."

"We'll put a bed for you in her room—and I want you to sleep for a few hours. You're going to have to be ready when she comes out of it—at your best. One wrong word—"

"I understand," he said, driving his fear away. It was

the one emotion he dared not have. Courage would not do for the task ahead, only true fearlessness.

When Sergi woke in the infirmary, he found his charge asleep, pale, her hair disheveled—and her arms laced into restraints. Remembering her horror of chains—of restrictions—he wondered how he could stand it when she woke. The restraints were to prevent her from hurting herself. Nonetheless, he hated them as much as Risa would.

Nedd entered the room, zlinned Risa, and said, "She'll sleep for a while yet. I'll relieve you so you can eat and get cleaned up—but be as quick as you can."

Sergi took the absolute minimum of time. When he returned, Kreg and Triffin were sitting outside the room. Risa wouldn't know—her room was draped with the heaviest insulation—but they obviously felt they had to be there.

Triffin looked up at him. "I didn't know," she said. "I thought she was already one of you. Risa gave me courage to come here. Don't let her die!"

"I don't intend to," he replied, glad they were Gen and could not zlin that his confidence was forced.

Kreg said, "Please take care of her. I'm learning, Sergi—someday I'll be able to do what you're doing for Risa."

"Yes." He smiled, wondering if it looked as false as it felt. "You will both be fine Companions one day."

Nedd left Sergi alone with Risa. The whole room was shrouded; although it was day, a lamp was lit so that Sergi could see. Hours dragged by.

Finally Risa woke. "Sergi?" It was a harsh whisper.

"I'm here." He wet her parched lips with the sponge Litith had supplied. "As soon as you're ready—"

She tugged at the restraints, tried again with augmented strength. Then she lay still. "I'm ready," she said, her eyes gleaming. "Release me, Sergi."

She was lying!

He could feel as plainly as a Sime ever zlinned that

she did not want him! Never in his life had he understood a Sime's motivations so plainly.

What she wanted was fear. For months her junct system had been denied the high of Gen terror, culminating in the kill—and now it rebelled, demanding satisfaction.

Sergi offered his eager desire to ease her need. Her emaciated body writhed, head thrashing on the pillow.

Then she forced herself to lie still. He could see her tentacles moving within the restraints. A grin of pure malediction drew her lips back from her teeth. It felt more like the hideous grimace of a Gen dying in terror than like the reassuring smile she intended.

"Come to me, Sergi," she whispered. "Give me transfer. It will be beautiful—but you'll have to let my arms free."

The rejection beneath her coaxing words was worse than if she had attacked him. Did she think he couldn't tell—?

Sergi put aside his hurt. *That is junctness speaking, not Risa. She must reject the kill. Then she will be mine.*

"Risa—forget the idea of escaping from me and killing somebody. You don't really want that—you know you don't!"

She writhed again in fury, augmenting, the restraints bulging with her agonized efforts to free her arms. "You lorsh! You want me to die!"

"No," he whispered, letting all his reassurance flow to her. Her need was deepening. Sergi's desire to serve her soared. He wanted to tear off the restraints and force his selyn upon her—and her response to his emotions was to struggle even more furiously, screaming incoherently.

Never since the day Nedd qualified him had Sergi been so helpless before a Sime in need. No Sime before had failed to respond to his field—yet Risa rejected his love, his caring, his need to give—

A junct must be tempted as a junct. Risa had to make a choice—had to reject fear and choose caring. He must entice her as he would any junct Sime he wanted to control. Let her attack—and if she did not reject the kill of her own accord, he could control the transfer, not allow her to kill him. Then there would be next month—

She could not survive another month. Her body was wasting away, and an unsatisfactory transfer would not give her strength to face another crisis.

Then it must be now.

He had real fear to give her—fear for her life, for Keon's survival without another channel, and most of all for his own life looming empty without her, if she died or if she failed. Either way, his future would be as half a person.

Sergi reached out to pull the bell, alerting Nedd and Litith that the crisis was here. They would come to the door and wait—wait for Sergi to call for their help, or for him to emerge in triumph.

Then he began to unfasten Risa's restraints, carefully working one side, then the other, so that he could finally release both her arms at once, all the while bathing her in his need to give—

The moment both her arms were free, as she tried to thrust him away, he let his fears surface. She turned from rejection to desire. She lunged for him, her fingers crushing his forearms—he let the pain join the fear—

Risa screamed.

"No! No! Wer-Gen! Sime-killer!"

With augmented strength, she threw him across the room.

Sergi hit the wall, the breath knocked out of him.

The door slammed open, Kreg barreled across the room, shouting, "Risa! Risa!"

She turned to the boy, a feral gleam in her eyes. She grasped him, laterals streaking his arms with ronaplin as they settled against him.

Kreg looked down in utter astonishment, then up at the face looming at him. Not his sister's face. The ravaged, mindless face of a Sime about to kill.

Chapter Eight

Risa felt pain and fear surge in the Gen she held—delicious promise of satisfaction at last. But there was something else—some other promise with the fear—

Her oversensitized nerves made her aware of other fields—Sergi climbing to his feet, his nager numb with despair. Nedd and Litith at the open door, Triffin dimmed by being thrust behind the channel.

Tension filled the small, insulated room.

Something about the Gen she held was familiar. Not possible. Along with the fear was love—

With incredible effort, she forced herself to duoconsciousness, looking at the Gen who promised her life.

Father!

The dark-lashed gray eyes blurred into the eyes of her nightmare father, then back to Morgan Tigue's. Her father was Sime. She held a Gen. Yet she held her father—enticing her back to the life she had known with him. He wanted her to kill—yet if she killed, she killed *him!*

The nightmare paradox resolved into recognition.

Kreg! As brave as their father, who would have given his life for his children.

Their eyes met. "Risa," Kreg whispered, "do you want to take transfer from me? I can do it for you."

But he couldn't. That small trickle of fear running

up his spine was enough to kill him. Yet she couldn't let go—she *needed* that fear. She couldn't survive without it.

Nor could she survive if she killed Kreg.

Only Kreg? The nightmare father's face blended into her brother's, her father's, Triffin's— "I don't want to kill!" she realized on a wave of agony. "Don't let me kill!"

Her hands and tentacles seemed paralyzed. Her efforts to release Kreg wasted even more selyn. "Sergi!" she whimpered, unashamed of her need of him.

He was there, his field flooded with relief and joy and promise. Her hands moved, laterals fixed themselves—then his familiar lips touched hers, and life poured through her devastated nerves, blissful renewal, and peace at last.

Risa felt as if she had just come through changeover— only better. Kreg was standing by the door, rubbing the bruises on his arms. But it was no time for apologies. The fact that her brother had established as a Gen— was technically adult—truly penetrated for the first time.

"Congratulations, Kreg," she said.

He flung himself into her arms. "Oh, Risa—congratulations! You made it, Sis! I knew you would!"

Nedd, Litith, and Triffin all hugged her; then Litith cleared everyone out, brought soup and fruit which Risa had no trouble eating, and insisted that she go to sleep.

She woke raring to go. Someone had placed her robe and slippers by the bed. She padded out, flicking a tentacle at the startled Sime at the desk.

It was a cold, clear morning. She inhaled frost and woodsmoke and an eager desire to get on with her life. She ran to the guest house, showered, dressed in woolens and boots—and found Sergi waiting.

He looked as good as she felt, clear-eyed and glowing, cheeks pink with frost.

"You should have waited for one of the channels to

check you out of the infirmary," he said, but there was no real admonition in his voice or field.

"*I'm* a channel," Risa replied, "and I declare myself to be in perfect health."

Risa received congratulations from everyone she met—and a sense of welcome, as if they all now considered her part of their family.

"I'm going into town," she told Sergi. "Coming along?"

"Haven't you forgotten something?"

"What?" she asked blankly.

"The schedule board? You are now a working channel."

For a moment her elation dimmed. *Tigues pay their debts,* she reminded herself, and followed Sergi to check the board.

Sure enough, she had a lesson with Nedd that afternoon, then donations—and transfers! Her heart leaped at the memory of the one time she had stood between a Sime and the kill. *I can do it now,* she thought. *I want to do it.*

Neither her name nor Sergi's appeared on the morning list, but she saw why her brother was not around: he was having a lesson with Rikki.

"We've got the morning free," Risa observed.

"You're supposed to be resting."

"I don't require any more rest, and neither do you. Come on—let's tell Verla the good news!"

Verla had wasted no time purchasing Laster's saloon. They had written up a contract, Verla trusting Risa that it said what she claimed, before Risa had been confined to Keon. She had withdrawn money, Verla had deposited it in the shiltpron parlor account, "And Tannen Darley can just go spit if he dislikes my backer," Verla said spiritedly.

When she and Sergi rode into town, Risa was amazed at the work already accomplished on the saloon. The front was freshly painted, the windows gleamed, and a sign proclaimed VERLA'S in lettering a bit too fancy for Risa's taste.

The bar was already open, although all the tables

had been removed, and a man and a woman were sanding the floor.

Verla was behind the bar, chatting with a Sime who leaned on one elbow while he watched the workers. Verla had softened the red of her hair to a much more attractive auburn. She wore a dress of turquoise material, a little bright in color, but covering her from throat to ankles, with sleeves to her elbows. There were no feathers or sequins, but the dress outlined every curve of her figure—and Verla somehow gave the impression of having more curves than the average Sime woman.

Risa was delighted at her partner's business sense. They did not want their establishment taken for a brothel, as they hoped to attract respectable customers. "My kids will be here lots of times," said Verla. And so she had changed her image.

"Risa!" Verla squealed, and ran to hug her. "Oh, you look wonderful! I'm just so happy for you! And Sergi—"

The ambient surged with malice as the proprietor of Verla's Shiltpron Parlor hugged a Gen. Verla turned to her audience. "These're my friends. You don't like it, there're other saloons. And you two—" she called to the workers sanding the floor, "I'm payin' you to work, not to gawk!"

Two of the three Simes at the bar walked out. The man and woman sanding the floor shrugged and went back to work. The man who had been talking with Verla zlinned Risa and Sergi with lazy insolence, and went on drinking.

"Verla," said Risa, "if we're going to chase your customers away—"

"Those two'll go over to Zabrina's and tell what they saw here, and pretty soon a dozen people'll come over to zlin the, um, householders. And they'll all have to buy drinks! So before I get really busy, come see how I'm fixing things up. Ambru! Ambru—get up here and take over the bar!"

From one of the back rooms came a Sime, hobbling

on a crutch. Not only was he lacking one leg, but his back was bent so that he did not come quite up to Risa's height. His face was as crooked as his body, jaw undershot, mouth toothless, nose hooked, eyes squinting. A woolen cap was pulled down almost to his eyes.

Verla said, "This here's Ambru. When he plays the shiltpron, you'd swear you could float on the ambient! Ambru, I've told you about Risa and Sergi ambrov Keon."

"How do, folks!" Ambru said cheerfully. "Any friend of Verla's is a friend of mine!"

Verla showed Sergi and Risa through a hallway, where storerooms on either side had been partitioned into small rooms. "Each one of these'll be a guest room," she explained. "I've built on more storage out back."

"Guest rooms?" Risa asked.

"Absolutely not killrooms," she said firmly. "But Risa, you mix porstan and shiltpron, and some people just gotta sleep it off—or maybe a man and a woman—"

"I thought you said—" Risa cut off her words; she had not told anyone at Keon that she was partners with Verla. Was the woman using that fact to turn the establishment into what they had agreed it was not to be?

"No, no—I'm not gonna have any girls. But people are people. Men and women are gonna come in together. Even married folk, away from the kids for a night. And some of the hands from the farms come into town, get drunk—they'd like a nice clean bed to sleep it off, and can't afford the hotel. I'll keep things respectable—just you wait and see."

As she led them on she added, "This last room's Ambru's, then some storage space. I've got glasses on order—Sergi, you better get to work on about a gross of glass holders."

"I'll tell Kreg," he replied. When Risa looked at him sharply, he explained, "Your brother took over production while I was too busy to work in the metal shop."

"And what *other* news have I missed?" she asked.

"Tannen Darley's little girl's sick," said Verla. "She got hysterical when Tan brought a couple new Gens from the choice auction last week. On his killday, I took Susi with my kids to Hanging Rock so she wouldn't be there when— Well, she's worked herself into a fever because one of the Gens is gone. Tan's looking for someplace else to keep them now."

"Why did he come up short?" Risa asked.

"Oh, he augmented like crazy. After what happened . . . I think he was trying to get rid of your selyn."

It sounded likely. But what about the poor little girl? Most children changed over between twelve and fourteen natal years; she should still have time to harden herself to the fact that Simes killed Gens to live.

But what if the banker's daughter should try to run for Keon at her changeover?

There has to be a way to make this community more tolerant of Keon.

Verla showed them her living quarters, similar to the apartment behind Tigue's that Risa had grown up in. The kitchen/parlor had a table and chairs from the saloon, a stove, and a sink. "Look," Verla said proudly, "a pump right in the sink—no more running outside in all weather."

"You'll have to get a boiler," said Risa. "Sergi, can you make one, instead of ordering one from Norlea?"

"If I can find enough tin for the tank," he replied.

"Good. We'll make you one, Verla—and then you let everybody know how reliable it is and where you got it."

"Risa," said Sergi, "I might be able to find tin for *one* boiler, but if we were to get orders for half a dozen—"

"We'll worry about that later," she replied.

Metal was always the problem. Keon craftsmen could hollow and filigree bits of metal into glass holders, bake enamel over thin sheets of metal at the core—but even those small quantities were scarce and expensive in Gulf Territory.

In Gen Territory, though, were ruins of Ancient cities waiting to be mined. Sime senses combined with augmentation had long ago stripped the Ancient city near Lanta of every scrap that could be reached without the Ancient ability to move mountains. But Gens couldn't zlin or augment.

Furthermore, the Ancient ruins in Gen Territory were often hiding places for berserkers, who fled to the labyrinth of fallen buildings at changeover, and might survive for months, preying on foolhardy prospectors.

Everyone at Keon must know these facts, yet no one seemed to have thought of a mining expedition to Gen Territory.

"Not to a *big* city," Risa told Nedd later that day. "Last summer Dad and I zlinned places overgrown with kudzu that must have been Ancient communities. You can't see anything now but lumps under vines."

"But what do you want to do about it?" Nedd asked suspiciously. "Risa, Keon cannot go raiding into—"

"Not raiding! We don't go *near* out-Territory Gens. I'm talking about salvage, which belongs to whoever finds it. That's the law, and it's part of the border treaties, too."

"The border treaties also say it is illegal for a Sime to enter Gen Territory, and any who do may be executed on sight."

"We can't let them see us, then. You don't let them see you when you cross Gen Territory for the Arensti competition."

Nedd sighed. "All right, forget legalities. How much do you think it would cost to equip such an expedition?"

She figured. "We've got horses, mules, wagons, and people. We'd require picks and shovels, block and tackle—"

"And what are the most important and therefore expensive components of those items?" Nedd prompted.

"Metal," Risa groaned. "But Nedd, that's just why—"

He flicked two handling tentacles in a "let's be reasonable" gesture. "I concede your point. Let's survive the winter, and discuss your idea next year."

"Next *year*! The time to do it is *now*."

"Yes, *right* now, between harvest and winter. But we cannot go in the next few weeks—and with the Year's Turning comes the worst weather of the winter. You must learn, Risa, that there is a time for everything—and now is the time for you to learn to channel, not go prospecting in Gen Territory."

Working on channel's functions, Risa forgot her frustrated plans—and when she was scheduled for a free hour, she found Kreg waiting for her. "I'm supposed to be your Companion for your rest period," he said with a grin. "Shall I make you some tea? Rub your back? Sing you a lullaby?"

Her brother knew perfectly well that Risa required no rest. She was eager to get on to her first assigned transfers. "Why don't I just take your donation while we're resting?" she teased, for Kreg's field was still high and growing. To her relief and satisfaction, there was not even a startled response, let alone fear at her words.

"Nedd thinks I can go right to transfer, the way Sergi did—but he has me working with Rikki. I'd love it to be with you, though, Sis. I can wait a month, if Nedd approves—and if Sergi doesn't object! I understand how he feels—Risa, I *would* have given you transfer yesterday, really I would."

"I know," she said. "I could feel that you wanted to—but you were nervous, too, and I could not have controlled if anything had gone wrong. I love you, little brother. I'm so glad I brought you here. I hope you'll be happy."

"I was mad at first. It'd be . . . convenient to be Sime. But when you touched me, and this morning with Rikki—there's the most wonderful feeling of being able to give—"

"I know, Kreg. You're projecting it right now."

"Yeah—but you should feel it from the *inside*."

She felt something of what Kreg and Sergi did when she began giving transfers that afternoon. All Risa's assignees today were nonjunct Simes with no physiological or emotional problems. Yet each one brought a new delight.

Risa imitated Sergi's need to give as each Sime entered nervously. The nervousness was need, not worry about her competence—if Nedd said she was ready, they trusted the Sectuib. She watched need tension drain away beneath her touch. It felt like magic—and when she actually gave selyn, projecting the sweet, bright fulfillment Sergi provided her, it was a blissful sharing, less powerful than what she knew with Sergi, but just as beautiful.

It was almost a disappointment when she came to Carlos, the last Sime on her schedule. When he entered and she let her field support him, he sighed and said, "Min's right. We really got lucky this month!"

Risa zlinned a delighted affirmation in Sergi's field. Min had been on her schedule about two hours ago—and she had felt in the woman an astonishment similar to her own in her first transfer with Sergi. Apparently she was giving more than they expected of a disjunct channel. She felt pleased.

When Carlos had left, Risa was scheduled to rest again. "This is ridiculous," she said. "I've worked four hours today, but it's been spaced out over six—there shouldn't be five or ten minutes between transfers, either. As soon as one of the Simes is ready to leave, the next one could come in. Nedd's got me scheduled like some kind of invalid."

Sergi laughed. "No, he's got you scheduled like one of Keon's normal channels. We're on again at midnight for infirmary duty, although there's not much going on there. *I* intend to get a good night's sleep. That's one advantage to being a Companion; I can perform half my duties sound asleep."

But Risa was annoyed at breaking her days up into

little chunks—a couple of hours of work, and then time off, but not enough time to *do* anything. For four days straight she had no stretch of daylight time long enough to ride into town.

She complained to Rikki, who told her he could not change her scheduling without Nedd's permission. So she accosted the Sectuib in one of his own rest periods, and told him, "I have these short rest periods when I sit around playing with my tentacles and waiting to *do* something."

Nedd opened one weary eye. "Didn't you just come off duty?"

"Yes. That's what I'm talking about. I'm back on again in thirty-three minutes. What am I supposed to do with thirty-three shidoni-be-flayed minutes?!"

"Rest!" he said, leaning back in his comfortable chair.

"But I don't require rest! Nedd, there is no reason I cannot do my own business and perform my duties for Keon—if only you would give me a sensible schedule."

As he forced both eyes open, she realized he was not exaggerating. He was indeed tired, his systems in recovery mode but not yet back to normal, although it was probably half an hour since his last function.

"Nedd—are you ill?" she asked, conscience-stricken.

He gave a wry chuckle. "No, I'm not ill. I've been working on and off since midnight, that's all. My last shift comes up in twenty minutes, and I will be fully recovered.

"*You're* unusual, Risa—not Rikki or Loid or me. I don't think even my father had your capacity. You belong at Zeor, not Keon—if Keon didn't need you so desperately I might be tempted to see what *they* could do with you."

His tone of voice and nager told her that his throat to send her to the "best"—and strictest—householding was not exactly a compliment.

"I'm sorry," she said. "I didn't realize—"

"No, you're right. I'll tell Rikki to reduce your rest periods to twenty minutes."

With an improved schedule, Risa felt better about her life. Kreg gave transfer to Rikki just before Risa's turnover, and came from the experience glowing. "I've never felt so good in my life." he told her. "Where's Sergi—I've got to tell him he was right."

"I couldn't tell the difference from what Sergi gave me, the few times I've had transfer with him," Rikki told Risa. "What Kreg doesn't know is that I couldn't really satisfy *him*. Someday I suppose he'll have to do what Sergi did—go find himself a channel up to his capacity."

The next day Sergi, who had been spending much of his time in the metal shop, began dogging Risa's footsteps. When he did not leave her side as she returned to her room after midnight, she realized it was her turnover day. She examined her systems, found that she was indeed on the descent toward need—and had not felt a thing.

"Sergi—I'm not junct anymore," she told him. "If you want your privacy—"

He looked up from turning the cover back on the second bed, unused since Risa had left the infirmary. Someone on housekeeping detail had made it up fresh today. "What I want is for you to sleep. You'll wake before I do. Just go on with your duties, and I'll see you at breakfast."

Risa shrugged. It wasn't worth arguing about.

Three days later Triffin gave transfer to Loid, and Nedd called Risa, Triffin, and Kreg to his office. Sergi was already there. "It's time for a celebration," said the Sectuib, "when the three of you pledge unto Keon. I don't believe we have ever had a three-way pledge party before—and certainly never one welcoming a channel and two Companions!"

Sergi said, "If you've wondered why I've spent so much time in the metal shop this month, here's the reason." He held out his hand. Three gold rings gleamed on his large palm, rubies winking. They were of graduated sizes—a large one like Sergi's for Kreg, one slightly smaller for Triffin, and the new, more delicate design he had been working on—

"No!" Risa said involuntarily, staring at the enameled white chain surrounding the stone in each ring.

Everyone stared at her, Nedd zlinning her concernedly. "Risa, this will only formalize what you already are."

"A member of Keon? I'm not—and I don't want to be."

"Sis!" Kreg said, stricken. "You aren't leaving?"

"I owe Keon far too much for that. You pledge, Kreg. You're happy with Keon's system. But I can't live under it."

"What are you talking about?" Sergi asked, his field under harsh control.

Nedd's field was numb. "What system?" he asked blankly.

"Your whole way of life," Risa answered. "There's no incentive here. All you have is duty, duty, duty, 'So burdensome, still paying, still to owe.' "

"What?" asked Sergi.

"It's from an Ancient poem," Kreg explained. "Dad used to quote it. But Risa, I don't feel that way. Why do you?"

"Maybe because I owe more than you do—and always will," she replied, surprising herself. "But Kreg, half the money I got from selling the store is yours. I've invested it."

"I trust you."

"What Risa is saying," Nedd suddenly realized, "is that she fears Keon is asking for all your worldly goods. And . . . she's right. All that you are and have will be Keon's, and all that Keon is and has will be yours." He sighed. "This is the first time I can remember that we have had someone come to us *with* worldly goods. Just how wealthy are you two, anyway? No, I'm sorry—that was a rude question."

"You have the right to know," said Kreg. "Risa, as a Gen I've lost inheritance rights. If you won't let me pledge my money, that's up to you. Sectuib, I will pledge myself, if you will have me."

Risa managed a rueful laugh. Verla planned to give half of *her* profits from the shiltpron parlor to Keon. Kreg's decision meant that his half of Risa's portion would also go to Keon. "Kreg, you know I would not cheat you of your inheritance. If that is your decision, half of all profits from the investment go to Keon—but Nedd, I think you will be surprised to discover what you own half of."

"Not me—the householding," he replied. "I'm sure you have made a profitable choice. I looked at our accounts yesterday, Risa. Keon made enough profit on those glass holders last month to buy metal for the new orders coming in and still pay our taxes despite acquiring two extra Gens. As for your own decision, we would never demand a pledge of anyone who does not want with all her heart to give it."

"You have my services as long as you need them."

"I would ask that you live here, please," Nedd added. "We are Gen high. Having another Sime in residence not only decreases taxes, but makes less likely the threat of confiscation for hoarding when there are shortages."

Risa could feel the deep hurt Nedd was trying to conceal, and wished desperately that she had been able to find a gentler way to inform the Sectuib of her plans. Shen Sergi and his shedoni-doomed rings, anyway!

If Nedd was hurt, Sergi was seething with indignation. "How could you *do* that to Nedd?" he demanded when they had left the office and were out of earshot of the others.

"How could *you* do that to *me*?" she challenged. "I told you I won't be chained!"

"But you're a channel. How can you even think of leaving Keon? Risa ... all of a sudden I don't know you!"

"I'm the same person I've always been. I told you I wanted to disjunct, and I did. I said I'd channel for Keon, and I will. What more do you expect from me?"

"Loyalty! Caring!" He seemed about to add something else, but cut it off.

"Sergi, I do care," she said softly. "I love channeling—but I can't earn a living at it."

"What?" He was bewildered.

"Look at you. You work as a Companion. You make objects that bring Keon money. If you did nothing but produce selyn, you'd deserve twice the payment of anyone else at Keon. But you are paid the same as everyone else: nothing!"

"Risa, you cannot talk about selyn in terms of money!"

"Why not? You *should* be paid for it."

His eyes flashed blue ice. "And then I suppose you'd have the channels sell it to the renSimes—at a profit?"

"Yes!" she said eagerly. "You *do* understand."

He turned away. "Is that all you think about? *Money?* How can you speak of life in terms of—of *profit?*"

"Because profit is important, that's why. Value for services rendered. Of course money isn't everything—but look what a little money has done for Verla. Do you think she'd be better off without it, selling her body for barely enough to pay her Gen taxes?"

"Verla is a junct living in a junct society. That society buys and sells people . . . and you grew up in it. I'm sorry, Risa. I don't know why we didn't realize that you were still thinking that way. But it can't go on. Perhaps—" he fixed her with angry eyes again, "perhaps if you pictured your little brother on the auction block, you would stop thinking of life in terms of money."

Sergi was not sure Risa understood, even when she went pale at the thought of Kreg auctioned off for the kill. He had thought she had adopted Keon as her family . . . and now he learned she regarded the householding as a necessary evil.

And their transfers as something to be paid for—

He traded the next duty shift with Triffin. Knowing what had happened in Nedd's office, she agreed. Loid seemed puzzled, but Sergi rarely claimed personal privilege.

Nedd, though, had heard about the trade by the time of his next conference with Sergi. "You quarreled with Risa?"

"Yes."

"When she is well past turnover?"

"Don't try to make me feel guilty, Nedd. I have just found out what a cold, unfeeling—"

"Sergi!" Nedd had not used that tone of voice with him since he was a small boy folding paper into airship models during changeover class.

But he was a man now, even if disillusioned and hurt. He calmed himself, determined to make Nedd understand. "Risa thinks life is to be bought and sold. Verla deserved to disjunct, not Risa!"

"Do you realize what you are saying?"

"Yes. Since she could not disjunct, Verla made sure her children will never kill. She changed her way of life. But Risa would buy and sell selyn! She regards me as providing a . . . commodity! I can't give her transfer, Nedd. I never want to touch her again."

The Sectuib let Sergi storm. When the Companion finally sat down, he said, "You saved her life when you knew she meant to kill you. You brought her through disjunction."

"And now she rejects everything we stand for."

"Not everything." Nedd smiled. "Sergi, how can you abandon Risa over a difference in economic philosophy?"

"You don't understand," Sergi said numbly.

"I know you're in love with her. That's why it hurts you so to think she sees you as a commodity. Son, Risa is on her last defenses. Give her time! She loves you— but she is not ready to make that final commitment."

"She still sees Gens as objects to buy and sell."

"That's not what you said," Nedd reminded him. "You said Risa sees *selyn* as a commodity. *I* said you think she sees you that way."

"What's the difference?" Sergi asked hopelessly.

"How does she perceive the role of channel?"

"She said—channels should sell selyn at a profit," Sergi said.

To his dismay, Nedd laughed. "Sergi, don't you see? Purveyors of a commodity! You may not like the way Risa perceives you, but she perceives herself the same way."

As Sergi studied his Sectuib, a thought surfaced that he had been suppressing since the day of Risa's disjunction. "Nedd . . . how do *you* perceive us?"

"Us?"

"Gens. You're a channel. You've never killed a Gen. Yet . . . you risked killing me at our first transfer."

"I judged that you were ready—and I was right. Such judgments are a Sectuib's duty, Sergi."

"Like your judgment that Risa would not kill her brother?"

"You think I *arranged*—?"

"Of course you did. Or at least let it happen. Two augmenting Simes could not prevent a Gen from running into that room? You held Litith back. You let Kreg risk his life—and Risa's! What if she'd killed her brother?"

"She did not kill him. She could not—and we *would* have aborted any try she made."

"If you could have in time," Sergi said flatly.

"She had to make a choice, Sergi. No choice, no disjunction. You are satisfied that she is truly disjunct?"

"I would stake my life on her," Sergi replied.

"Then my judgment was correct. Such decisions are the Sectuib's burden. Be grateful they are not yours."

Sergi was astonished—not so much at Nedd's revelation as at the fact that in all the years he had worked closely with the channel, he had taken such decisions for granted. Nedd had always been right . . . for the first time he was wrong, it would mark the end of Keon.

Nedd broke the silence. "Go find Risa and make up—you'll be giving her transfer again in a few days. And if you two should decide to take your relationship beyond that of channel and Companion, it would be the best thing that could happen to either of you."

Two days before transfer, Risa decided to ride into town. At the stable, she discovered Nedd saddling up. "I was beginning to think you never left the grounds," she told him.

"I was beginning to *feel* that way!" he replied. "It's become such a habit, I almost gave you the bank deposit—then I realized I had time to do it myself. Mind if I ride with you?"

"Not at all." Nedd could hardly call more attention to Risa's status than Sergi did.

When they were on the road to town, Nedd asked, "Are you and Sergi getting along better?"

"We work together just fine," she replied.

"That was not what I asked. A channel and her Companion cannot afford to be at odds."

"Nedd, Sergi and I have the same differences you and I have. I'd rather not argue with you, either."

"There's nothing wrong with arguing, as long as it doesn't turn into fighting."

Risa smiled. "My dad always said the same thing to Kreg and me. All right. What do you want to argue about?"

That drew a low chuckle. "Actually, I'd like some information. Kreg will pledge to Keon day after tomorrow. He still doesn't know how you've invested his inheritance."

"When we get to town, I'll show you. Before you decide to withdraw Keon's support, consider what you would do to someone you have been helping to change."

"Verla? I heard something about her starting a business, but I don't remember that she said what kind."

"A profitable one. Nedd, it could be Keon's financial salvation."

"We have never invested outside the householding," he said thoughtfully. "I wouldn't expect juncts to accept the householding as an investor."

"Some poeple are going to be prejudiced forever," Risa said, "but most are like Verla: make their lives more comfortable, and you will soon have them on your side. Too many people in this area can't find work—and can't pay their taxes. So you get drifters and unlicensed raiders. Still, I'm amazed at the way people around here can't seem to count."

"What do you mean?"

"The local pen carries enough Gens to supply roughly three-quarters of the people on the rolls. Not counting Keon's Simes, either. A good number of the local Simes must either raid across the border or be involved in some sort of scheme with Nikka, the Gendealer."

"Scheme?"

"There was a scandal at one of the Lanta pens. The local dealer was siphoning off Gens, selling them as extra kills. In bad times some local citizens couldn't pay their taxes—so why keep surplus Gens? The food money went into the dealer's pocket, along with extra funds from illegal kills. People who couldn't pay their taxes turned raider, stole other people's kills—or died. A small shortfall could be kept under wraps—but the dealer got greedy, and sold off more and more Gens illegally. Soon there weren't enough for people who *had* paid. My dad—" Risa choked over the memory.

"Risa—are you all right?" Nedd asked in concern.

"Yes. I was fifteen; Kreg was nine. Dad took us to Lanta to see the dealer, publicly caged. Execution by attrition. Shedoni." She shuddered. "I couldn't zlin— but it was bad enough. Dad said it was an object lesson, in case we ever considered being dishonest in business."

"It's barbarous," said the Sectuib.

"To steal people's kills, force them to raid or steal or die horribly? Yes. It's barbarous."

She felt Nedd zlin her. "The method of execution is equally barbarous."

She looked over at him. "I agree. And it will happen right here in Laveen if the quiet conspiracy continues to support Nikka's greed. Tannen Darley knows what's going on—or at least suspects it. He'd like to get rid of Nikka, but if *he* doesn't have the influence, who does?"

"Not Keon," Nedd replied.

"No. Not Keon. Not Darley and other honest business people. Not the farmers. None of us alone. But think of what we could do together."

"Risa—that is a lovely dream, but it won't happen. No junct will have anything to do with us."

"Oh? Let's go in here for a drink," she said as they approached Verla's, "and see how we're welcomed."

Verla had finished her remodeling. The bar had been moved to the other side of a highly polished floor. The tables and chairs were back in place, also shining with polish.

Ambru was seated on a platform at the back, playing a lively tune on his shiltpron. He played on the audial level only for the afternoon crowd—but crowd it was, more than twenty people right in the middle of the day.

There were dusty farmhands at the bar. The usual gamblers sat around the largest table, concentrating on their cards. Drifters loitering away a few hours in the warmth for the price of a drink or two occupied the small back tables.

Verla was sitting with three other women at a table near the door—but wonder of wonders, these were neither prostitutes nor townswomen, but modest farm wives, one with a baby on her knee. Such women never set foot in Laveen's saloons. How had Verla wooed them in?

"Didn't I tell you someone from Keon would stop by soon?" she asked the other women as Nedd and Risa entered. "Here's the Sectuib himself—the very man to ask!"

Some of the women looked startled; others shy, especially a young woman Verla introduced as Melli Raft, whose strong Gen accent placed her as a refugee from across the border.

When the introductions were completed, and Nedd was served porstan and Risa tea, the explanations came. The three wives ranged in age from Melli's three years past changeover to Miz Frader's some thirty years past, showing in her stooped shoulders, lined face, and sparse silver hair. Joi Sentell, the one with the baby, was somewhere between—this was her youngest of four children. Children were what they had in common—and grandchildren in Miz Frader's case.

"I got no learnin'," she said, "so my kids got none. They been grubbin' in the dirt all their lives. Cain't do much fer them no more, but I got six grandchilder, an' ain't one of 'em can read nor write. T'ain't right, no schoolin'."

"I've been telling them about the school at Keon," Verla explained. "Look at that," she said with a proud gesture toward a plaque on the wall. It was brightly painted, and lettered in a child's large but clear printing:

HOUSE RULES

1. NO KILLS ON THE PREMISES.
2. YOU START A FIGHT, YOU TAKE IT OUT-SIDE.
3. ANYTHING YOU BREAK IN A FIGHT, YOU PAY FOR.
4. NO SOLICITING.
5. YOU DON'T LIKE THE COMPANY—LEAVE.
6. GAMBLERS WELCOME. CHEATERS WILL BE THROWN OUT.
7. NO CREDIT.

"My Dinny wrote that," Verla said proudly. "His teacher helped him with spelling, but he did the lettering himself."

The women were suitably impressed, but Miz Frader asked, "If we was to send our children to your school, how do we know you wouldn't teach 'em . . . perversion?"

Nedd began, "Well, we couldn't change our—"

Risa interrupted. "Ladies, you are asking *us* a favor." Zlinning Nedd's consternation, she extended her show field to blur his. "Keon would never force its ways on anyone. What your children *observe* there, however, will be the way we live. We will hide nothing—for we have nothing to hide."

Joi's nager became a wall of revulsion. "You mean you would let little children see—?"

"Transfer?" Risa supplied the forbidden word. "No, of course not. You don't let your children watch kills, do you?"

The woman blushed furiously. "No. But would you teach them that the kill is wrong?"

"Nedd?" Risa asked. When he did not answer at once, she continued, "I don't see why you could not enroll your children in classes in reading, writing, arithmetic, history, crafts . . . and not have them attend our changeover classes. But many of Keon's teachers are Gen."

The three women looked at one another, two in horror, but the third—

Melli Raft spoke up at last, her voice so soft and frightened it could hardly be heard above the music. "I have three children. Two of them are my husband's, but I love them as my own. They took me in when I ran across the border, thinking my life was over. Except for having to—to kill, people aren't that different here." Tears rolled down her cheeks, and her field shook with agonized shyness, but she continued, "I dind't *know* there was a place where I wouldn't have to kill! I stayed on Hal's farm for over a year, just learning the new language, afraid to be away from people who accepted me—and when I learned about Keon, it was too late."

Verla put a sympathetic arm about the sobbing woman. In her own need, Risa throbbed to their regret. It was only chance that she had met Sergi when there was still time—barely—for her to disjunct. Two or three months later—

Melli leaned against Verla, swallowed hard, and looked at Joi and Miz Frader with as much defiance as her painful shyness would allow. "I don't want my children to kill. I want them in *all* the classes, not just reading and writing. If Hal objects—" She squared her thin shoulders. "I don't care. I love them too much to let them go through what I do."

Joi looked at Miz Frader. "If my kids have Gens for teachers . . . how do I stop them from growing up to feel—like her?" she gestured at Melli.

The older woman gave a sad smile. "When you've watched two sons buried, and a daughter and a grand-daughter dead tryin' to birth babies—mebbe you'll start thinkin' 'bout what kids you got left. I took Billijo to the border last summer, an' I ain't afraid t'say so. If I'd of took him to Keon—I'd *know* he was safe, an' I could see him. Some six years back, my first grandchild, Sharla, turned Gen—an' her own daddy kilt her, tryin' t'help her get away when he was in hard need hisself. That was my boy Larens, an' I allus thought he grieved hisself to a early grave over killin' his firstborn." She sat back in her chair, the weight of years bowing her shoulders. "Nature's kind to most Simes—they don't live long enough t'see what I seen. Don't make no sense t'kill what you love." She shook her head. "Just don't make no sense."

Joi licked her lips, outnumbered. "My husband'd whup me if he thought our kids—"

"Your husband whups your kids," said Miz Frader. "You oughta whup *him* a time or two—teach him what fer! He give you any argument, you give me a holler!"

Risa sat in amazement, watching the three women persuade themselves that their children belonged in Keon's classes. This was the best possible way to have Keon accepted by the community: educate the children. Train them to increase the produce on their farms, or give them a trade. That ironmongery Nedd had said was impossible—with the cooperation of the community—

When the women had gone, Verla ordered more porstan for herself and Nedd, and a fresh glass of tea for Risa. "This is . . . your investment?" Nedd asked. The clientele had changed, those who had left during the discussion replaced by others. The two channels were being zlinned curiously, but only a few people bore resentment in their nager.

"You told him?" Verla asked.

"Keon owns Kreg's share," Risa explained.

"You seem busy for this time of day," Nedd observed.

"You ain't seen nothin' yet!" Verla replied. "We're ready for a grand opening. Risa, you'll have transfer soon—"

"In two days."

"Fine! Then we'll have it that night. You come post for the best time. Nedd, please come, and bring your wife—and any of the other channels that can get away. And Gens. Risa, don't you dare come without Sergi! You folks are gonna be a big attraction."

"Verla," said Nedd, "what if people get drunk and mean?"

"Rule Two. You start a fight, you take it outside. Those rules are gonna keep this a nice place where families can come. A place where people can cut loose and have a good time—and have nothing more than a headache in the morning!"

Even in her approaching need, Risa was excited about the official opening. "We'll be there," she promised.

Sergi, too, was pleased at the prospect of a party—a double party, for Keon would have the pledge ceremony for Kreg and Triffin early that evening. Most of the householders would remain on the grounds, and probably celebrate well into the night, while Risa, Sergi, Nedd, Litith, and Gevron went to Verla's grand opening.

Kreg wanted to go, too, but he and Triffin were the guests of honor at Keon's celebration, so Risa promised to tell him everything that happened, and to take him to the shiltpron parlor soon. Actually, she was glad to delay his first excursion off Keon's grounds as a Gen; a shiltpron party was not the place for him to test his new abilities.

In her brother's honor, Risa wore one of Keon's red capes, a floor-length ritual style in lighter material than the ones worn outdoors. When she walked, it floated impressively behind her—a fun garment until she walked through the swinging doors into the dining hall, and they closed on the cape, bringing her up sharp, to the giggles of the children eating an early supper.

Risa laughed, too, as she untangled the cape and joined Sergi. They had just had transfer, all their differences forgotten in the joy of sharing life.

As they got up to stack their dishes, Risa caught her cape under her chair leg, and sat ungracefully at the tug.

"This is ridiculous," she said as she extricated herself again. Sergi picked up her tray and deposited it on the counter, unhampered by his cape. "How come you don't catch your cape on things?"

"Oh, Gens are just a little smarter than Simes," he replied with a grin, "but since you're so useful to us, we try not to let you know it."

The schedule had been juggled to allow everyone a free evening. The dining tables were removed, the chairs set against the walls. A platform was set up and draped in red—and the hall filled with Simes, Gens, and children in red capes as the hour of pledging approached.

Sergi brought out a length of lightweight white-enameled chain. Risa watched in revulsion as he measured lengths of it to fit about the necks of all the channels and Companions—symbolic of the heavy white-painted chains raiders used for makeshift collars on the Gens they captured.

She understood intellectually that the chain represented the choice of being bound to the householding—but when she saw it clasped tightly about her brother's throat, she shuddered. Thank goodness the householders wore them only for ritual occasions.

Risa's heart caught in her throat as she watched her little brother pledge his life to the strange ideals of Keon. When Nedd placed the ring on Kreg's finger, and embraced him, she blinked back tears.

Then it was Triffin's turn, and Keon's two newest members turned to face their new family. A cheer went up, and music started. Fiddle and banjo broke into a lively reel, and dancers whirled onto the floor.

Kreg fought his way to Risa's side, and hugged her against him. She felt his tears on her cheeks as he murmured into her ear, "Oh, Risa, don't turn away from us. Please!"

She noted the "us." "Kreg—I'm very happy for you," she told him.

"Give Risa time, Kreg," Sergi said. "She'll discover that her place is here, too."

Then Triffin came to hug Risa and Sergi, saying, "Now I've got a real home and family—oh, thank you for giving me the courage to come here!"

Then she and Kreg were pulled into the circle of dancers, laughing as they fumbled through the unfamiliar steps. Soon they had the figures, though, and Risa was startled to find herself thinking that Kreg and Triffin looked good together. Were they interested in one another? Kreg was too young . . . she thought.

Risa didn't know when a Gen's sexual interest began. For a Sime it was usually three months after change-over. She had had her first experience then, kind of sweet and fumbling, but nothing to make her want a permanent relationship. That all seemed so long ago now, in another lifetime!

She hadn't given sex a thought since then. She had suffered shortings and unsatisfactory kills, then gone off with her father on their trading expedition. After that, disorientation, disjunction . . . she had been in no condition to feel strange sweet yearnings that now ran through her as she tapped her foot in time to the music.

Risa took off her cape as most of the other dancers did, and lost herself in the music. The changing figures brought Sergi to her side. When he swung her, he picked her right up off the floor, and she felt safe in his arms, just as she felt safe leaning on his field in her time of need. To think of a Gen as strong was foreign to everything she had grown up with, yet Sergi's strengths were undeniable.

The patterns of the dance separated them again, and when the musicians took a break, parents began gathering children to put them to bed. The party would continue, but Risa and Sergi had other obligations. Nedd and Litith were ready, and Gevron was going with them, no other Gens. Everyone in the party but Risa wore heavy red wool capes. She put on her old brown cape against the light stinging snow.

They arrived at Verla's red-cheeked from the cold, to find her party in full swing. Here, too, people were dancing, but the music was Ambru's shiltpron—ringing on the nageric level as well as the audial. When the Gens arrived, the ambient shifted markedly. The dancers halted, zlinning. Every eye in the place focused on the group from Keon as Verla hurried to greet them. "I've saved you a table," she told them. "Gigh! Drinks for my friends!"

The bartender set porstan before them, his nager a forced neutrality.

Ambru kept playing. The stares continued, but the Gen fields echoed the nageric pulses of the shiltpron, soothing the ambient into pleasing harmony. Joi Sentell was there, with a man who must be her husband. He stared resentfully at the Keon party as they entered, but made no move.

At a back table, Tannen Darley sat drinking porstan, his daughter Susi beside him. Her pink party dress was crisp, but the child herself was pale and uncertain. Darley's eyes followed Risa's every move, but he, too, remained where he was. There were too many people between them for her to read his field clearly; she wondered what he was thinking. Did he know that half this place belonged to Keon? How could he not know, since all the monetary transactions went through his bank? But he was here, lending his considerable authority to their venture.

Eventually the novelty wore off. People went back to drinking and dancing. Verla, circulating as a good hostess, came by and asked, "Why don't you folks dance?" and Nedd and Litith took the floor. No one objected. When they sat down, Verla approached again, urging, "Risa—Sergi—show us your style. Come on, Gevron—dance with me!"

Poor Gevron's embarrassment burst upon the ambient like a wash of cold water. Verla laughed. "Now you've done it—no one will be satisfied until you strut your stuff."

The Companion realized that all eyes were on him, and judged rightly that the quickest way to lose their attention was to dance. So he got up, bowed to Verla, and led her onto the dance floor. As everyone else backed off, Risa quickly grasped Sergi's hand, and they joined the other Sime/Gen couple. Ambru struck up a waltz.

The musician's artistry turned the dance into magic. Risa melted into Sergi's arms, moving to the sweeping rhythms as Ambru charged the ambient with nageric tones in rhythm with the two Gens' heartbeats—until the rhythms blended into one. Counterpoint of iambic heartbeat—selyn production rhythm—and dactylic waltz cadence came together, reflecting the impossible blend of Sime and Gen.

When the music ended, there was absolute stillness in the room. As the couples returned to the Keon table, only hushed whispers broke the silence.

Then the ambient was shattered with brutal force as a harsh voice demanded from the doorway, "Hey! Where's yer killroom?"

Chapter Nine

Risa recognized Nikka, proprietor of the local pen. She was dressed to kill—quite literally, for she tugged along a shivering Gen in a stained white smock. The loose garment hid sexual characteristics, and the Gen's features were hidden under windblown hair. It was a Gen as Risa had known Gens all her life—until Sergi. It was frightened and miserably cold, its legs bruised where Nikka had kicked it along.

Nikka wore a gaudy dress. In contrast, her field rang with hard need. She wanted to kill that Gen—immediately.

Verla stepped forward. "No kills on these premises. After you have killed at home, come join the fun."

"I thought this was a shiltpron parlor," Nikka said with heavy sarcasm.

"It is," Verla replied. "Porstan, shiltpron, dancing—everything for a good time. But no killing."

"Ain't no fun without kills! Hey—I got some extras. Lemme bring 'em up, we'll dance 'em around, beat 'em up—"

"Nikka, you will leave quietly or I will remove you." Tannen Darley had moved up behind Verla.

"Shen and shid, Tan—you goin' over t' the perverts?" Nikka gave an obscene giggle. She gestured toward

Risa and Sergi, dripping ronaplin from her lateral orifices. "Them two's post as post. What you folks been zlinnin' 'fore I got here? An' where *you* gettin' yer selyn these days, Tan?"

Unknowingly, the woman had hit a nerve. The banker stepped forward as Verla said, "Tan—no!"

"Daddy—make her go away!" Susi Darley wailed.

Darley stalked menacingly forward. "This is a family place. Everyone has acted with courtesy—until *you* arrived. Go take your kill in private, as ladies and gentlemen do. We will not allow you to spoil our pleasant evening, Nikka."

The woman looked past him, toward some of the other local people. "Hey—you gonna let this spoilsport—"

Tripp Sentell got up, and stood shoulder to shoulder with Tannen Darley. "You been asked nice to leave. Now git!" He raised a threatening hand. Other people joined the two men.

"Shedoni-doomed fools, all of you! You'll be sorry fer protectin' them perverts—they'll steal yer children, turn 'em into wer-Gens an' use 'em fer dirty, disgusting—"

"That's enough!" said Verla. "No one insults my guests. Take your Gen, and don't come back."

Nikka finally recognized that she had gone too far. She turned sullenly, with an ineffective, "You'll be sorry!" and dragged her Gen off into the darkness.

Embarrassed relief flooded the ambient. Darley told Verla, "Maybe it's a good thing your rule was tested. Now everyone knows this is the family entertainment place Laveen's been lacking."

A murmur of agreement rose, making Verla blush and smile. As the others who had gone to her defense returned to their tables, Verla moved toward the Keon party, Darley following.

Nedd rose. "We'll leave before any further incidents."

"You sit right back down!" said Verla. "Nobody's got the right to drive you out of your own place."

"You will soon make enough profit to buy out Keon's

share," Nedd told her. "Meanwhile, no one has to know—"

"Everyone knows already, Mr. Varnst," said Tannen Darley. "Verla has made no secret of it—nor has it harmed business. Zlin the ambient. If you should decide to sell, I will gladly purchase your share at any time."

"Well, I—" Nedd fumbled.

Darley said, "I suggest that you consult Miz Tigue. I cannot help noticing that Keon has achieved solvency since she began handling your finances." Then he turned to Risa, who was fighting the urge to kick Nedd under the table.

"Risa," said the banker with a slight bow, "would you join my daughter and me? I have something to say to you."

Ignoring the warning in Sergi's nager, Risa joined Darley and his little girl at their table. When they were seated, he said, "I apologize, Risa—although my exposing your association with Keon has done you little harm."

"Actually, it led me into this very profitable venture."

"Which will pull money from the pockets of transients and into my bank, so everybody profits," he said with a smile. "Nonetheless, I do apologize. Susi told me everything. The Gen tricked Susi into helping it escape."

Risa wondered how he could refer to Triffin as "it." Even the poor creature Nikka had killed by now was a person.

The junct defense mechanism became glaringly obvious. Risa felt a surge of sympathy toward Tannen Darley and all his kind: good people who could not survive if they acknowledged that their lives continued at the expense of other people's.

Darley misinterpreted Risa's sympathetic reponse. "Susi's been ill. I hoped you would explain to her—"

The child's huge blue eyes fastened on Risa's. "Why can't you give my daddy selyn every month, so he won't ever have to kill somebody?"

Darley waited in painful silence for Risa's answer. With equal directness, she replied, "Because if your daddy tried to stop killing now, at his age, *he* would die."

Shock rang through Susi's childish nager. Then she flung herself onto her father's lap, hugging him tightly. "Oh, Daddy, I'm sorry! I love you. I don't want you to die!"

Darley looked over the girl's head, and mouthed the words, "Is that true?"

Risa nodded solemnly, wondering why Verla hadn't told him, then remembering that her profession included listening to men's troubles, not telling them her own.

People were looking at them from the corner table. Darley said, "It's time to go home, Susi—past your bedtime."

Susi stretched out her hand to Risa. "Please," she said, "come home with us. I have to ask you things—"

Darley added, "Please, Risa. And tell her the truth. I'd rather lose her to Keon than to kill trauma."

Kill trauma was a leading cause of death in changeover. A child who saw a kill—especially of a family member or close friend—might become hysterical during his own changeover, using up his last reserves of life force before his tentacles emerged. Unable to draw selyn, he died of attrition. Susi might never have actually seen a kill, but she had all the warning signs of traumatic changeover.

It could have happened to Kreg, after he saw Alis killed.

So Risa went home with the Darleys, ignoring the flare of denial in Sergi's nager when she stopped at the Keon table to tell them not to wait for her.

She helped Susi get ready for bed, explaining that a Sime need never kill if started on channel's transfer at changeover. "But even if you kill them, you don't have to continue. You have First Year to disjunct—to stop killing. It's much harder, but it can be done. I did it."

"You killed?"

"Yes—but in First Year I decided to stop. You can make that decision, too, Susi—if you want to."

"I won't ever kill at all," the girl said determinedly.

Her father, who was standing in the doorway listening, said, "I'll take you to Keon, Susi—I promise."

Risa expected Darley to tuck his daughter in, but he left the room after his painful promise. So she pulled the covers up to the girl's chin and kissed her on the forehead, saying, "Sleep now. Your daddy will take care of you."

With an angelic smile, Susi fell at once into the deep sleep of childhood.

When she had been in this house before, Risa had had only a quick impression of the elegant parlor. Now Darley stood before the fireplace. Sparkling crystal tea glasses gleamed on the mantel in Sergi's silver holders. Darley was looking up at the portrait of a woman . . . obviously Susi's mother.

"Tan—"

He turned when she spoke, and she saw tears on his face. "Oh, Tan, *don't!* You're not going to lose your daughter—now you can't possibly lose her." She looked into his troubled eyes and added, "Not even if she turns Gen."

His last control gave way when she voiced every loving parent's greatest fear. He sat down on a small, elegant sofa, and cried—deep, cleansing tears.

It didn't last long; he was not a man to indulge emotions. He wiped his eyes, and looked at Risa. "I can't go with her," he said flatly.

"No . . . but you wouldn't want to. After all you've built here—"

"What good is it? All my money couldn't save Lita's life. It couldn't do anything for Susi. Risa—are you sure I can't stop killing? What you did to me—mostly you scared shen out of me. Why can't you—?"

"We can't do it *to* you, Tan. Even if you were young

enough, you couldn't do it because Susi rejects the kill. Only because *you* do."

"I could learn. I had almost made up my mind—"

"Susi accepts the facts. Now you accept them, Tan. You cannot disjunct, but your daughter can be nonjunct."

She felt his emotions normalize. He was very much her kind of person, a realist. She liked him—and he felt it. He took her hand, his handling tentacles sliding over her skin.

He was lonely. How easy it would be to slide into his arms and ease his loneliness, her desire—

But he was zlinning her deeply, and a rueful smile curved his lips as he said, "It's not me you want, Risa."

"I'm sorry," she whispered.

"Don't be. I'm going to need a friend much more than a lover." She noticed his deliberate use of the word "need."

"I'll be your friend, any time you want me. Susi's friend, too."

"I'll take you back to Verla's," he said.

"Susi—"

"One of my men is outside. And for the first time in two months I know she won't wake up with nightmares."

As they walked through the cold, crisp darkness, Darley commented, "That shiltpron parlor may be the best thing that's ever happened to Laveen. I thought it would be disruptive—you know the kind of goings on they usually have."

"What Nikka expected."

"Yes. But Verla will keep the riffraff out." He laughed. "I never thought Tripp Sentell and I would stand shoulder-to-shoulder. That a shiltpron parlor owned by householders should bring the farmers and the town together."

"I'd like to see even more cooperation," Risa said, and told him her idea for mining in Gen Territory. "Keon has the knowledge, but not the funds to build an ironmongery, or access to enough metal to make it worthwhile."

"Now *that* is an idea worth exploring!" said Darley as he opened the door to Verla's for her.

Ambru was playing and singing, the audience spellbound, listening and zlinning. Only Sergi remained at the Keon table. Risa was momentarily indignant that he had assumed she would come back for him—but the music was too beautiful to spoil with opposing emotions.

Ambru's voice was as worn as his body, carrying an overload of experience. He sang an outlaw ballad in which the hero outwitted the law time after time, only to end his life by fleeing into Gen territory, shot down by Gen militia rather than facing death by attrition if captured by Simes.

Shifting mood, Ambru broke into a rollicking change-over celebration song, setting feet tapping all around the room. Sergi's nager pulsed in rhythm to the joyful music. People turned toward them, encouraging more.

Ambru changed the mood again, to a love ballad. Sergi's field amplified the emotions flowing on the nageric level. Risa felt a pang of sympathy that his Genness cut him off from experiencing the combination of audial and nageric music.

Risa was seated to Sergi's right. He put his right arm around her, taking her hand, then took her left hand in his.

Risa was overwhelmed. She seemed not only to hear and zlin the music, but to feel, see, taste, smell it. They became performers and work, building their own world.

When the music ended, Risa looked up at Sergi, and realized that he had missed nothing.

Always she had thought, *He does amazing things . . . for a Gen. He's very perceptive . . . for a Gen.*

She had thought she accepted Gens as people—but she had perceived them as handicapped, incomplete people . . . or as children. No wonder she had not seen Sergi as a man.

Without a word, they got up and went outside. On the porch, Sergi drew Risa into his arms, wrapping his

cape about both of them against the sharp wind. He
kissed her, his lips warm and yielding. Risa, balancing
on her toes, became breathless and had to break the
kiss, although she wanted more. "Let's go home," she
murmured.

He smiled and replied, "This place belongs to us.
One-quarter yours, one-quarter mine. We'd better hurry
if we want to find an empty room."

Sensing her shyness, he led her around to the back
door. They went through Verla's kitchen, where one of
her employees was boiling up hot water to wash glasses,
and into the hallway lined with bedrooms. The insulation was entirely adequate; Verla had taken Risa's sensitivity as her standard. Risa ducked into the first empty
room, watched with great relief as Sergi closed and
latched the door, then felt herself blush violently, her
heart pounding, as he turned to face her.

He was so large, so masculine . . . nervousness prick-
led her skin as she felt his desire. He paused, puzzlement in his nager. "Risa . . . don't tell me you've
never—?"

"O-only with a Sime," she managed.

He laughed, but it was in delight, not derision. He
took off her cape and his own, hanging them on the
pegs provided. Then he kissed her again—and again as
he began to undress her, layer by layer of winter clothing giving them time to become accustomed, to become
aroused. . . .

Caught up in Sergi's desire, Risa participated in the
unveiling, her tentacles undoing all his shirt buttons at
once, sliding cloth over skin until at last skin met skin,
the full length of her body pressed to his cool/warm
Gen strength.

He laid her down—but when he put one knee on the
bed to lie down beside her, she said, "Wait. Let me look
at you."

Not only had she never seen him naked before—he
had never been so much as shirtless with her, even in
summer.

The night they had met she had stripped and bathed in the rain, unselfconscious because he had been Gen, not person, to her then. But he had preserved his dignity and her growing sensitivity. Thus his nudity was new to her, in keeping with her new perception of him. She smiled in appreciation.

"You're beautiful," she said. "Like one of your own sculptures." She laid her head on his shoulder and let her hand and tentacles play across his chest.

He pulled her close and kissed her again, then murmured, "I love the way you see me. I love to look at you. I love you, Risa."

Passion surged quickly, then grew again more slowly, with time to explore and experiment until they lay quivering in each other's arms. Sergi said, tightening his arms around her, "I can't imagine anything better."

"There isn't," Risa said, snuggling closer.

"Lortuen—the LOT relationships. They're supposed to be better."

"What's a lortuen?" Risa asked languidly.

"What a Sime and a Gen are perfect matchmates nagerically, and also happen to be of opposite sexes, their transfer relationship carries over into their sexual relationship. It's supposed to be beyond anything we mere mortals ever know."

Risa lifted her head so she could look into his eyes. "But that's what we have," she said.

"No—although I never *want* to have transfer with anyone but you, it is still physically possible. In a LOT relationship, the systems of the Sime and Gen become so perfectly attuned that they *cannot* touch anyone else. If they can't have one another for transfer, they will die."

Sergi was speaking dreamily, a soft smile curving his lips. "You'd *like* that!" Risa said in astonishment.

His smile changed to a laugh. "Lortuen's probably just a myth anyway." He kissed her. "We have love—and that's enough for anybody. Nedd was right not to pressure you. Now we can have your pledge ceremony and our wedding at once."

With a hard shove against his chest that knocked the breath out of him, Risa sat up, staring. "Shen and shid! If you can't chain me with some weird nageric thing, you want to tie me down with vows! I'm not ready to get married—and certainly not to a—"

"Gen?" he asked, his nager as icy blue as his eyes.

"To a householder," she said, hoping he could tell she meant it. "Is that why you seduced me? Was this all Nedd's idea? Won't you people *ever* trust my word? I gave Keon a promise—and that's bloody-shen good enough for a Tigue."

Sergi was too stunned to move. Risa pulled on her clothes, and with the thick braid of her hair hanging down her back like a child's, she grabbed her cape off the peg and stormed out, slamming the door.

As if released from a spell, Sergi grabbed his clothes. It was one time he desperately wished for tentacles, as his fingers fumbled at buttons while his feet met no success at getting into his boots without the help of his hands.

By the time he reached the front door, Risa was gone. His horse was still tied where he had left it—but he could not even hear the hoofbeats of Risa's.

His impulse was to ride after her, but it was nearly midwinter; dawn would not break for several hours, and the overcast sky provided no light.

He turned—and faced a roomful of junct Simes.

The shiltpron parlor had emptied out until only about twenty people remained. Several were still drinking. Ambru was sitting at the largest round table with Tannen Darley and almost a dozen other men and women.

Before someone noticed him and started trouble, Sergi went up to the bar and told Verla, "I'm afraid I've lost my escort. Nedd will send someone for me, but. . . ."

"Don't you worry," she told him. "You're my guest. I'll escort you to Keon later this morning. I'm gonna close up pretty soon anyway." She leaned across the bar. "What happened? Risa ran out of here like her tail was on fire."

"We . . . had a misunderstanding."

Verla sighed. "That girl! Don't worry, Sergi—she'll soon realize that you're the best thing ever happened to her."

Verla began doling out steaming glasses, saying, "No more porstan, folks! We'll reopen at noon—have a nice glass of tea now and go home and sleep it off. Anybody want fosebine?"

There were ritual protests, and one man proceeded to pass out, but no one was angry or vicious.

Verla collected empty porstan glasses at the big round table, and without thinking Sergi picked up the tray of tea glasses and started passing them out, mindless work to keep his attention off his latest rift with Risa.

He sensed that he was being zlinned. He kept his thoughts, and hence his field, neutral. He was low-field, but he knew perfectly well that he far outshone any pen Gen.

Any abrupt change could provoke a junct. He continued smoothly setting out glasses, as if he had noticed nothing. The tray empty, he started to retreat to the bar, intending to try to blend into the furnishings—

"Sergi." It was Darley. A junct calling him by name? "Come join us. You can probably answer our questions."

"How may I help you?" Sergi asked warily, taking the empty chair between Darley and Zabrina, owner of the largest saloon in town. What was she doing patronizing Verla's?

"Risa says Keon could make many useful implements, if you had a good supply of metal."

"That's true," said Sergi.

Darley picked up a glass holder. "We've all been using these the past few months. Beautiful craftsmanship. Applied to plowshares, wheel-rims, knives, ax-heads. . . ."

There were nods all around the table. "Good money in all that," said a man dressed as a farmer. "I pay enough for it!"

"Sergi, can Keon do it?" Darley asked.

"Make knives and plowshares? We could, but—"

"No more buts," said Darley. "We'll get you the metal. But Keon has to cooperate."

"Cooperate?"

"We're going into Gen Territory—Risa's idea. Mine those deposits the Gens aren't using. People we've got—there's not much work till spring planting. The farmers have wagons, horses, and mules. Zabrina, Quent, Brevit and I will put up money for mining tools. Will Keon do its part?"

"What part is that?" Sergi asked, quelling astonishment.

"Keon has Risa, to guide us to where she zlinned those metal deposits . . . and Keon has Gens to front for us."

"Front—?"

"How's your English, Sergi?" Darley asked in that language.

"Supposedly perfect," he replied in the same language. "My teachers came from Gen Territory—I've never lived there."

"But some Keon Gens have?" Darley switched back to Simelan, both because his English was not particularly good and because several people around the table obviously understood nothing of the exchange. Sergi followed suit.

"Yes, but . . . I have no authority to involve Keon," he explained. "Only our Sectuib can make such a decision."

"Well," said Darley, pushing his chair back, "*we're* all agreed."

"I'll get my friends together this evening," said the farmer. "This is the best deal we've had in years!"

"I'll ride out to Keon today," said Darley. "Sergi—will you ride with me, so they'll let me in?"

"Of course," Sergi replied, holding in utter incredulity.

"Good. Finish your business with Verla. I'll go check on my daughter, and be back for you at dawn."

Darley seemed to think Sergi was doing him a favor, and the Companion did not disabuse him. When they reached the hall outside Nedd's office, though, the truth was driven home very quickly. The office might be selyn-shielded, but shouts came through the door rather well. It was Nedd shouting, angrily, a sound Sergi had rarely heard before.

"I don't care *what* he did—you had no right to desert a Companion in a town full of juncts! Now you hie yourself back there, young lady—if anything's happened to Sergi—"

"Nedd—Nedd, I'm perfectly all right," Sergi said as he pushed open the door and let his field soothe the emotions pulsating in the small room.

Risa turned to him, anger outweighing relief. "Why did you risk riding out here alone? You were safe with Verla. Shen it, Sergi—I'd just changed my whole perception of you—I forgot you were in danger without an escort."

"I found my own escort," he replied as Tannen Darley entered. Then he had the pleasure of watching their growing amazement, followed by the amusement of watching Risa and Darley run roughshod over Nedd to make him agree to their plan. All in all a scene worth a few nervous moments in town.

Within the hour it was settled—as soon as the special implements could be brought from Lanta, they would go prospecting in Gen territory.

Risa enjoyed the excitement of planning, even though it overloaded her schedule. Nedd balked at her assumption that she would lead the expedition, and had to be reminded daily that she was the one who knew where the metal deposits were.

Those more affluent put up money or supplies; many other town and farm Simes contributed labor. The juncts grumbled at the condition that no one be close to need—and that there would be no raiding of out-Territory Gens. Companions were the only Gens going from Keon. Sergi would accompany Risa, of course. Sintha, whom Risa had gotten to know only slightly before, drilled everyone, Sime and Gen, in English.

"If you can shout to someone in unaccented English," she told the Simes, "you have more than doubled the chances that he won't come close enough to see that you're Sime."

Kreg insisted on going. When Risa objected, he said, "I know I'm not completely grown up yet. If the Gens see kids in our party, we'll look even less suspicious."

"But your English—"

"Has improved considerably," Sintha put in. "Kreg can pretend to be a Gen recently escaped from Sime Territory. Get Sergi to carve you a starred-cross, Kreg. Many escapees wear them all their lives for good luck."

Sintha was a woman of middle age, her skin creased, her hair streaked with gray. She had the robust good health of everyone at Keon, and a motherly air compounded by her role as teacher. Risa asked her, "Won't you be tempted to stay on the other side of the border, once you're home?"

"No. There's nothing for me there but terrible memories. The raiders who captured me killed my husband and his parents, and murdered our two children. That was all the family I had. I suppose I could have gone back, and claimed that burnt-out house on forty acres— but I didn't want to live with ghosts. Keon is alive, Risa, and you've made it even more so. I don't understand why you still refuse to pledge."

The question came up time and again, from Kreg, from Sergi—only Nedd never asked it, and the junct Simes who assumed that Risa was ambrov Keon already. But something held her back from pledging— and from marrying Sergi.

She could no longer deny that she found him attractive. If she would not admit it in her waking hours, her dreams made it very clear. But they had resumed their post-transfer schedule, and with preparations for the mining expedition they hardly saw one another except when they were working.

Finally the day came. Before dawn, the party from Keon rode into Laveen. It was their last chance for such a journey this year. Another month, and snow would keep the wagons from getting through. With the first expedition only begun, there was already talk of making it an annual event.

There was another reason to make their expedition now: if the Gens didn't know the reasons, they knew the patterns of Sime raids. Harvest brought work, and tax money for the fall quarter. At the beginning of the new year, though, many were without funds—and the year's worst weather found Simes raiding in desperation, one by one.

"It's the most frightening time of year," Sintha recalled. "In summer, between planting and harvest, licensed raiders strike—but they can be seen. People get guns and fight back. The winter Sime strikes in the dark, without warning. My father died that way.

"The first months of the new year," she continued, "the border patrol is doubled. If we're there and back before year's turning, chances are we won't be noticed."

Risa zlinned the people gathered at Verla's—and found three men and two women within a week of hard need. "You were supposed to take early kills," she reminded them. "We won't be back in time. Go over to the pen—"

"Nikka won't give us no Gens," protested Tripp Sentell.

"She can't refuse when you're in need." The law said any Sime past turnover could claim his Gen for the month—although he could have no more than twelve government-supplied Gens per year. In winter people took them as early as possible.

"Nikka is claiming a shortage," Tannen Darley explained. "She's trying to undermine our plans, Risa. She doesn't approve of the cooperation between the town, the farmers, and the householding."

"A few days ago she claimed to have extras."

"She's sold them. I checked. She can't be hiding any extras in that place. She's invoked the two-day rule."

"When did this happen?"

"Yesterday," Sentell replied.

"Well, come on," said Risa, "you know what to do."

The man bristled. "If you mean take selyn from *you*, that's goin' too bloody-shen far!"

"No, of course not! All of you close to need—go load up the wagons. Augment, while the rest of us conserve. Get yourselves *down* to a two-day supply of selyn, and then claim your kills. Hurry, now—we don't want to be late starting!"

The five looked at one another. The Sentells and one of the other men were farmers; the others worked as hired hands. None were ever in a position to waste selyn, lest they have to buy an extra kill they couldn't afford. But augmentation was fun, and the expedition promised money—

Five augmenting Simes easily rearranged the supplies brought by the three groups of people in the time it would have taken if everyone had worked at a conservative pace.

All five were in Nikka's killrooms by the time the wagon train passed the pen. Nikka was outside, her resentment an ugly smear on the ambient. Several other Simes were with her, three of whom had been refused a part in the expedition because Tannen Darley said they could not be trusted not to run off to raid Gens.

"You'll be sorry, Tan," Nikka shouted, "takin' up with them perverts! All a you—you just wait! It ain't smart to insult yer Gendealer."

There was some nervous reaction to her words—the Gendealer held the power of life and death in a small community like this one—but as the train moved on, soon joined by the five stragglers now post and in high spirits, the excitement of high expectations returned.

They proceeded northward to their first obstacle: the small river, a tributary of the Mizipi, which formed the border here. It was easy enough for a rider, but the wagons had to be pushed and hauled, their wheels bogging down even now. Their greatest challenge would be getting those same wagons back across the river laden with metal.

By the time they were across, it was growing dark, but they went on for several hours before making camp. If they hadn't had Gens with them, they probably would not have stopped at all—but even the juncts knew that those Gens were their safeguard against recognition and capture.

They made only a small fire to prepare tea and soup. People doubled up to keep warm, Risa and Sergi snuggled up together for the first time since that fateful night at Verla's. In heavy winter garments, they could hardly feel romantic, but Risa enjoyed the feel of Sergi's arms about her, his nager warming her very soul.

When it was Risa's turn to stand guard, Sergi accompanied her, as silent as a Sime while she zlinned in every direction and reported no one within her considerable range. Then, for the first time since the shiltpron party, he asked, "Risa—I believe you when you say you refuse to marry me because I'm a householder, and not because I'm Gen. But I still don't understand why you refuse a householder."

"I won't be chained," she replied for what seemed the thousandth time. "Sergi, Keon claims its virtue is freedom, yet your symbol shows clearly that it isn't so. I don't understand why the Simes don't see it. You, I can understand. You are free from fear at Keon—"

"I am at Keon because I am free from fear," he replied. "You've got it backwards."

"No, I haven't. Outside the householding some Sime

would slit your throat just for existing. Keon is the only place you can live. No wonder you feel a false freedom there."

"Risa—I am as free as you are," he told her. "I'm young and strong, I know the Gen language, I have skills. Why—I could ride off today, find a Gen community without a blacksmith, work at that until I made enough to start silversmithing—in five years I'd be rich as Tannen Darley."

"Why didn't you do that years ago?"

"Ask Kreg," he replied, his nager a strange combination of satisfaction and frustration. "There's no life for a Companion away from Simes. Would you want to stop channeling?"

"Not entirely," she admitted. "I just don't see why I can't trade services with Keon."

"For my 'services,' you mean?" he asked indignantly.

"Why do you always act as if that would be a form of prostitution? I don't see anything wrong with your being paid for your talent as a Companion. You expect to be paid for your talent as a jeweler."

He hunched up against the cold, sinking his hands deep into the pockets of his heavy Gen-style jacket. "We're back to symbols—and perhaps I do react as irrationally to that one as you do to Keon's chain. Risa, do you remember reading about the first Sime/Gen community, before householdings?"

"Freedom Township? Yes—but it's mostly legends."

"It's still a good example of choosing one's chains. Before Zeor was founded, when Simes and Gens first started living together without killing, they just lived in a town like any other in-Territory. That is history, not legend."

"So?"

"The Gens of Freedom Township had to wear tags identifying them as Sime property. On the other hand, they traveled freely, not requiring Sime escort. But neither Simes nor Gens in that early community had protection under the law. The government labeled it a Genfarm, called all children with at least one Gen parent preGens subject to property laws and taxes—and to escape those chains, the first householders had to choose other chains of their own making. To *choose*, Risa. They chose to separate themselves from junct society, so that within their walls Gens could have equality. Eventually they won rights for us outside the walls, too. I have no tags, no papers saying I am property."

"You're taxed like property," Risa pointed out. "I know—I keep Keon's books."

"Look up the law," Sergi told her. "A householding is not a Genfarm, nor are its Gens property—we are taxable people. It's a compromise. The government still gets its money—but householding Gens get their dignity."

"Symbols," said Risa.

"The householdings gained more than mere symbols. All householding children have the same rights as children of Simes; none are labeled preGen, and cannot be counted as property. To gain those freedoms for their children, householders accept other restrictions—chains, if you will."

"I see what you mean," Risa admitted. "None of us is completely free; we can only choose some of the restrictions on our lives."

"Exactly!" Sergi's nager rang with relief and joy.

The first pale gray of dawn was lighting the sky. The Simes were all up, breaking camp. Risa looked at Sergi's face, so eager and hopeful . . . yet she had to tell him the truth. "I am not sure I want Keon's restrictions. I don't like being shut in, Sergi. Let's dissolve the barriers between Keon and Laveen—and maybe someday, if we can't get rid of Keon's walls, at least the gates can be open!"

The barriers dropped steadily. The farther from the border, the more farms they passed, although they carefully avoided settlements. Late that morning they met a couple of boys herding cows along the road. The

Simes huddled in the wagons or rode in the middle of the group, hoping their thick winter clothing would disguise them. The Gens moved to the edges, waving cheerfully to the boys and exchanging guesses as to when the first "sticking snow" would fall.

If Gens could zlin, thought Risa as the ambient pulsed with nervous tension, *we'd be caught in no time.*

But when boys and cattle were left safely behind, tension eased. The fear that the Gens would betray them was assuaged. Halting conversations began, first between the juncts and the householding Simes, then between juncts and Gens.

At their destination, the barriers dropped even farther. It was a treasure trove! Gens stripped frozen vines away, and Simes dug into the mounds, peeling away dirt, rotted wood, ancient brick, and pulling out rusty beams, green copper wire, whole sheets of metal encrusted with crazed enameling. They even found cooking utensils of the strange Ancient metal that did not decompose—a thorough scrubbing, and those items would pay half the cost of the expedition!

High spirits and good fellowship prevailed as they loaded the wagons, and covered the traces of their digging. If no one came here before the kudzu grew back next spring, all signs of their excavation would be covered over.

Risa's patrol encompassed a wide perimeter, prepared to sound a warning if anyone came near. Of course no one did—what would Gens be doing in the frozen woods at this time of year? Sintha had assured them that the deer hunting season was over. All they had to worry about was someone following the path they had cut for the wagons—but that hadn't happened yet.

Sergi and Sintha rode out to Risa, their Companions' peculiar senses leading them straight to her. How fortunate out-Territory Gens, living away from Simes, never developed such sensitivity!

Both Gens were rosy-cheeked with cold and excitement. "We're almost ready," Sergi told her. "Ride on ahead along the trail, to zlin that no one's coming in from the road."

As Risa rode ahead of the Gens, her laterals extended for greatest sensitivity, she zlinned a strange metallic deposit beneath the woodland floor near the road. There were hundreds of such sites in Gulf Sime Territory, a frustration to the Simes who could zlin that they were composed of a thin, wide layer of precious metal, oxidized and intermixed with loam and debris. But there was no way to separate the powdered iron from the other material.

Risa pointed it out to the Gens, who could of course see nothing but more forest. Sintha said, "Up in the northeast, Gens mine that material and turn it into steel."

"Yes," Sergi replied casually, "with a blast furnace."

Risa pulled up her horse so abruptly that the two Gens almost ran into her. "What did you say?!" she demanded as she turned her horse on the narrow trail.

"I said only a blast furnace can smelt metals out of that stuff," Sergi answered, surprised by her vehemence.

"Do you know how to build one?"

"Well, I know the *theory*—" he said with a shrug.

"Sergi ambrov Keon, you *lorsh*!" Risa gasped. "Here we are risking our lives for a few piddling wagonloads of metal, while *you* sit on the secret of making a fortune right at *home*. With stuff that's free for the digging all over the territory! Shen and shid—just when I had started to believe that Gens had brains."

Sintha intervened. "Risa—Keon hasn't the manpower to run a steel mill, let alone money for the equipment—"

That was true. "I'm sorry," she said. "Of course you'd do it if you could. Forgive me, Sergi."

"You're forgiven. You didn't understand," Sergi replied. "It's much too big a project for Keon."

"For the moment," Risa agreed, but she was already planning. The metal they had gleaned on this trip would be worked by Keon's metal shop, and sold at huge profits in metal-starved Gulf Territory. Keon's share of the profits could buy equipment to build that furnace. At last householders could command economic power—

Risa planned on as the party of Simes and Gens wended its much slower way back toward the border with the heavily laden wagons. Wheels broke and wagons had to be unloaded, repaired, and loaded again. Mules and horses moved at a monotonously slow pace along the rutted road. Fortune frowned and smiled on them at once, in the form of freezing rain. While it slowed their progress, it kept other travelers off the road. The few they met were too eager to get to warm, dry destinations to investigate the plodding wagon train.

The persistent downpour penetrated the thickest clothing. The Gens shivered and sneezed, and Risa had to exercise her new healing skills to prevent pneumonia. The Simes augmented to keep warm, expecting their share of the profits to buy extra selyn.

The morning they finally reached the river, wearily contemplating their hardest task yet, the sun came out from behind the clouds as if to encourage them. Once across they would be safe—and soon home to warmth and riches! They began working the first wagon across the ford. It bogged down almost at once, and Simes waded into the water to free it.

Kreg rode out to guide the horses while Simes steadied the wagon. "It's too heavy," he said as people and animals strained to no avail. "Here—hand me some of that stuff. Form a line across the river—we can hand the metal across piece by piece, and reload on the other side."

"Good thinking, boy," said Tannen Darley, fighting the current to guide his horse up beside Kreg's. Others joined them, and the first wagon's goods were slowly but surely passed across. Unburdened, the wagon jolted across.

While two men began reloading that wagon, the second was drawn up, and the line of riders formed again. Risa watched, proud of her brother. She zlinned mechanically along the river bank—

Gens!

A whole mob of them, riding hard in their direction!

"Take cover!" she shouted, flaring a nageric alarm.

But most of the mining party were out in the cold water, up to their horses' withers in the swift current—

Shots rang out.

Horses screamed and reared. Chunks of precious metal fell into the rushing water, but Risa zlinned no pain—no one was hit.

The mules pulling the wagon being unloaded took fright. A wheel caught. The wagon overturned, spilling people into the water.

The Gens drew closer—nearly fifty of them! Bullets splashed in the water.

"Run!" Risa shouted to those still on the Gen side of the river. "Cross the river! Hurry!"

Where had fifty Gens with guns come from? The border patrol should be ten or fifteen men—

Ambush!

Risa and Sergi rode to the end of the train, urging those who hesitated to leave the loaded wagons.

"Our mules!" wailed Joi Sentell. "We have to have them on the farm!"

"Save your *lives*!" Risa insisted, pulling the reins out of the woman's hands. "Run! Swim for your life!"

Husband and wife finally jumped down from the wagon and ran for the river.

The Gens were on them!

A scream and a flare of pain—one of the swimming Simes was hit.

Risa couldn't tell who it was—but across the river eager hands reached out to help people ashore. Everyone else was off the bank now. "Sergi—come on!"

"Halt! You're under arrest!"

But no Sime would stop for the Gen patrol. Better a quick death from a bullet than torture in a Gen prison.

Risa pushed her horse forward, into the swiftest current.

Sergi was right behind her, his big bay horse stronger than hers. He tried to maneuver to cut the worst of the current for her mare—

Sheer agony sliced through Risa's head—jolting white pain—

Not herself.

Sergi!

Sergi was hit!

She turned to see him falling toward her, blood staining his yellow hair.

His huge, heavy body sagged against her, and fell into the rushing water.

Chapter Ten

Risa dived off her horse, reaching for Sergi.

She could zlin his field—he was unconscious and bleeding from a head wound—but alive.

As she struggled in the freezing water, she remembered her father dying in the river—

Not Sergi too!

Someone bore down on them—Gens on horseback with guns.

Risa pulled Sergi under water and let the current carry them. When she surfaced, the puzzled Gen patroller was looking around for his target—

From behind him, one of the town Simes leaped, twisting the man's gun out of his hands. The Gen flared fear.

That was all the Sime needed. He hauled the man off his horse, forcing his mouth to the screaming face—

Killbliss!

Keon's nonjuncts flared intil—but controlled it.

The juncts did not control. Several had passed turnover on the journey, and were close enough to need—

The Gens who had ridden into the river realized their mistake—too late—and their panic made them targets. Kills splintered the ambient.

Risa dragged Sergi ashore. Still unconscious, he was shivering uncontrollably. His skin grew paler.

She had no way to warm him. He was going into shock.

Despite her terror, she remembered her lessons. Channel's mode. Imitate hard need—

She extended trembling hands over his head, laterals seeking the wound, concentrating on encouraging selyn production—

His field was flatter than she had ever zlinned it. Selyn was there, unmoving—almost like the wisps of flat selyn pluming off a corpse!

He stopped shivering and lay motionless, skin gray.

"Sergi!" She grasped his arms, seating her laterals, and pressed her lips to his, trying to waken his need to give. Nothing. His lips were cold beneath hers.

She lay down on him, trying to will her own warmth into him—but she was cold herself.

She heard a wagon roll, and horses ride off. They were being deserted! How could she save Sergi? The Gens would cross the river and—

A Gen presence—and a Sime. Tannen Darley and Kreg had cut through the woods to them.

"Is he dead?" Kreg asked as he knelt beside Risa.

"No—it's shock," she replied. "I can't get him warm."

"Here." Darley produced a small flask. Risa smelled the sharp tang of brandy. "It's a stimulant."

"But he has a head wound—"

"His body's shutting down with cold, Risa. Do you have anything else to give him?" Risa shook her head.

They pried Sergi's teeth apart, and poured a small quantity of brandy down his throat, Risa zlinning carefully that it did not go into his lungs. He swallowed reflexively, but did not cough or come to. His heart rate increased.

"That won't last," said Darley. "We've got to get him dry and warm before the stimulant wears off."

Between them, Risa and Darley picked Sergi up and moved through the trees at a diagonal toward the road. Despite their burden, they caught up with the single plodding wagon.

Hal Raft was already in the wagon, bleeding from a bullet in the shoulder. Sintha held his head in her lap, her field soothing—Risa spared a moment to zlin that the bleeding had amost stopped. A flesh wound, not serious.

But Raft, too, was cold and wet.

"Who's got dry clothes?" Tannen Darley stripped off his jacket. Those who had ridden their horses across were soaked to hips or waist, but their upper garments were only damp.

Risa and Kreg stripped Sergi. Others did the same for Raft, despite his protests and the pain when he was moved. Darley gave him some brandy, which he swallowed gratefully.

They wrapped the two injured men in the dry clothes. "Kreg—get over there with Sintha," Risa directed. "One of you on each side of Mr. Raft."

Risa tried to take Sergi in her arms, but she was too small against his bulk. "He needs body heat—and stimulation to produce selyn. Who's close to need? Help me warm him up."

But most of the Simes were fleeing ahead.

"Hey—you fools!" Tannen Darley shouted after them. "Get back here!"

His authoritative voice was enough to make them hesitate. He added, "That's how the Gens got us—we were spread out! Stick together so we can fight if we have to!"

The riders, several doubled up on horses now, returned to the wagon. Risa asked, "Did everyone escape?"

"Where's Tripp Sentell?" someone asked.

"He stayed to see if the Gens followed," his wife replied anxiously. "He should have caught up by now."

"Fivvik—Quent—go back and—"

"No—he's coming," Risa zlinned.

Sure enough, Sentell came out of the woods onto the road. "They're not following," he reported in a voice heavy with sarcasm. "They're too busy claiming their loot—*our* wagons, *our* animals, *our* metal!"

"Why did we ever go along with perverts?" Joi Sentell complained. With an angry glance at Risa and the Gens in the wagon, her husband joined her, and they rode ahead.

Tannen Darley's attention returned to Risa and Sergi. He plucked one of the Simes off his horse. "You're close to need, Fivvik—get in there and warm up that Gen."

Gingerly, the man entered the wagon. Risa placed him on one side of Sergi, herself on the other, imitating need.

The momentary stimulation of the brandy had worn off, and Sergi's heartbeat slowed. "No!" Risa gasped as she zlinned his blood vessels contracting against the cold.

"What's wrong?" Kreg asked. "Can I help?"

"Stay where you are," she told him. "He'll respond to our need!"

It was more hope than fact when she said it . . . but slowly she felt Sergi's field recover. Production began, pulse by pulse, his field meshing with hers. Without regaining consciousness, the big Gen began to shiver again.

They were leaning against some slabs of metal. Despite the layers of clothing they had wrapped Sergi in, the metal was conducting warmth from his body. "Fivvik," said Risa, "help me lift him away from this stuff. Can you hold him?"

Darley zlinned what was happening, and swung off his horse and into the wagon with a grim laugh. "Pretty crowded back here, but it's one way to keep warm!" He slid between Sergi and a sheet of enameled iron. This put the two junct Simes, both past turnover, under Sergi, and Risa virtually on top of him—she could zlin warmth transfusing into his body as his own system began producing selyn steadily.

Risa smiled at Darley. "Thank you. And thank you for the brandy earlier—I don't know if he'd have survived without that stimulant. How did you know it would work on a Gen?"

Surprise rippled through Darley's nager. "I didn't," he replied. "It works that way on Simes. I forgot he was Gen."

"Yes," Risa observed, "Sergi has that effect on people. I'm certainly glad you had the brandy." She tried not to let her misgivings show, for Simes rarely drank anything stronger than porstan. Brandy was for the jaded, along with choice kills. Was Tannen Darley, for all his superficial good sense, overstimulating himself toward an early grave?

"My wife was a healer," Darley explained. "She would never have let me go off in cold weather without a flask of brandy." He swallowed hard. "She healed other people all her life—but no one could do anything for her."

"Did you try the channels at Keon?" Risa asked gently.

"She wouldn't let me," he said in a tight whisper. "I don't know why—something Nedd had told her once. I could afford extra kills for her. She made me promise not to call for Nedd." He looked at Risa out of pain-filled eyes. "I should have anyway. If I had known you people then—"

"We can't change the past," Risa said, remembering what her father had always told her. "We can only learn from it to change the future."

"Susi's future," he said. "Shen—I wish this trip had come off better! What rotten luck that the patrol was out. At least we're alive. I've never *seen* so many Wild Gens!"

She let him change the subject, which soon came around to what they had salvaged. What was in the one wagon, they calculated, might pay for the wagons, horses, mules, and mining tools they had lost. "All that effort for nothing," said Darley. "We can't go back—the Gens will back-trail to where we found it, and dig up the rest for themselves!"

"Well, it is their territory," Risa pointed out, and told him about Sergi's revelation concerning smelting metal.

"All the more reason to keep him alive," said Darley.

On the road to Laveen, Sergi came to enough to broadcast a sick headache. Risa's horse, with her medical kit, had been lost to the Wild Gens. But Darley carried fosebine as well, and Sergi drank down the foul-tasting stuff without protest, falling into a restless sleep.

When Verla zlinned Sergi, she wanted to put him to bed at her place. "No," Risa said, "I want him in Keon's infirmary. We've got him warm enough now."

Melli Raft claimed her husband. The single wagon went on to Keon. There they would do what they could with the metal they had salvaged, to make it sell for the highest prices.

Only Keon members traveled on along the road, as snow clouds gathered overhead. Gloom lowered like the clouds as Risa waited to face Nedd's "I told you so."

But there was none. Instead, he examined Sergi, said, "You handled it exactly right," and helped Litith install the Companion in the infirmary.

"It could have been such a *disaster*!" Risa confessed to Nedd over trin tea. "If those Gens had better aim, or better guns, we could all be dead!"

"But you're not," said the Sectuib. "Risa—that wagonload proves that your *idea* was sound."

"I don't think the local Simes will cooperate with us soon again."

"Not until we sell what we make from that metal in Lanta and Norlea—and everybody gets his share. Much as I hate to admit it, money does break down certain barriers."

Risa looked up sharply, and Nedd smiled at her. "You've really shaken up this old place, Risa. Now get some rest—you're back on the schedule at midnight."

"I want to check on Sergi first," she replied.

As they walked back toward Sergi's room, Risa asked, "Nedd . . . what did you tell Tannen Darley's wife, so that she would not accept your help when she was dying?"

"So she never told her husband. She was a channel, Risa—a junct channel. It's amazing she lived as long as she did."

"Why?"

"You remember being shorted. That's only the beginning. Untrained, improperly exercised, a channel's dual system is nothing but trouble. It's especially bad for a woman, since pregnancy complicates everything.

"Lita Darley managed to survive childbirth, but her systems were in chaos. She needed extra kills—and of course she went to the junct remedy of choice kills. Do you understand why that is the worst thing for a channel? "

"Combine a channel's sensitivity and a self-aware Gen—" Risa shuddered. "How could she help feeling guilt?"

"But in junct society one doesn't feel guilt over killing Gens. I told Miz Darley she was a channel, and that we could help her control some of her problems. She refused. In fact, she called me a liar."

"But why?"

"She came from a very old, very wealthy family near Lanta—you know the kind of people. Claim there hasn't been a child turn Gen in their line for ten generations?"

"I never did understand how being rich kept kids from establishing," Risa said, "but I've heard those claims."

"Sime, junct, and proud. Lita defied her family to marry Darley, a self-made man. She married the man she loved—but she could not face being something, physically, that her family considered shameful. Ironically," he added, "her family is probably *full* of channels—and so are all those other families that have been intermarrying for generations."

"Then it does run in families," Risa observed. "That . . . that could be why my mother died in childbirth. She had me, then Kreg—but the third pregnancy—"

"She bore a channel and a Companion," Nedd agreed. "She would have to have been a channel to survive those births. But don't *you* worry. You're disjunct, you're in control of your systems—and you've got Sergi. When you're ready for children, you'll have the best possible care." A warm glow suffused his nager. "Which reminds me—we haven't made the announcement yet. Litith and I are going to have a child."

Blushing, Litith accepted Risa's congratulations, then left her with Sergi. He was sleeping peacefully now, healing rapidly. His field was lower than it should be at her turnover, but rising steadily.

Satisfied that Sergi was all right, Risa let her thoughts turn elsewhere. Litith was considerably younger than Nedd. She had no idea how long they had been married—knew so little of the private lives of Keon's membership. *And I walked in here and started trying to change everything—*

The infirmary was well-insulated in every way—not just selyn-insulated, but sound-insulated as well, to guarantee the patients their rest. Thus Risa did not know what was happening outside until Rikki threw open the door. "Risa—bring Sergi. It's an attack!"

The only other patient in the infirmary just then was a child with a broken arm. Litith was hurrying him out the back door as Risa helped a very groggy Sergi down the hallway. "Where are we going? Who's attacking?"

"Into the main house!" Litith called over her shoulder. "All channels, Companions, children, and pregnant women!"

"But who's—?"

The cold night air revived Sergi, and he ran with her, his arm about her now for protection rather than support.

Buildings were burning. People ran in the lurid light, shouting. There were no gunshots. Not Wild Gens. Instead, the sound of cracking whips shattered the cold night air.

Pain seared the ambient—whip lashes on a frightened Gen—then the kill! Sime pain—a Keon Sime who had tried to rescue the Gen, being slashed by the same whip—

Pain and death blossomed on every side. From the burning buildings, Simes and Gens ran screaming with burns, suffocating from smoke inhalation.

Killust followed them—killer Simes come over the wall and moving in a band through the householding grounds.

Kreg and Triffin charged past, carrying knives from the kitchen. "No!" Risa cried. "They'll murder you!" She darted after the young Gens, caught Triffin, wrested the knife from her, and shoved her toward Sergi. "Take her inside!"

Risa augmented and caught up to Kreg—just as a Sime loomed out of the night at him: Tripp Sentell!

The junct was not in need, but the pain in the ambient had spurred him to a fever pitch. He grabbed Kreg, squeezing his forearms with a shock of pain. Kreg dropped the knife—but did not flare fear. "You can't kill me!" he sneered.

"I c'n slit yer throat!" the man growled, wrapping the tentacles of one arm about both the boy's wrists.

But as he started to bend for the knife, Risa poised to throw the one she held into his back—

Sentell froze. "So. The little troublemaker! You want the Gen, pervert?" He held Kreg in front of him as a shield, shoving him backwards toward Risa as he squeezed his arms bruisingly, causing Kreg to gasp with pain.

Risa zlinned, for she could not see well enough in the flickering firelight to throw the knife at his head—and Sentell knew it. He laughed, ducking behind Kreg, who already had enough Gen bulk to shield him completely. "You'll have to get the Gen first, pervert!" he taunted. "Gen lover! I wish it was that big buck o' yourn—I'd fix him so's he'd never touch no Sime woman agin!"

He squatted down, still using Kreg as a shield, and picked up the knife. "Think I'll fix this one." With one quick flick of the knife, he slashed through Kreg's belt. The boy jerked reflexively, and the Sime laughed.

Risa circled to find a target before Sentell really hurt Kreg, zlinning other Simes coming up behind him— two channels, holding their show-fields so the junct would not perceive them over the high-field Gen. They were supposed to be safe inside the house! But only channels could sneak up on another Sime.

She forced her own show-field high, and tried to soothe the junct before her, dilute his rage so that he would not take out his hostility on her helpless brother!

But Kreg was not so helpless. Over the junct's shoulder, he spotted the two channels approaching. His field suddenly flicked with a painful shock! Sentell released him with a yelp, and he fled into Risa's arms.

The two channels, Rikki and Nedd, hit the junct, one high and one low. They went down in a heap, arms, legs, tentacles thrashing— Sentell still held the knife. Nedd reached for his arm—and in a flash of terror, the junct threw all his augmented strength into wresting it free—and plunging the knife into the channel's heart!

Risa screamed.

Everything but the flickering flames came to a frozen halt.

Sentell leaped to his feet. "That'll teach ya to try yer pervert's tricks on *me*!" he shouted into the silence. "You shedoni-doomed lorshes pack up and get out of here! This town don't allow no perverts no more."

He turned and stalked off. Other town and farm Simes abandoned the field. Keon Simes ran to where Nedd had fallen. Gens, seeing the crowd gathering, came to see why. Risa and Rikki knelt over him, searching for signs of life.

Then the crowd parted, and Litith came through the ranks. She knelt, zlinned her husband, and sat back on her heels, her field ringing with grief as she looked up at the assembled householders. Then, her calm voice belying the chaos in her nager, she announced into the crystalline silence, "The Sectuib in Keon is dead."

*   *   *

"It's my fault!" Kreg sobbed. "Gevron taught me that trick days ago, but I didn't remember it!"

"No, Kreg," said Rikki. "That junct murdered Nedd. Come now—there's healing to do. Pleth—Liana—get those fires out. Risa—start treating the burn victims. Sergi—no, you're in no shape to work. Go to bed. Where's Gevron?"

The young channel assigned tasks, just as he did daily on the schedule board. Each person turned away as his name was called, until Litith knelt alone beside the body of her husband, now able to express her grief without an audience.

Risa turned her mind to healing the wounded. Never before had she faced the agony of burns. Gevron put aside his grief as they moved the victims into the infirmary; the old Companion didn't have Sergi's strength, but he had many years of experience. Snow was falling by the time the last of the injured were indoors, and it was gloomy gray daylight when an exhausted Risa emerged from the infirmary.

The snow was up to her ankles and falling steadily, its purity covering the scars of the night's raid. But snow could not cover Risa's guilt.

For hours she had worked without rest, Rikki and Loid using their breaks to instruct her—driving home how incomplete her training had been. Two people had died in her care. Despite the dozen they had saved, the negative thoughts forced aside during the night assaulted her tired mind.

In her room, Sergi slept in the second bed. He woke when she entered, took one look at her, and said, "To bed with you right now—no arguments."

"I won't argue," she replied, "but I can't sleep."

"I'll put you to sleep, and stay to see that you don't have nightmares. I'm sorry I couldn't have been with you—"

"You can't work with that head injury." She zlinned him. He still had a slight headache—and he wasn't hungry. It was the first time she had ever known Sergi not to wake up practically starving. "Will you please make us some tea?" she asked. "I think there are biscuits in the kitchen."

The guest quarters had a small communal kitchen. Sergi returned with steaming glasses and a plate of biscuits. By unspoken consent, neither mentioned Nedd's death. They had a day to get through before they could use the energy in sorrow—for Risa was back on the schedule at noon.

Just as Sergi was carrying the tray back to the kitchen, the bell at Keon's front gate began to ring. Fear lanced through Risa. Eviction notice? So fast?

They pulled on boots and threw capes over their pajamas.

The guard atop the gate flared astonishment. She turned as Risa approached. "Hajene Risa—I don't know what to do!"

Risa leaped up to the platform, and looked out at a dozen people—townspeople and farmers loaded down with bundles. And children! What in the world—?

Verla and Tannen Darley rode forward. "Risa—we heard what happened. We're here to help."

Risa's tears broke loose despite the fact that she was past turnover. Sergi climbed the ladder and took her in his arms. "What's wrong?" he demanded.

"They—they've come to help us!" Risa sobbed.

"Well—let them in," Sergi told the guard.

"What if it's—?"

"Our enemies don't come to the gate and ask politely to be let in."

Miz Frader rode in, saying, "These here's my granchilder. 'Bout time I got 'em in yer school."

"And my children," Melli Raft said softly.

Susi Darley hung back until Triffin came out—then she ran to the Gen girl to hug her excitedly. "I'm coming to school here every day—I'll see you all the time!"

Darley sniffed the sour smell smoke. "Risa—I didn't

know it was happening. Please believe me! I went home to Susi. I never dreamed— I'm sorry," he finished lamely.

"Oh, I am, too," said Verla. "Tripp Sentell got to drinking with some of Nikka's cohorts last night—and I threw them out when they got rowdy. If I'd let them stay, I'd have heard what they were planning—"

"And they were wrong!" Darley added angrily. "Those Wild Gens were set on us!"

"What?!"

"I'll tell you," he said, "but first, we brought medicine, clothes, blankets, bandages. What did they destroy? We'll help replace it. But we can't do anything about . . . people. Only what you told me, Risa—make the future better."

Not knowing what else to do, Risa called some of Keon's renSimes over. "These people have come to help us rebuild. Put them to work."

Among the townspeople and farmers, Risa saw— could it be?—Joi Sentell! The woman's face was bruised— half-healed injuries, possibly from last night, and a very fresh black eye. Miz Frader leaned toward Risa conspiratorially. "Joi finally stood up to that brute she married. He beat her last night when she tried to stop him, but when he come home braggin' he'd murdered ol' Nedd—that done it. Hear tell she busted his nose, which is a whole lot less than he deserves!"

Darley and Verla accompanied Risa and Sergi to Nedd's office—that was where conferences were always held. The desk was its usual mess; Risa had not been there for days to bring the books up to date.

Risa would not sit in Nedd's chair, so she sat on the edge of the desk and listened to Darley. "Nikka left town early this morning. You may have noticed that she didn't come out here—just set her henchmen to stir up the folks who lost their horses and wagons. She stayed at Zabrina's until they came back, bragging about what they'd done.

"Zabrina says she zlinned something funny—Nikka

was just too pleased with herself. Zabrina tried to open her up with whiskey, but Nikka just passed out."

"Then why do you think Nikka set the Gens on us?" Risa asked.

"Because when she came to, she ran. She's afraid she let something slip," said Darley.

"And that means she *had* something to let slip," Verla affirmed.

"By the time Zabrina sent for me, the pen was locked up and Nikka was gone," Darley told them.

"So all of us there in town appointed Tan sheriff right quick," said Verla, "so he could break in."

"Her office was a shambles," the banker said. "The safe was standing open, empty. Papers were burning on the floor—she must have meant the whole pen to burn down, but it was so damp they were still smoldering. It's obvious she was keeping double books—but they're burned too badly to lead us to her source of extra Gens."

"I think she was dealing with Genrunners," Verla said positively.

"Genrunners?" Risa asked blankly.

Sergi supplied the definition. "Wild Gens who ... sell their own people across the border. Orphans, drifters, tramps—they promise them some kind of work, maybe driving a herd of cattle to market. Only when they get to where the cattle are supposed to be, licensed raiders are waiting instead—and it's the people who are herded off to market."

"The raiders pay in gold," said Darley. "The Genrunner takes the risks. We suspect that Nikka alerted her contact across the border, and he diverted suspicion from his own activities by reporting us to the border patrol as a raiding party. They knew we'd move quickly and be back to ford the river at that one shallow point. We were ambushed."

"It's all speculation," said Risa.

"Then why did Nikka run?" asked Verla. "She's gone,

and so's that gang of no-goods used to hang around the pen."

"And Laveen is left without a Gendealer," said Risa.

"I'm taking the pen," said Darley. "I can get bonded and licensed faster than anyone else." He looked into Risa's eyes. "I don't want it. But that's how Nikka got the power of life and death: high principled citizens don't want the hard, dirty work of running a pen—we leave it to people like Nikka. Shen! We should have run her out of town years ago."

Darley went on to Nashul, leaving Susi at Keon. Risa watched the girl's shyness dissolve. Susi could cook and sew, do fine embroidery, write with elegant penmanship—but she was more comfortable with adults than children at first.

When Tannen Darley returned from Nashul, though, Susi ran to greet him with her hair mussed, her face dirty, and her child's nager happier than Risa had ever zlinned it. She was dressed in borrowed denims and a flannel shirt, and said excitedly, "Daddy, I'm helping in the metal shop. Come see!"

Susi and several other older children were making wire—bales that would go off to Nashul within the month to begin recouping the losses from the out-Territory expedition.

Keon Simes and Gens took some of that wire at various stages and made spikes and nails . . . and chains. Artistic objects brought more money for less metal—but the scarce practical goods could be made more quickly and would sell much faster. "We'll repay the farmers first," said Risa, "so they can replace their wagons and animals. And those who have no other source of income, so they can pay their taxes—and won't go raiding. Tan—did you get everything settled?"

"I've got a temporary license, and there's a shipment scheduled next week. If my people cleaned up that pen as they were supposed to while I was gone—"

"They did. Verla told me everything's in fine shape."

"Good," he said, but he was preoccupied, watching

his daughter working. "Risa, what is Susi doing here? I thought you were going to teach the kids to read and write."

"Susi knows how," she replied, as they left the shop. "You just happened to arrive when the older kids are in the shop. Did you ask her what she did all morning?"

"No."

"English and mathematics. We didn't know if you wanted her in our changeover or history class, so we've been having her help teach the farm kids to read during that time."

"She knows territory history," said Darley.

"It's householding history, from the time of the first channel," she told him as they entered Nedd's office. Risa had gotten over her reluctance to sit behind Nedd's desk; she sat there to do the accounts and fill out the endless tax forms—this time complicated by the deaths of Nedd and four other Simes, as well as two Gens. Litith sat there to write up her journal. It was just a desk, in the Sectuib's office . . . although for the moment Keon had no Sectuib.

Darley slumped into a chair. "I promised Susi," he said. "You were there, Risa. If she decides to live here, she should know the history. It's propaganda, I suppose—"

"I'll give you the books, and you can decide. What about changeover training? I've been worried about that, Tan, since you sheltered her from knowledge of the kill—"

"Do you think I'd risk her life? I was going to start her training on her birthday—but because of Triffin it got started a bit early. Put her in the class—the more practice she gets, the better off she'll be when the time comes."

Susi went into the regular changeover class, as did Melli Raft's oldest stepson, at her insistence. Other non-Keon parents, though, did not want their children taught about channel's transfer. Most of them tried to consider those "perversions" the householders' private business as long as they did not touch them or their children.

So there was a separate changeover class, to be sure these children at least had the knowledge to prepare themselves. The kill was not mentioned, but it was an unspoken assumption that their parents would provide them with Gens at that terrible-wonderful moment of First Need.

Winter had set in. Although there was much more snow here than Risa had been used to in Norlea, it rarely accummulated more than ankle-deep around Keon and Laveen. The roads, though, turned to mud, then froze, melted into more bogs and ruts, then froze again.

The Gen shipment from Nashul was three days late because of the bad roads, and its arrival eased tensions greatly. Nonetheless, half the people in Laveen still kept their distance when householders were in town, and many others were only coldly polite. Verla's business suffered. The warm camaraderie of the shiltpron party seemed a dream now, a fleeting glimpse of what might have been, gone forever.

And then on a miserably cold day, with snow blizzarding in sharp ice bits, Tannen Darley fought his way through the storm to Keon. Risa, overloaded since Nedd's death, did not have time to see him for over two hours. It was one of the rare times when she could have used her rest break to rest, for she was approaching need and had been working steadily since dawn. Beside her normal channel's duties, she had spent a frustrating time in the infirmary, attempting to get a grip on the fields of four children down with fever and a rash. One boy was on the verge of pneumonia, and Risa had used every bit of her need-sensitized strength to affect his field—but his child's nager would not respond, and she had finally had to go on to her other duties, leaving him in Litith's care.

Nedd's widow was bearing up well, but Risa worried that she exposed herself to the children's illness while she was pregnant. Litith insisted Simes could not catch children's diseases, and went on with her duties ... and Risa had to recognize that the woman needed her work as much as she needed selyn. So she simply asked Rikki to assign her a Companion, since Keon had an oversupply of talented Gens.

And that was why Tannen Darley had come. He was sitting by the fire, an empty tea glass beside him. But he was not drowsy, as might have been expected after waiting in a warm room after a cold ride. His nager was charged with worry and frustration. "Risa—Sergi—we've got bad trouble this time."

"What is it?" Risa asked.

"My latest Gen shipment arrived this morning—thirty-three Gens short. The roads are closed over Eagle Mountain, so the supplier at Nashul can't get his shipments from the big farm at Lanta. But ... he says we're lucky." Darley's voice and nager rang with angry sarcasm. "Look!"

He held out an official document. Risa took it, and she and Sergi read it together.

"Since Householding Keon now has an illegally high ratio of Gens to Simes, we are invoking ordinance GTS 56.318, reverting all Gens on said premises to the status of property until the balance is corrected. The director of the local pen may confiscate thirty-three Gens from Householding Keon at his discretion. It is recommended that those Gens known as 'Companions' be avoided, as they do not make satisfactory kills. The director of Householding Keon is hereby informed that once the illegal imbalance has been corrected by the removal of said thirty-three Gens, the Householding will revert to its previous status."

"They can't *do* that!" Risa gasped.

"Oh, yes they can," Sergi said. "We've broken the law—and like any other criminals, we've lost our rights until we repay our debt to society."

"Shen and shid!" Risa swore. "What are we going to do? Tan, do you intend—?"

"I don't *know* what to do!" the man replied in frustration. "People on my rolls are entitled to thirty-three more Gens than I've got. I can't take Gens from Keon— but where else am I to get them? Even the Nashul Choice Auction has been closed. I can't encourage people to raid across the border. They're *entitled* to those kills." He sat down again, in total defeat. "You tell me, Risa. What are we going to do?"

Chapter Eleven

Sergi had seen Risa frustrated before, and angry, and sorrowful. He had never seen her defeated.

As she slumped in the big desk chair, she looked like a child again—a misperception he had long since forgotten in the face of her tireless strength. She looked tired now.

Her helplessness reflected Sergi's. Ever since Nedd's death, he had been waiting for Risa to recognize her place as Sectuib in Keon. But she refused to confront her destiny.

If Risa—the only channel with the strength to be Sectuib—let Keon be defeated by government regulations, the householding would die. Oh, Carre would absorb many of the members—but Keon's members had left Carre a generation ago because they felt the call of freedom. The drive that, paradoxically, prevented Risa from pledging Keon. The same drive that would send Sergi to an empty, lonely life across the border rather than pledge to anyone but Risa.

Tannen Darley was saying, "I can save one Keon Gen, Risa. If you will give me transfer again. And Verla—"

"And where do we find thirty-one other people willing to endure perversion?" Risa asked hopelessly.

"Will you give up without a fight?" Sergi asked.

"How do we fight something like this?"

"First we buy time," he replied. "The weather will change. Tan, what will be your time shortfall?"

"About five days."

"Then we have approximately three weeks to make up the Gen supply . . . or find another solution."

Risa said bleakly, "The tax inspector will show up when the weather breaks. If we're still thirty-three Gens high—"

"That's the least of our problems," said Darley. "They can hide out in the pen. It's easy enough to fool government flunkies—but there's no fooling thirty-three Simes in need."

"Hide Gens . . . in a pen?" Risa was surprised, but too deep into need to appreciate the humor.

"And I'll put through an emergency order citing weather-caused augmentation," said Darley.

"Isn't that illegal?" Risa asked dubiously. "You're operating on a temporary license; they'll be watching you."

"As carefully as they watched Nikka. I can tell whose tentacles require a bit of gold to keep them off the books." He gave her a strange, sad smile. "You're just a little too honest, Risa—which is why you're well off instead of rich."

"That's what got us into this predicament," added Sergi.

"What?"

"Risa, if you had consulted me, I'd have told you not to report that we were Gen-high. By the time an inspector gets here, we won't be. Carre will take some of our Gens or send us some Simes to put the ratio back to normal. Just a couple of changeovers would do it, without outside help."

"You want me to . . . cheat on *tax forms*!" Risa's round-eyed astonishment set both men chuckling.

Then, "It's not cheating," said Darley. "You just don't tell the government what it doesn't have to know."

"It's not as if we would *keep* an illegal Sime/Gen ratio," Sergi added. "It never occurred to me that you'd report it."

"Oh?" Her dark eyes flashed in anger. "Because I was junct when I learned bookkeeping, I must have learned to do it dishonestly?"

"No, I didn't mean—"

"My father was the most honest businessman in Gulf Territory. As long as *I'm* keeping Keon's books they will be kept honestly and accurately."

Keon's bookkeeper seemed to be Risa's image of herself that winter. She worked long, hard hours without complaint, but she did not participate in any of the householding's ceremonies. Her first refusal had been the Year's Turning celebration, this year including a memorial to those who had died in the attack on Keon. Nothing Sergi could say would persuade her to participate, or even attend. She had spent the time on the household accounts. And, Sergi now knew, that fatal tax report.

Risa's reluctance to accept Keon frustrated Sergi. It seemed the more donations she took, the more transfers she gave, the more sick and injured she healed . . . the more aloof she remained.

Nor did their next transfer put her in a friendlier mood. She would not make love again, asking, "Do you want me pregnant just when I have to be at peak performance?"

"Risa, there are precautions—"

"All of which can be totally forgotten in a moment of passion. And afterward, my routine would risk the child's life. No, Sergi, I will not chance it."

So she left him frustrrated, and not only sexually. When he tried to broach the topic of Risa's future at Keon, she changed the subject at once. That was easy in the work-packed days of late winter—she could legitimately bring up schedules and illnesses and the progress they were making in turning the salvaged Gen metal into salable goods.

Then one day Melli Raft's stepson, Prence, gave his fellow students a graphic lesson by going into changeover in the middle of the training class! His parents were sent for. Melli pleaded with her husband for the boy to be left at Keon. "Hal—you know they've got the best skills to help him here ... if anything should go wrong."

"Nothing's going to go wrong," the man insisted.

Sergi assured him, "Everything is normal. But if he reaches breakout here, he will receive channel's transfer."

"Hal—please!" Melli was more forceful than Sergi had ever seen her. "Prence doesn't want to kill—we've talked and talked about it. Please don't make him leave, Hal."

It was clear that the man desperately wanted to humor his wife, but he said, "Melli, what am I going to do without Prence's help on the farm if he lives at Keon?"

Risa, emerging from the insulated room where she had been checking the boy's progress, gave the answer. "Prence doesn't have to live here. He can just come to Keon for transfer."

Horrified, Sergi said, "Risa, we can't—!"

"You'd turn away a nonjunct Sime and force him to kill?"

"No—no, of course not, but— We've never done anything like that."

"Carre has. Remember your friend Prather Heydon, who runs the inn on the eyeway? If he can be nonjunct and live outside a householding, so can Prence."

Sergi didn't dare argue, for Melli Raft was saying, "Oh, yes! Hal, you *can't* object, since it's what Prence wants!"

"I'll ask him," the man replied. "If it's not just something you've talked him into—"

The boy was certain. Even as he descended into First Need he insisted he wanted channel's transfer. His father left the room immediately after the breakout of Prence's tentacles, but Melli stayed, her stepson shielded from her joy/guilt/pain by Sergi's nager. Risa whispered, "Congratulations, Prence," entwined their laterals, and pressed her lips to his.

Risa had never before given First Transfer. Her eyes

met Sergi's with the first spontaneous smile she had given him since the night of the raid.

But if Risa was more content as a channel, she showed no inclination to take on any more formal role. Tannen Darley appeared as promised, to take transfer as Verla had done a few days before. Kreg was scheduled to relieve Sergi, who walked Darley outside afterward.

The banker said nothing until they reached the point on the muddy pathway where he would go toward the stable for his horse while Sergi went on to the metal shop.

"Would you like to see our latest progress?" Sergi invited. "We'll have the last shipment ready to go to Nashul in a few days. We'll be able to pay everyone back."

"What?" Darley dragged his attention back from somewhere far away, then said, "I know you're working day and night. So am I. I finagled an emergency shipment of fifteen extra Gens, but they're a sorry lot." He added, "I almost couldn't make myself come here today. If I had not given my word—"

Never trust a Sime in need, Sergi had always been taught, but he was learning that there were Simes who kept their word even under that duress. Even juncts. "You didn't expect to be satisfied?" he asked.

"Satisfied? Oh, it was satisfying even that first time, when Risa forced me. But this time it was much more!"

Sergi chuckled. "I know. My nager is having no effect on you at all—now *that* is post-syndrome."

Darley smiled in response, his post-transfer emotional high making him more congenial than usual. But there was sympathy in his voice as he said, "You love her— and you can never know what she can give, because you're Gen."

"No, Tan, you're wrong. I have transfer with Risa every month—I *do* know."

Just as he knew that Risa was holding back at their next transfer. Even though she was out of First Year, her systems were growing with her increased workload.

Still she would not let herself go in transfer, controlling the flow so that although it was as wonderful as ever, it was *only* "as ever," the promise of something more held tantalizingly out of reach.

Sergi could have overcontrolled her, grasped that elusive joy and shared it with her—but he feared that Risa would perceive it as forcing rather than sharing. So he endured the piquant frustration of the best transfers of his life, knowing they could be so much better.

But the problems not only remained, they grew. Rain fell incessantly. It penetrated every kind of clothing, making it harder to keep warm now than in the snowy weather.

Keon's Gens sniffled and sneezed. Under house-holding regimen simple colds went away in a few days, but it seemed that every Gen at Keon was coughing or aching—and working in spite of it.

The Gens in Tannen Darley's pen fared worse. Despite new stoves, the old buildings remained drafty. Leaks sprang through the roofs with every rain. The Gens fell ill—and, having been raised as drugged animals, had no will to live.

When Risa received Darley's message that his Gens were sick, she pounded her fist against the desk in frustration.

"Don't!" Sergi said, taking her hand. "Jolting your laterals won't solve anything."

"But I can't help!" she said angrily. "I can't be spared, and neither can Rikki or Loid."

"Tan will understand."

Her huge dark eyes studied his face. "I got the town involved with Keon. We owe them, Sergi—and we can't pay!"

"Life doesn't operate like mortgage payments."

"Doesn't it?" she asked grimly. "If you miss your mortgage payments you lose your property. If we miss this payment, Sergi, we'll lose everything—and we can't ask for an extension, because the juncts need those kills *now*. If the pen Gens die, or can't provide adequate selyn—"

He knew the consequences: more raids. Or Darley might execute his confiscation order. "Very well," he said. "Since we cannot send a channel to heal the pen Gens, and most of the juncts will not come to Keon for transfer—what *do* we do?"

Suddenly Risa's expression changed. "But the juncts *will* come to Keon," she said, "if their Gens are here."

"What?" Sergi asked in amazement.

"We've got an infirmary better than anything in town—and warm, dry quarters to keep the healthy Gens well."

"We don't have enough channels to care for the sick Gens and our own people," Sergi protested.

"We have something the town doesn't: nonjunct renSimes. Gens will respond to any Sime in need. Don't look so horrified," she added. "I won't put anyone in *hard* need in with them—but all post-turnover Simes will take turns in the infirmary. I'll tell Rikki. You go into town and tell Tan."

"You know I can't go into town alone."

Exasperation firmed her lips into a thin line. "Will you stop acting like a pen Gen? Go round up some renSimes, ride into town, and help Tan move his pen!"

In the next few days, the Gen dormitory was cleared out, the healthy pen Gens housed there in brief comfort. Sick Gens filled the infirmary, but responded quickly to warmth, medication, and the ambient of need. Only one Gen, far gone into pneumonia, died soon after being transported to Keon. The rest survived, then thrived.

But their numbers dwindled as juncts claimed their kills. Keon's members tried not to watch the green pennant flapping soggily over the main gate, but no one could forget it. Tannen Darley respected Keon's rule that there would be no kills on the grounds, delivering them to the gate so that no junct Simes in hard need set foot inside the householding. Unless they came for transfer.

Melli Raft refused her kill, and so did Miz Frader. Joi Sentell told her husband she would claim her Gen, but instead took transfer in angry defiance. Several of Darley's employees sheepishly explained that they'd rather not kill the ones they'd cared for—they'd accept channel's transfer now and wait for a new shipment.

As a result, the community squeaked through the month with barely enough kills. "But only because some people went raiding across the river," Darley observed.

A new shipment filled the dormitory—but there were still not enough to go around. And then the river flooded. There was no crossing that raging torrent; every Sime on Darley's list would have to be supplied with selyn . . . somehow.

A windstorm demolished a temporary storage building. The next day Sergi was on his way to meet Risa as her brother Kreg came out of the infirmary, yawning mightily. "You on duty with Risa now?" the younger man asked.

"That's right," Sergi told him.

"Say hello for me. Rikki's got me scheduled with him for the next few days—and you know what he did?"

"No, what?"

"Scheduled Triffin and me on opposite shifts. We *never* get any time together!"

"Rikki is simply rotating the Companions for efficient use of their time," Sergi explained. "He hasn't arranged your transfers to put you off-schedule from each other, has he?"

"No, and I guess he'll put us back together at the end of the—" He broke off, blushing. "How did you know?"

"As you are learning, Gens are as perceptive as Simes."

"Yeah . . . but you're lucky, Sergi. You get to be with Risa all the time."

If Kreg only knew! But Sergi murmured something sympathetic and was about to move on when one of Darley's men, Fivvik, approached. "Hey—Sergi. The boss told us to help rebuild that barn. But the Keon

Simes're augmenting like crazy. We got no extra kills if we waste selyn like them."

"You can have transfers," Kreg spoke up.

"Huh?"

Sergi looked from Fivvik to the group of Simes lagging behind him. Kreg was right. "We have plenty of selyn. You can have all you want, as long as you take it from channels. If you're willing to do that, go ahead and augment."

The juncts looked at one another uncertainly. Under augmentation, work did not feel like work, but like joyful play. Denied that experience for two months, they could not resist. Sergi saw the look pass from one to another, the grins break out—as one they turned and darted for the construction site on a burst of joyous release.

Thus profligate use of selyn solved the problem of the Gen shortfall. Word quickly spread that anyone helping at Keon could augment and receive extra selyn— and they were inundated with volunteers. Dozens of people went into a three-week need cycle, persuading themselves that getting extra selyn between kills wasn't "really" transfer. The effect was to extend their kill cycle to *six* weeks. As spring sunshine brought the daffodils to bloom, Tannen Darley reported the startling news that he now had surplus Gens!

The pen was moved back to town, into new, well-built quarters. The town was thriving again, spirits high because even those who would not go to Keon's channels had the security of knowing a Gen was available every month, no matter what the weather. As the hard work of spring planting, cleaning, and rebuilding began, more juncts set aside principles for practicality. Keon could not find work for all who came seeking selyn, but they turned no one away, promising they would call for their help when the right time came.

"The right time," Darley observed, "is as soon as spring planting's done."

"For what?" Risa asked. "Let them owe us until we have reason to call in their promises."

"You haven't forgotten your plans to build a steel mill!"

Sergi had long since forgotten—but Risa sat forward in sudden animation. "Tan—you're right! People who work only at planting and harvest will be glad of steady jobs! Where are those plans? We have to figure costs, find backers—"

"I'll back you," said Darley. "In fact, if I knew anything about making steel, I'd probably try to beat you to the punch. But Keon has the expertise."

With the diagrams in front of them, though, as they began figuring materials, labor, and a mining expedition, they quickly realized that Darley's funds combined with Keon's added up to barely half the estimated cost.

"A loan?" Darley asked. "I have connections in Lanta—"

"No," said Risa and Sergi in unison.

"That would make it *your* steel mill, Tan," Sergi explained. "If I do this, it will be for Keon. No Lanta bank will lend money for a project sponsored by a householding."

"We'll sell stock," said Risa. "I'll put my personal funds in. Verla's making some profit now. I'll bet lots of local people can afford a share or two. If Keon Steel Mill has hundreds of small stockholders, that's hundreds of Simes with a motive to keep Keon safe from harm."

"No one will buy stock in a householding," said Sergi—but he knew he would be glad to be proved wrong.

Their planning session was cut short, as Risa was due to take donations. Distributing selyn to the juncts added to the load on Keon's already overburdened channels. Only the nearly empty infirmary let the schedule work at all.

As Risa and Sergi hurried toward the collectorium, Risa looked up and stretched out her arms, extending her handling tentacles. Taking a deep breath of warm spring air, she said, "Oh, it's such a *beautiful* day! I don't want to go inside again. How am I going to *stand* missing springtime?"

Four high-field Gens waited on the steps, Keon members but not Companions. A young woman named Bess said, "We don't want to go inside, either. Why don't we stay here, Hajene Risa? We're just giving donations, not transfer."

The others nodded, and Risa laughed. "Why not?"

Her good mood was improved even more by the arrival that day of Dina, a channel from Carre who would stay with them until they found another permanent channel or reduced their membership somehow. Rikki put Dina right to work, and for the first time in months Risa and Sergi had free time.

They walked to the top of the hill to watch the sunset, then hand in hand to the dining hall—where Sergi noticed that the pinkness in Risa's fair skin was not due entirely to the reflection of the sunset. She was slightly sunburned, and freckles were popping out across her nose.

"Look—you even have freckles on your handling tentacles," Sergi said as Risa picked up her tray.

"And you are turning gold again," Risa said in mock envy. "It isn't fair. I've always wanted to tan the way you do."

Their banter could have turned into flirtation—but Litith came looking for them. "Hajene Dina wants to pay Carre's respects to the Sectuib in Keon."

Sergi saw Risa pale, then set her jaw determinedly. He wished he could read her mind, or even zlin her—for she could not now avoid the issue of her rightful place here.

Dina was waiting by the desk in the Sectuib's office. She was tall, blonde, cool—looking as if she belonged in the frozen north, not the steamy south.

She turned when they entered, and her glance grazed across Risa's ringless hands. "Who speaks for Keon?"

"I do," Sergi replied quickly. It was his place as First Companion until a Sectuib was named.

"Carre's respects, Naztehr," Dina said formally. "How is it that you have not yet named your Sectuib?"

"Nedd's heir—" Risa began, but subsided when Sergi placed a hand on her shoulder.

"Nedd's heir was unnamed at his death," Sergi explained. "The reason you are here is the same reason we have had no time to discuss this matter in-householding. Keon accepts Carre's respects, and extends a grateful welcome. Dina, your presence relieves a critical situation. Thank you for coming."

The woman warmed to his sincerity, and accepted Triffin as escort to the dining hall. Dina had risked traveling without her own Companion so as not to add to Keon's surplus of Gens. Sergi foresaw a contest among Gevron, Kreg, and Triffin at the end of the month as to who would give her transfer, for Dina was a channel of Nedd's ability or better.

When she had gone, Risa turned to Sergi. "Why did you stop me from saying that Litith is carrying Nedd's heir?"

Litith gasped. "Oh, Risa—no! I didn't know you thought I would oppose you as Sectuib. Please forgive me for not realizing sooner."

Risa stared blankly at Litith. "What do you mean?"

Sergi said, "The office of Sectuib is not hereditary. Upon the death or retirement of the Sectuib, the best channel in the householding assumes the title. In some cases there may be a dispute as to who is the best channel, but otherwise. . . ." He let the statement trail off, hoping for a positive response.

But Risa said, "There is no reason to assume Nedd's child won't be as good a channel as he was."

"There is no guarantee that his child will be a channel at all," Litith responded. "The child's selyn-consumption rate is higher than that of a renSime—but not a channel of your abilities, Risa. I might carry a

Companion like Sergi—they often consume as a lesser channel would.

"But whether or not my child is a channel, Keon cannot wait twelve years or more to find out. You have been sent in our time of need. I will pledge to you gladly. You have been Sectuib in all but name since Nedd's death."

Risa had paled during Litith's speech so that her new-sprung freckles stood out in sickly contrast. "I can't!" she said in a choked whisper. "Find someone else—Rikki, Loid, anyone!"

"Risa, Keon *needs* you!" Litith insisted.

Risa gripped the edge of the desk as if to keep from falling. "Then . . . I will have to arrange it so that Keon does *not* need me anymore. Tigues pay their debts. I will pay mine, I vow—but no more, Litith. No more!"

Risa set about paying her debts with a vengeance. The more interdependent Keon and the community of Laveen, the safer the householding. The steel mill would bring money into the area. Men like Tannen Darley, with strong ties to the householding, would become the local representatives to government—and make changes that would make life easier.

And Risa would be free.

The future she envisioned was to live in Laveen, channel to local people who did not want to kill. The local juncts found channel's transfer acceptable when it meant they could augment freely. Darley's pen was well supplied; no one had to risk raiding. Keon's channels stripped selyn from the surplus pen Gens as demand grew, and the Gens simply produced more.

The mill was not on Keon's land, but on a large wooded area between the town and the householding, a sort of no man's land between the two communities. Now they cleared the forest, building the first of the mill's buildings, selling some of the wood to a paper mill for ready money, and turning the rest into charcoal for the blast furnace.

With bunkhouses going up and the brick foundations of the furnace being laid, the dream took on substance. Tannen Darley brought some business acquaintances from Lanta to observe. When they saw an investment likely to bring in a solid return, they, too, sacrificed principle for profits.

With the money from the new investors, Keon Steel hired more laborers, and work proceeded faster than ever. The blast furnace would be ready for operation by autumn.

Life was good in Laveen that summer. Between planting and harvest, the farmers earned extra money building the mill. Every evening Verla's and the other saloons were full of happy people with money in their pockets. Verla laughingly told Risa that she was now earning more with less work—and left Ambru in charge in the slower daytime hours while she joined one of Keon's classes to learn to read and write.

All who worked for Keon Steel were entitled to free education for their children. The classes filled. Most of the newcomers had been held back all their lives by illiteracy. Perhaps they told themselves that they would leave the "perverse" influences of the householders after they got a nest egg together—but attitudes changed with time and exposure ... and the freedom of augmentation.

Three times that summer changeover victims were rushed to Keon—children whose parents accepted their determination never to kill. Two others were held at home, killed once—and then walked out on their families, determined to disjunct.

So far as Risa heard, no local children who turned Gen were killed or escorted across the border. But three were brought to the householding by parents who dared to go on loving them.

In late summer, the first mining expedition returned to heap red ore mixed with Ancient metal into a man-made hill to feed the furnace. Explosions echoed through the hills as a quarry was blasted out and a hill of white limestone grew beside the red. The furnace rose. They were ready to set the firing day, the day they would complete the blast stoves, the crucible furnace, and the shops where the steel would be turned into salable goods.

The mill was considered an extension of the house-holding, even though it was a separate legal entity under the papers Risa and Tannen Darley had registered with the territory government. On the grounds, Keon's Gens were treated as if still inside householding walls. Soon they were treated the same way in town, although Risa was not conscious of it until one day when she was called to help one of Zabrina's employees, who had been attacked by a horse in Skif's stable.

"It was my own bloody-shen fault!" gasped the woman, Jasteen, when Risa hurried into the back room of Zabrina's saloon to zlin her injuries. They were bad—a broken leg, several cracked ribs, and a dislocated shoulder. Still, a Sime would heal quickly once the bones were set.

"Just lie still," Risa said. "How could a horse do this to you?" A Sime should have been able to augment to duck even a horse's flying hoofs.

"I was stupid—I believed Skif!" Jasteen replied in frustration. "He said the horse was broken, and I just went right into the stall, never thinking— Oh, that lorsh! I knew it was too good a horse for him to afford; should have known there was something wrong!"

"Hush, Jassie," said Zabrina. "Risa'll fix you up."

Risa asked, "Do you have any fosebine?" She and Sergi were in town on other business, and she was not carrying her medical kit.

"Naw—the gang in here last night cleaned me out. I'll go down to the pen; Tan always keeps some on hand."

But Zabrina did not return, and Jasteen's pain increased as her wounds swelled; the longer they waited, the harder it would be to set the bones and the more it would hurt. "Sergi," Risa said, "run over to Verla's and see if she has fosebine. I don't want to try this without it."

Without thinking, Sergi walked out into the saloon. It was only when she heard the words, "Hey, fancy Gen—where ya think yer goin' all by yerself?" that Risa realized what she had done. There were transients around—and malcontents who either wouldn't work or wouldn't behave around householders.

But before Risa could reach the door, at least three different voices had responded, "He's with me!" She reached the doorway in time to see her bewildered Companion standing in the middle of the saloon while three local Simes placed themselves between him and the troublemaker at the bar. Others edged their chairs out, ready to join the fray.

Prence Raft was one of Sergi's defenders. "You plan to spend much time around here," he told the man at the bar, "you gotta learn the local rules. Any householding Gen in Laveen—you just consider him escorted. Understand?"

There was a murmur of assent from the small group of local Simes. The offender stared at them, his nager radiating disgust, but he was outnumbered. He turned his back on them, and ordered another porstan.

Prence turned to Sergi. "Want me to come with you?"

"It appears," Sergi said incredulously, "that that will not be necessary, thank you."

Once they could dose Jasteen with fosebine, which both Sergi and Zabrina brought back, it was easy enough to set the woman's fractures and start her healing. That was not the surprise of the day; Keon's channels had long since become healers to the entire community. But on the way back to Keon, Risa reached across from her horse to take Sergi's hand. "You're not imprisoned behind Keon's walls anymore," she said.

But his impervious nager told her that he was not as pleased as she was by the day's events—probably because Risa saw it as a step toward leaving Keon's walls forever. He would come to accept it, she decided. He was dedicated to Keon's virtue of freedom—but perhaps anyone's first true taste of it seemed bitter after a lifetime behind walls.

As the summer drew to a close, Keon Steel began hiring permanent employees. All required training, for there had never been a steel mill in the territory before. Even Sergi had no practical experience with a full-scale mill, but he knew more than anyone else—and anyone who could not accept a Gen as boss was eliminated from consideration.

The atmosphere in the community shifted again as those who were turned away flooded the saloons to voice their complaints. A few local farmers who had not worked on or invested in the mill joined them, Tripp Sentell among the most vocal. Some of the new employees resigned.

The camaraderie of the summer disintegrated under the impact of hundreds of juncts never before exposed to Sime/Gen cooperation. Many had made a long trek to seek work, and now their pockets remained empty. Petty thievery became a nuisance.

If those who would not work under Keon's conditions had moved on, the problem could have been contained. But they had no place to go. A few found work on harvest crews, but most just hung around town, making trouble.

Risa's frustrations increased on all sides. Despite Dina's presence she was back at the work-work-work routine of last winter, because those Simes building the mill needed extra selyn. The new business increased her paperwork, filling every minute, it seemed, when she was not channeling.

Her two reliable supporters were too busy to help, Tannen Darley snowed under with tax and kill records for the hundreds of newcomers, and Sergi too busy with the mill to be with her, even after her turnover. There was a Companion in the second bed in her room any time she was scheduled for a few hours of sleep—

but it might be anybody now. Sergi was there with her only the last day before transfer. Afterward, he hardly eased her into post-syndrome before rushing off to solve some problem with the rolling mill.

When Risa reached turnover the last month of summer, Rikki approached her. "Risa, you're not going to like this, but please think before you bite my head off. I've scheduled Triffin to give you transfer this month, and Kreg next month."

She nearly panicked, but maintained control. Once the mill was in operation new problems would take up Sergi's time. She managed to say as much to Rikki, forcing intellect to overrule emotion.

He smiled. "That's the spirit. Both Triffin and Kreg need a transfer with a channel of your capacity to bring them to the peak of their abilities."

"Why bother?" Risa asked. "We're overflowing with Companions."

"We won't be low on channels forever. At least five kids close to changeover age are possible channels. We cannot afford not to train Kreg and Triffin while they're young. And it's not good to rely on only one Companion, Risa. You have had Sergi for a whole year now. While you're healthy and in control, accept someone else. That way you'll be able to if you must in an emergency."

He went on to explain that the second month would be harder than the first, which was why he had scheduled her brother for that time.

Triffin was eager and solicitous, a bit awkward at times, but dependable and steady. Risa was glad of the opportunity to get to know her better. One day this girl, born in a Genfarmer's stock pen, might marry her brother. That was certainly a change in the world ... but only the world inside Keon's walls.

Their transfer was nothing like what Sergi gave her emotionally, nor did Triffin have Sergi's speed. Yet she had plenty of selyn and good will, and Risa was left content enough. It was still better than any kill she had ever had—and if she had come to Triffin instead of Sergi as her first experience of transfer she would have been overwhelmed by the pleasure of it.

As Triffin was overwhelmed. The girl's pale blue eyes sparkled as she whispered, "Oh, thank you, Risa! It's never been as good with the other channels. I'll envy Kreg next month . . . and Sergi, that he has this almost every month."

Sergi was odd Companion out that month, Loid taking his field down to keep him in synch with Risa. But he obviously missed giving transfer, and the few times Risa saw him she suspected that his frustration stemmed as much from being unfulfilled as from last-minute problems with the mill.

Kreg joined Risa the day after her transfer. It was good to have time with her brother; they hadn't had a family talk in weeks. On her turnover day, despite her protests, Rikki scheduled her for afternoon and evening off. "And I mean *off*," he insisted. "No working on the books or going down to help with the steel mill. Kreg, you try to get some food into her, and then make her lie down. Put her to sleep if she won't be still."

Knowing her brother would try just that—and almost curious enough to see if he could—Risa let herself drift at his command. They ended up in her room, drinking tea and eating apples while Guest purred on Risa's lap. "I'm going to ask Triffin to marry me," Kreg said suddenly. "Maybe next spring. I think she'd like a real wedding feast—she's never had anything like that. I don't know if she'd want to celebrate her establishment day, like they do here—'cause on *her* day they put chains on her and sold her to a dealer." He shuddered. "Oh, Risa, I'm so glad you made me come to Keon!"

"So am I, Kreg."

"Then why won't you pledge? This is *home!* You love Sergi. Why not marry him? We'll have a double ceremony!"

"I'll consider it," she replied, "once we don't have to live behind barred gates. I can't live chained, Kreg—

any more than Triffin could. She fought and won the right to live. But it's not enough, not for her and not for you."

"But we *choose* it," Kreg insisted. "Triffin and I could go into Gen Territory—where Gens live behind locked doors for fear of raiders or berserkers. Come on, Sis— life can't be perfect. But we keep making it a little bit better."

"Dad always said that," she said, remembering, seeing once more the image of their father in her brother.

"Dad was right," Kreg asserted. "I've thought a lot about it, Sis. I think he'd approve of what you've done. I know he'd approve of the steel mill!"

"I'm not so sure he'd approve of a Gen running it."

"He'd approve of me," Kreg said positively. "Risa—I can feel your need now. And I can ease it. If Dad could see his children complementing each other that way—oh, Risa, I *know* he'd approve."

But Kreg and Risa were not fated to have their transfer together. A few days later, Rikki was waiting when Risa finished one of her transfer sessions. He handed her a note, saying, "This just came for you."

The message was in Tannen Darley's bold scrawl: "Risa—Susi is in changeover. I can't move her. Come at once—please! She trusts you. Tan."

"Kreg—go saddle our horses while I get a medical kit," Risa instructed.

"Wait!" Rikki exclaimed. "Risa, our best channel can't be spared for one child in changeover! It's much easier to shift my schedule—"

"I'm going, Rikki. Put *that* on your schedule."

"Shen it, I know Darley's your friend, but—"

"Yes, he's my friend. I would go for that reason alone—but he is also the best friend Keon has in Laveen. If his child dies because we couldn't free the channel she trusts for a few hours, Keon is a lorsh in the basest meaning of the word: someone who would abandon a friend in changeover! Now get out of my way and go fix your shidoni-be-damned schedule!"

Risa and Kreg arrived to find Susi already in the last stages. Her father looked up with worried eyes. "She keeps passing out," he said. "I've never seen a change-over go so fast—and she's so helpless. Zlin her selyn drain—"

Risa zlinned the unconscious child. She had depleted much of her energy, but the new tentacles were forming nicely in their sheaths along her forearms, and her selyn systems—systems!—were already clearly delineated.

"Tan—it's perfectly normal," Risa assured him. "Susi is a channel."

"A . . . channel?"

"That's why it's going so fast. Her systems are developing normally. All we have to do is keep her from using up her last selyn before breakout. Kreg—you come over here now, and take Tan's place. Control the fields—we can't have any sudden disruptions—"

"Risa—you want me to—?" Kreg was bewildered.

"She has to have First Transfer from a Gen to develop her best potential. She couldn't do better than you, little brother."

"But—what about you?"

Risa shrugged. "Rikki won't be pleased. Sergi will."

It didn't take long for Kreg's joy at the opportunity to serve First Need to overcome his reluctance. He carefully edged onto the chair by the bed as Tannen Darley vacated it, then zlinned Risa. "You and your brother—?"

"We were scheduled for transfer a couple of days from now. Don't worry—Kreg is plenty high-field; Rikki deliberately had him ahead of me."

The man stared at Risa as if he had never seen her before. "Risa—I do not believe what I just zlinned. You relinquished your Gen to my daughter just like that!"

"Susi needs him. Stop worrying, Tan—you're disturbing the ambient. Susi's going to be fine."

Under the impact of Kreg's field, Susi regained consciousness—but when she saw a Gen by her bed she reached out, trying to push him away. "No!" she sobbed. "No—I won't kill! Won't kill! I want a channel, Daddy!"

"Susi!" Risa moved quickly to Kreg's side. "Susi, you *are* a channel. Kreg is going to be your Companion—he'll give you transfer. You can't kill a Companion, remember?"

The girl stared at Risa, her lips trembling. Fear was devouring her last reserves of selyn. "Risa? Can't you—?"

"We want you to be the best channel you can be. Think of it! You saved Triffin's life—now you'll save other lives, every day."

Risa could zlin the moment Susi finally understood what she was being told. Excitement blossomed through her weak nager, and tears slid down her cheeks. "I'm a channel!"

"That's right," Kreg told her, letting his field entice her again. She turned toward him reflexively, and he took her hands. "Now relax. It's not time for your breakout yet. Let's try some breathing exercises, all right?"

Risa's regret at not having Kreg for transfer this month was far overshadowed by her pride in her brother as he coached Susi through to breakout, then, with her new tentacles clutching his arms spasmodically, held her gently for the moment of penetrating realization before he whispered, "Congratulations, Susi," and touched her lips with his.

Although Risa was shielding Darley, to keep his emotions from interfering with his daughter's First Transfer, he zlinned enough to dissolve into tears of mingled joy and grief. Risa, too, felt the piercing delight of that transfer, echoing what she had with Sergi. But Susi would never, ever, have her transfers haunted by the specter of the kill. *If only I could have had that the first time!*

But Risa had put the kill behind her—her true first time was with Sergi in the Shrine of the Starred-cross. She pulled the symbol out from under her shirt and held it tightly, remembering. And thinking gleefully that soon she would know that pleasure with Sergi again.

Susi, meanwhile, laughed aloud in the pure innocence of the nonjunct, and threw her arms around Kreg, kissing his cheek. Then she held out her arms to her father, saying, "Daddy! Oh, Daddy, don't cry! I'm all right!"

Darley wiped his eyes and went to hug his daughter. "Yes, baby, you're all right. Congratulations, Susi!"

But when Risa and Darley went into the parlor, leaving Kreg to encourage Susi to rest until morning, Darley looked up at his wife's portrait and asked, "Why did she have to be a channel? I had resigned myself to losing her to Keon only if she'd turned Gen."

"Tan—Susi has to train at Keon, but after that she can live here in town. There *should* be a channel nearby, so children in changeover don't have to be rushed to Keon."

Darley shook his head. "People will never accept it. The newcomers already think Keon is too open about its . . . perversions." He sighed. "I'm being ungrateful. You saved her life, and it's not your fault she's a channel. Do you have time to come over to Verla's for a drink?"

"I'm sorry. I've already been away for hours. I'll take it as a promise for another time."

"All right. You go on back to Keon. In the morning I'll escort Kreg—" He broke off with a grim smile. "Susi can escort him now, can't she?"

"Yes—and let's hope that once the mill is operating and the local population settles down to prosperity, it will be the way it was in the summer, when householding Gens could move freely without escorts."

"I'm afraid that will take a long time. Too many people are afraid now to associate closely with the householders."

Risa rode through deepening twilight, and met Sergi at the turnoff from the mill. "Where's Kreg?" he asked her.

"You're going to have to take his place, I'm afraid," she said, and told him what had happened.

"Susi Darley a channel!" Sergi exclaimed. "Well, we certainly need another one. Risa, you know how to pick your friends." He was cheerful. "I have news, too. As soon as we turn the water into the soaking pits—one more day's work—we'll fire up the blast furnace and try our first steel!"

"Sergi! That's wonderful! We'll make it a big occasion. Invite everybody to come and see the first steel poured."

But there was no time to plan that night. Risa's defection had thrown Keon's schedule into chaos, and there were Simes in need waiting anxiously for Rikki, Loid, and Dina to get to them. Risa spent four hours straight giving transfers, insisting that she had had enough rest at Darley's, with Kreg doing all the work. With Sergi by her side again, she did not feel at all tired, and shortly after midnight the schedule was in order again.

By that time she was feeling weary—or was being affected by Sergi's tiredness, for he had worked at the mill dawn to dusk before taking up his role of Companion again. Just as they were walking back toward Risa's room, they heard a distant noise—a chanting, rising rhythmically outside the gates, too distant for words to be made out.

Then the guard at the gate was shouting, "Attack! We're being attacked!" and Risa could hear voices and hoofbeats on the other side, zlin people marching on the householding—

The voices coalesced into a chant, "Perverts! Perverts! Perverts!"

Something pounded on the gates, paused, and hit them again with a resounding crash. The guard clung precariously to his perch, then leaped to the ground as the gates crashed open and a mob of junct Simes heaved through them, dropping the tree trunk they had used as a battering ram.

Keon's members came running from every side, and for one moment there was a pause, the two parties facing one another. Tripp Sentell stepped forward. "This is the end, perverts! Today ya brung yer filth inta town—right inta Tan Darley's house. Well, we ain't takin' no more! We found that blastin' powder." He held up a sack of it. "We was gonna blow up the mill first, but then you might escape. So we're gonna blow alla you up *with* the mill."

The juncts fanned out, attempting to surround Keon's Simes and Gens. Whips cracked, and fear and anger burst through the ambient. Sergi's dogs, Leader and Feathers, snapped at the intruders, barking and growling.

Risa saw one of the juncts grab for Gevron. The old Companion gave him a nageric shock that made the man yelp and fall to his knees, then calmly kicked him in the throat and left him choking on his own blood.

Sergi grasped Risa by the upper arms. "Come on! Channels into the main building—"

"Shen it, Sergi—you want them to blow us up in there?" She shook him off and leaped for Tripp Sentell.

The junct was startled enough to let her wrench his whip out of his hand, and she slashed him, saying, "You sniveling coward! You beat your kids! You beat your wife! You pick on helpless people! Well, we're *not* helpless, you lorsh!"

Sergi was at her side, trying to calm her rage with his nager, impossible because he was so thoroughly angry himself.

She squirmed in his grasp, only vaguely aware that the tide was turning about her—that the mob of juncts, not expecting Keon to fight back, were retreating toward the gates, shouting, "Blow up that mill!"

Keon's Simes and Gens pounded after them, leaping over the tree trunk still lying by the gates with something tied to it—something large and tattered and limp—

A shriek of agonized grief ripped the air and the ambient, shocking Risa into stillness. It was Triffin, kneeling, screaming in horror.

Sergi dropped Risa and ran to Triffin. Risa leaped after him, and he turned, catching her to himself, choking, "No—don't look!'

But Risa could not help looking—and zlinning the object the juncts had carried with them, tied to the tree trunk: the bloody, tattered, and very dead body of Kreg ambrov Keon.

Chapter Twelve

Sergi held Risa, unable to comfort her because of his own sorrow and outrage. Close to hard need, Risa could not grieve—her emotions burst forth in rage.

"I'll kill them!" she shouted, squirming out of his grip.

Risa's berserk fury shocked Sergi. "No!" he cried as she eluded his grasp. His field was enough to make her pause for an instant—and Sentell ran like the coward he was, augmenting as he plunged through the gates and into the darkness.

Risa turned on Sergi. "Why didn't you let me murder him?" she demanded, striking him with the whip she still held. "He murdered my brother!"

Sergi caught the whip and pulled Risa to him with it. "You said 'kill,' not 'murder.' Don't you know that a channel *could* kill a renSime?"

Triffin, who had remained weeping beside Kreg's body, came to life at Sergi's words. "Oh, no!" she pleaded. "If you revenged Kreg by killing—what would his life mean?"

Risa jerked the whip from Sergi's hand. "I won't kill," she said. "But my brother will be revenged!"

Just then the air shook with an explosion. Flames shot up over the treetops, and quickly died away.

"The mill!" Sergi exclaimed.

Risa ran for the gate with augmented speed, the two Gens racing after her as fast as they could go.

A supply shop had been the target of the first blast—but Sergi saw people attacking the furnace and the rolling mill, machinery they could not afford to replace.

A brief explosion flared at the base of the furnace—but fizzled out without damage. The attackers were discovering that sprinkling the powder and lighting it caused flashes, not the destruction they intended.

Junct employees from the bunkhouses joined the fight, but those trying to save the mill were losing ground. A wooden bunkhouse went up in flames—and in the glare Tripp Sentell appeared from the direction of the distant explosives shed, arms laden with supremely dangerous blasting sticks.

"Here, boys!" he shouted, passing them out to his cohorts. "These'll do the job!"

"You'll blow yourselves up, you fools!" Sergi shouted—but no one was listening.

One of the metal shops exploded with a thunderous roar. Debris rained down on the fighters—debris that included pieces of human bodies.

Unable to find Risa, Sergi followed Tripp Sentell.

Sentell's target was the blast furnace. His people surrounded it, parting to let him through. He grabbed a torch and leaped atop the foundation.

The junct shoved several blasting sticks between the foundation and the furnace itself. "Get ready to run, boys! I'll blow this thing sky high—an' them perverts with it!"

"Murderer!"

From the other side of the ring of juncts, Risa hurled herself toward Sentell—but she was stopped by six or eight juncts piling on top of her.

Sergi barreled toward the line—and through it with a flick of his nager.

As he reached the center of the circle he saw the blasting stick Sentell held aloft. The fuse was perhaps a double handspan long.

"Sentell!" Sergi shouted. "That's a fast fuse!"

Sentell laughed, holding the torch in one hand, the blasting stick in the other. "Grab him, boys! Knock him out and leave him here—him and his pervert girlfriend!"

Sergi fought physically and nagerically, working toward where Risa had disappeared under a heap of bodies.

Sentell looked out over the struggle, peering into the distance. "Hurry up!" he shouted, stretching out the hand holding the blasting stick, extending his laterals to zlin.

Sergi grabbed the forearms of a Sime attempting to throttle him, and squeezed his laterals viciously. The man let go with a scream of pain. Sentell's voice rose in pitch. "Leave them be and run! I'm gonna blow it now!"

"No!" Sergi shouted. "Don't do it!"

But Sentell lit the fuse, waving the sputtering explosive with a howl of triumphant laughter.

The junct was not watching the fuse, did not see the spark racing faster than imagination. The others saw, and broke ranks to flee.

Sentell turned, meaning to place the sputtering stick atop the others—

His scream began as he tried to throw the stick from him—too late!

The world exploded!

The noise resounded off the furnace—sound and blast wave hit Sergi together, followed by the impact of something impossibly heavy in the middle of his back.

He was flung to the ground, and pain clawed up to pierce him. Total silence enveloped him in waves of fiery pain—and then even that ceased.

Risa was pinned to the ground under Sime bodies. Her head seemed to explode. Her ears rang with shrieks and sirens as she fought her way out of the crush.

The two directly on top of her were unconscious. The other four were dead.

But Risa had no care for the juncts. She leaped to Sergi's side, shouting his name, her voice hollow and distant.

Her Companion lay face down in a pool of blood.

She flung aside the thing that had knocked Sergi to the ground: the headless, armless body of Tripp Sentell.

Sergi was unconscious, bleeding from ears and crushed nose. The impact of Sentell's body had broken three of his ribs, but had also protected him somewhat from the blast.

Sergi's field weakened with loss of blood, selyn pluming from his wounds into the night air. Risa let her need flow to him, and felt both bleeding and selyn loss slow.

She zlinned Simes running toward them and leaped up, prepared to defend Sergi.

Verla was hurrying toward her—and Susi Darley, in her nightdress with a cape thrown over it.

Zabrina appeared, torch in hand—and Jasteen, wielding a whip with practiced ease.

The town was converging on the mill.

Risa dared not leave Sergi. Her fury was burnt out, her whole attention on her Companion.

Her ears still rang from the explosion. When she zlinned Tannen Darley's attention on her, she looked at him before she realized he was saying something.

"I can't hear you," she told him. "The explosion."

He shouted, and she heard his voice as if through the whine of a metal polishing machine. "It's all over. We'll help you get the wounded back to Keon. Is Sergi all right?"

"He will be," she shouted in return, then realized that she didn't have to shout at Darley.

Risa's hearing slowly improved as the night passed.

On the road, Sergi came to with an involuntary moan.

Risa quickly bent over the litter, saying, "You're all right! Don't try to move—you've got broken ribs."

Sergi stared at her, startlement shattering his nager. At Risa's wince, his nager calmed, but he said something she couldn't hear. Then he put a hand to his ear and repeated it, and she knew he was saying, "I can't hear."

She nodded, trying to make him understand that she had the same problem, but that it was already getting better. She wasn't sure he understood.

Even though his injuries had weakened Sergi's selyn field, it still blazed out beyond bearing when they worked on his injuries. Every breath was searing agony when they bandaged his ribs—and that was the least of his problems.

Susi Darley, looking far out of place in her silk and lace gown and velvet cape, worked like a renSime, carrying the injured, running errands—until Risa remembered the girl was a channel, and put her to work balancing the fields.

Susi caught on quickly, and in the crowded infirmary gave Risa a bubble of privacy. Now she dared treat Sergi's facial injuries. His nose was broken and his left cheekbone cracked. The swelling made it both painful and difficult to work—and fosebine seemed to have no effect on his pain at all.

What had both Sergi and Risa in a state of anxiety was not his broken bones; both knew those would heal. The trickle of fear Sergi fought down over and over stemmed from the fact that he could still hear nothing—nothing at all.

The fact that Risa's hearing improved steadily only made her fear more that Sergi's deafness was permanent. But she gritted her teeth, while he was in pain, and tried to mold the cartilage of his nose to its proper shape. At least he began to breathe more easily, lessening the strain on his ribs.

When all the injured had finally been treated, Risa started through the crowded ward, sending home those who were both awake and well enough to be on their feet. Litith had to be chased off to bed in the middle of the night, when Risa caught her working just as if her baby were not due any time.

Sergi had been moved into an insulated room, Susi with him, with instructions to report any change in his condition. Risa, feeling need now that she had let her concentration lapse, started toward the doors.

Rikki, who had spent the night giving emergency transfers, had just joined the healers. He zlinned her sharply. "Why are you walking around in that condition?"

"What condition? I'm tired, that's all." And irritated, she might have added, from straining to understand through the ringing in her ears.

Rikki hurried to her side. "You were scheduled for transfer two hours ago—and last night you augmented and then worked all night. What's the matter with you?"

"Nothing!" she snapped. "So I'm in need. I'm going to sit with Sergi for an hour—my need will speed his healing. Meanwhile you can round me up a Companion, all right?"

His nager rang with astonishment. "Uh . . . all right," he said reluctantly. "Triffin's still in phase with you, and another hour's sleep will do her good." He shook his head. "You're hours into hard need and completely in control of yourself. Disjuncts are not supposed to be able to do that."

"Nonsense!" she told him. "A person does what he has to do—Sime, Gen, junct, nonjunct, disjunct. There were no kills last night, Rikki. We had junct Simes all over the place, and Gens in pain—there were deaths, but no kills."

Rikki smiled. "Maybe you're right. I'll send Triffin for you in an hour."

Susi rose when Risa entered. "He finally fell asleep," she reported. "I didn't notice any other changes."

She hovered anxiously as Risa zlinned her patient. "Everything's fine, Susi. Thank you."

When the girl had gone, Risa sat down and gave in to her need. Immediately Sergi's field responded, his cells increasing their selyn production, speeding healing.

He looked absolutely stricken, his face purple and

swollen, yet the moment her need washed over him he awoke, forcing open his swollen eyelids to peer at her owlishly.

"Go back to sleep," she said automatically, and felt sharply his moment's fear when he did not hear her.

Sergi quelled the fear, and held out his hand. "Are you all right?" he managed.

She wrapped handling tentacles about his hand, for it was too big for her to envelop even in both of hers. Squeezing, to offer comfort, she told him, "You'll be all right, too."

His swollen lips curved slightly in what was meant to be a reassuring smile, but it was not reflected in his nager. Then he closed his eyes and concentrated on Risa; her need subsided as Sergi's field enveloped her.

By the time Triffin arrived, Sergi had fallen back to sleep, but his body was healing steadily. Risa let her show-field rise slowly to mask her need. She had hoped not to wake him, but his eyes struggled open again, went from Risa to Triffin. "Go on," he said, quelling his own need to give. "You need a transfer, and I can't give it to you, Risa. Next month—I promise."

Risa's transfer with Triffin was bittersweet. The girl gave with all her natural Companion's desire and skill— but both women were acutely aware that this transfer was supposed to have been between Risa and Kreg.

Afterward, Risa wept with Triffin, who had loved Kreg as much as Risa did, if in a different way.

When they finally washed their faces and re-entered the world, Triffin went back to the infirmary and Risa met with Tannen Darley and his daughter in the Sectuib's office.

Darley told her, "Susi and I rode over to the mill." They had obviously ridden into town, too, as Susi was now dressed in a neat riding outfit.

The girl said, "There's really not much damage, Risa."

"One of the shops was destroyed, and one of the bunkhouses," Darley added. "People are rebuilding them. The furnace foundation is cracked—but we'll build a new one and set the furnace back on it. Maybe two extra weeks of work. As far as I can tell, the furnace wasn't harmed. Risa—they didn't get anything we can't replace with a few days of work."

"I don't care about the mill," Risa said glumly.

"Of course you do!" Darley exclaimed. "It's not just buildings and machines. Look what it's done for this community already!"

"Turned family against family, husband against wife."

"Tripp Sentell? He was mistreating his wife long before you got here."

"And now he's dead," she said bitterly, "and look what's happened to Sergi. And Kreg—" Her voice broke.

Susi jumped at the opening. "Where *is* Kreg? I didn't see him all night. Risa . . . what did they do to him?"

Risa looked into the young channel's anxious blue eyes, zlinned that Susi suspected the truth but didn't want to know it. But she had to be told. "Kreg is dead. Tripp Sentell and his men murdered him."

"It's my fault. He was protecting me!"

"Susi, what happened in town?" Risa demanded.

"After you and Daddy left, I fell asleep. When I woke up people were yelling in the parlor. Kreg was at the door of my room." The girl's eyes were focused far away. "He locked the door—but someone started pounding on it. Kreg told me to go out the window—go to Verla's and get Daddy."

"Everyone at Verla's came," Darley took up the story. "Those lorshes set my house on fire. We got it out pretty quickly—it didn't even get to the back of the house."

"But whoever did it was gone," Susi added. "I looked for Kreg. The door to my room was smashed in, but there was no one in the house except—" She choked.

"Except Fivvik," Darley said bitterly. "They murdered him." He paused, then added, "People started helping clean up the mess—and then we heard the first explosion at the steel mill. You know the rest."

"Who broke the gates in?" Susi asked suddenly. "Did they come here—?"

"Yes," Risa replied, "to deliver Kreg's body." Then she softened as the girl wept. "Susi, Kreg died as a Companion protecting a channel. When you come to understand what that means, you will know it is the death any Companion would ask."

Risa's words became Kreg's epitaph, carved into the stone memorial along with those of other Keon members who had given their lives for the frail dream of Simes and Gens living together in peace. "Kreg ambrov Keon—Companion."

Keon's stone memorial, a householding tradition, housed books with the names of the martyrs from all the householdings over the centuries. Their own members' names were carved into the stone walls—as all those other names were carved in stone in other places, eternally remembered.

Keon's cemetery was high on the hillside, overlooking the householding—and now the steel mill beyond. Clearing the trees had brought the town into view, and as she stood alone beside Kreg's grave, driving in the trefoil marker, Risa thought, *You look out over unity, little brother . . . as much unity, I fear, as this world will ever see.*

Each mourner walked alone and in silence along the path back to the householding complex. Risa had wept out her tears earlier. Now she doffed her funeral cape and set to work—to set Keon free of her.

It meant training Susi. It meant training a bookkeeper. But most of all it meant separating herself from Sergi.

He was on his feet for the funeral, in pain, but moving. But for his size and his nager, he was unrecognizable, his face still swollen and discolored, his bright hair hidden under bandages. He could not shave, and in a few days golden stubble covered the lower part of his face. But he healed steadily. If his nose always showed that it had been broken, it would not detract much from his rugged handsomeness.

But Sergi's appearance was not Risa's worry: his hearing was. When three days had passed after the funeral, he found her at the collectorium and said, "I'm going back on duty."

"You can't," she said, shaking her head.

"I have to," he insisted. "Risa—if I'm permanently deaf, the sooner I start coping with it the better. I can't abide sitting in silence, doing nothing!"

Reluctantly, she allowed him to join her in her work. There were times when he didn't understand, but other times when he refused to understand what he didn't want to.

On her turnover day, after she had snapped at Susi, Sergi, and Gevron, Rikki took Risa off the schedule, saying, "Go do something else—anything!"

Sergi said, "Let's check the steel mill," and started toward the stable before she could refuse. Bundled up against the frosty autumn air, they rode in bright sunshine, the leaves dancing in brilliant colors along the roadside.

The buildings at the mill had been rebuilt, and rugged scaffolding surrounded the blast furnace. The metal bell of the furnace had been hoisted up with sturdy winches while the foundation was restored.

When Sergi rode in, a cheer went up—Simes, mostly junct, cheering a Gen's recovery.

Once it would have warmed Risa's heart. Now it ate at her insides . . . it was so futile, so fragile—once those Simes came into hard need, Sergi would be prey, not friend.

Against her will, she was drawn into the consultation between Sergi and the Simes repairing the furnace, for he understood her better than anyone else. She was becoming accustomed to compensating for Sergi's deafness when they were alone together; now she was reminded that he was suffering because she had gotten him into this crazy project. The enthusiasm of the work crew only served to dampen Risa's spirits further.

She was glad when they finally left the mill, but she

did not look forward to what she had to do: tell Sergi at once, write it out and make him read it, that she was leaving Keon as soon as the householding could operate without her.

But as they rode through the opening the gates had formerly filled, the guard (*What are we guarding now, with no gates to close?* Risa wondered) called down to them, "Everyone's looking for you! Litith is having her baby!"

Nedd's widow was in one of the insulated rooms in the infirmary, Dina and Sintha with her. The child was drawing far too much selyn from its mother's system in a last-moment demand for the life substance it could not produce or obtain again until puberty.

Dina's field rang with relief as Risa entered. "I was afraid to give her selyn," she said. "She needs your touch, Risa—her nerves are raw."

Litith, like any pregnant Sime woman, had had a shorter and shorter need cycle for the past several months—but now her storage nerves were oversensitized by too-frequent selyn movement. The process of obtaining life became as painful as the process of giving birth.

Risa zlinned Litith. A contraction set her writhing, but then she smiled weakly as Sintha wiped her forehead. "Risa," she whispered, "save Nedd's child for Keon."

Risa replied, "You and the baby are both going to be fine. Sergi—" she gestured to him "—come sit here opposite Sintha. Rest on the Companions' fields, Litith."

She zlinned the baby, strong and healthy and properly positioned. The only problem was Litith's weakness—and Risa's lack of experience. She had never helped to deliver *any* baby before, let alone a child who might be a channel. Dina had, though, and so had both Sintha and Sergi.

"Dina—how long yet?" she asked.

"Two or three hours," the Carre channel replied. "First babies always take longer than later births."

Risa had been hoping that delivery was only a few minutes away. Litith's nerves could not take two transfers in rapid succession—but if Risa forced a full transfer into her now, she might be unable to resist augmenting in the contractions, crushing the life from the child. Yet if Risa waited too long, the baby could drain her so far into attrition that she would abort out of transfer—and die.

The Companions eased Litith's need; she was not suffering, but she was also not improving. "Dina," said Risa, "have you ever given selyn directly to the unborn child?"

"No—have you?"

"Shen! Where are the transfer points on an infant?"

"Head, throat, heart, navel," Litith said. "I know the theory, Risa—but I've never seen it done, either. Zlin for the nerve centers," she continued, as calmly as if she were lecturing in a classroom, "The draw will be through the umbilical, but the other points are necessary, just as a fifth point is for an adult. Do it before the child starts to breathe—drawing air into his lungs starts his child's metabolism, and his ability to assimilate selyn ends."

Risa was astonished at the confidence Litith placed in her. It was as if once the procedure had been discussed it was given that Risa would use it—and the child would be safe.

The contractions came closer together. Because of the Companions, Litith did not sense her need as acute, and relaxation delayed attrition. But the final contractions forced Litith to use selyn voraciously—and at the same time the child drew desperately as it entered the birth canal.

Risa reached for Litith's arms.

"No!" the woman gasped. "Save my baby, Risa!"

She could zlin the child's need. If she provided it with selyn, it would stop draining Litith. She reached carefully into the birth canal, easing her handling tentacles around the baby, zlinning for the nerve centers Litith had mentioned—

One hand lay on the child's belly, laterals drawn to the area over the heart and to the pulsing umbilical. The other hand cradled the child's head, preventing it for the moment from emerging to breathe before she could give it the selyn it craved. Her laterals found the nerve centers—

Selyn flowed into its starved system—only an instant and it was brimming, squirming, ready to be born—it rode from its mother's womb on Risa's hands!

Risa handed the baby to Sergi and moved to grasp Litith's forearms, pressing the lateral extensor nerves to force the small, weak tentacles to emerge. Shrieking pain brought Litith back to awareness as Risa forced selyn into her depleted system. Risa let the flow subside to a trickle, tantalizing—Litith found her pace and drew, painfully but surely, taking enough to last for several days.

The moment Risa raised her head, Litith whispered, "The baby!"

"It's a boy," Dina replied, joy in her voice and nager. "A fine, healthy boy!"

Joy swelled Risa's heart, and a strange sense of her place in the universe. The thought of leaving Keon became unbearable. *I'll stay if they'll have me*, she decided. *But will Keon want me after all the trouble I've caused?*

Risa turned, and saw Sergi still holding the infant as Sintha wiped its tiny body clean. Little fists waved and feet kicked, and an angry wailing filled the room. Sergi stared, and tears started down his cheeks. He looked over the squirming child and met Risa's eyes. "I hear it!" he said in utter astonishment. "I hear the baby crying!"

Sergi's hearing improved dramatically in the next few hours, as Keon celebrated the birth. The channels theorized that as his facial injuries healed and the swelling went down, perhaps aided by his ride in the cold air, the pressure on the delicate inner-ear mechanism eased. After that day, though, there was little change. It appeared that he would always suffer impairment— but he was able to participate in conversation, and was grateful for that.

He even joked to Risa, "If it's something unpleasant, I don't want to hear it anyway."

His face healed as the days passed, too. Each time Risa saw him he looked more like himself—but he could not spend much time with her as she approached need again.

Two days before her transfer day the blast furnace was fired. Both the town and the householding turned out to watch the steel being poured, white-hot, sparks flying. A cheer rose, householders and townspeople celebrating together the results of their long, hard effort.

There were minor problems, of course—and Sergi stayed at the mill all night instead of returning with Risa to Keon as planned. But when he did return, late that afternoon, he was grinning in triumph.

Not stopping to wash off the grime, he tracked Risa down at the dispensary to announce, "Everything's working perfectly—and now I'm all yours!"

"Not until you get that soot off you!" she protested, short-tempered with approaching need.

"The steel mill was your idea, Risa. You'll have to live with the consequences!"

But he did leave her, to reappear an hour later scrubbed clean, his hair a shining golden cap, his blue eyes sparkling in anticipation of their transfer. And he had shaved off his beard. He looked like himself once more.

Like Risa, Sergi had been denied proper transfers for the past two months—in fact, because of his injury he had skipped one month entirely.

When their last duties were completed, they left the transfer room they'd been working in—but when Risa started toward the better insulated one where channel's transfer took place, Sergi steered her away.

"Where are we going?" Risa asked.

"My room."

"*Your* room? Sergi, what—?"

"No more excuses, Risa. I want you for transfer . . . and afterwards. It's been too long, for both of us."

She didn't care. She just wanted to be alone with him.

He led her past the Sectuib's office and up the stairs. Risa had never been above the ground floor of the main building, although she knew the channels and Companions had living quarters there.

On the top floor, Sergi opened the door to a large, beautiful room with windows looking out over the center of the householding complex, and beyond to the autumn hills.

But Sergi lit the lamp and drew the curtains closed. The room was as well-insulated as a transfer room, Risa noticed—but of course, Sergi had to have a place where he didn't have to be in constant control of his nager.

His field throbbed with infectious joy. When he touched her, they resonated in such perfect pitch that it seemed her need disappeared, so filled was she with his nager.

She leaned against his hard chest, feeling as if she could sink right through his skin, to be one with him.

"Sergi . . . what are you doing?"

"I'm not trying to control at all—just loving you."

He kissed her. To Risa it was merely a pleasant closeness; she could feel no sexual desire, or even response, until after transfer.

"Let's lie down," Sergi said, unbuttoning her shirt.

"Before transfer?" she asked bemusedly, letting him strip her.

"*For* transfer. We might as well be comfortable." He placed her in the bed, shrugged out of his own clothes, and lay down in the big double bed, sliding an arm under her.

She cuddled contentedly against him, trying to avoid lateral contact, for the eager, moist tentacles were unsheathed despite her lack of intil. But Sergi lifted her arms and put them around his neck.

"Be careful!" she said. "You're getting ronaplin all over you."

"I'll only feel more," he replied.

"You're outrageous."

"You expect me to be sober and solemn when I have everything I need right here in my arms?"

Risa laughed, recognizing how incredible it was to feel amusement at the depth of hard need, a need not properly satisfied for months. She drew him close, unmindful of the selyn-conducting fluid smearing him everywhere her laterals touched.

Sergi held her, waiting for the right moment. Then his hands slid caressingly over her forearms, knowing the touch that brought exquisite pleasure on the heart-stopping edge of pain. Her tentacles instinctively sought the proper grip. Sergi studied her, laughter dancing in his eyes. "Care to try for a different fifth transfer point?"

"Oh, Sergi!" she said in amused exasperation, and pulled him into lip contact.

Sergi poured selyn into her as fast as she could accept it, like no other Companion. Today, though, there did not seem to be a flow through nerves at all—it was as if all the barriers were gone—as if they were one and the same, filling and filled, satisfying and satisfied, healer and healed.

It did not end until she was beyond any former satisfaction, as if he opened new depths in her simply for the pleasure of filling them.

Stunned, Risa stared at Sergi, seeing him, as always immediately after transfer, with only those senses they had in common. But his eyes were unfocused, and he seemed to be drawn within himself, one with her on that awesome nageric level. Then he blinked, and his eyes focused on her.

He could not speak, nor did he have to. They reached

out to one another, clinging, crying with a joy too strong for laughter.

For a while they lay quietly, absorbed in one another. Then, tenderly, his hand caressed her hair. Desire flowed from him to her, awakening her own.

She kissed him deeply, her body yearning for his. Where he was smeared with ronaplin, contact was even more intense. They moved together, their rhythm matching as easily and naturally as their fields resonated together. Risa could not sort out her responses from Sergi's—nor did she care.

Such sweet passion led inevitably to the moment of fulfillment, and they lay panting, Risa cradling Sergi's bright head on her breast, his cool skin a tender pleasure on hers. Finally she had to speak. "Sergi, what's happening to us? I've never felt like this before."

"Torluen." The word was muffled against her.

". . . what? You mean lortuen?"

"When the man is Gen and the woman Sime, it's called torluen." He pulled her down into his arms. "I don't know why there are two different words. Who cares which one of us is what?"

"I don't care," she replied, not yet realizing the implications. "I just love you."

His arms tightened about her. "Would you like to have our marriage celebration right away, or wait until the householding has pledged to you?"

"What?" She sat up in sudden horror. "Sergi, I—I'm sorry!"

"Sorry for what? Risa, everything is perfect now!"

She got up and moved away, picking up his shirt and draping it over herself against a sudden chill. The strange new connection between them did not lessen with distance. "Don't you realize what I've done to you?"

"We did it together."

"We shouldn't have! Oh, my love, I know I can't stay at Keon without committing myself—but Keon won't have me as Sectuib. Not after all the trouble I've caused."

"Of course we will. Risa, you have been Sectuib in all but name since Nedd's death. We'll put it to a vote of the membership, if it will make you feel better."

She nodded. "But what if they vote against me? What will happen to you, Sergi?"

"I stay with you, whatever happens. But I know what will happen," he added serenely. His confidence was so great that Risa barely knew her own fears. Sergi watched her, then got up and handed her her clothes. "Let's go set up the vote for tomorrow—you won't be happy until the whole householding lets you know how we feel."

"They know how *I* feel, and I can't change. Keon's traditions are not my traditions. I don't believe in community property—"

"Which is why Keon's members are now individual stockholders in Keon Steel."

"I can't live closed in behind stone walls!"

"And we have no reason to rebuild the gates. You have changed Keon, as every Sectuib does. If people didn't like what you were doing, they would leave—but no one has left."

"They have no choice. Where else could they go and be safe as Gens, or not kill as Simes?"

"Gen Territory!" Sergi answered as they went down the stairs. "Carre. Other householdings in other territories. My brother is at Imil, over in Nivet Territory. No one is forced to stay here. Keon's virtue is freedom—and we have never been so free as since you came here, Risa."

"Risa—Sergi!" Rikki came out of one of the transfer rooms with Dina. "I wasn't going to disturb you—but we could use your help! We've got two changeovers going on at once."

"Where do you want us, Rikki?" Risa asked resignedly.

Loid's son, Dron, was expected to be a channel like his father, so Rikki sent Sergi and Risa to help the boy through. The diagnosis proved true; Gevron provided First Transfer, and Keon had enough channels again, even with its added work load—or would have as soon as both Dron and Susi completed their training.

It was another occasion for a party—it seemed that Keon had done nothing else for days!

Risa tried to put aside her worry about the future. Then, as she stood watching the parents of the two new Simes toasting each other in porstan, Dina came up to her and asked, "Will you send me back to Carre now, Risa?"

There was something hidden in Dina's nager, but Risa could not fathom it in the crowd of happy people. "It's not up to me," she replied. "Rikki—"

"No. *When* Keon can operate without my services may be the controller's decision, but whether or not you allow me to stay is the Sectuib's. After what I have seen here—I want to stay, but only if I can pledge to you as my Sectuib."

Loid joined them, saying, "Dina is right. Risa—my son cannot pledge unto Keon until you accept the title. There are a dozen others houseless—all who have changed over or established since Nedd's death. We must have a Sectuib in name as well as in deed."

All around them, people took up the theme. "It's time to take the title, Risa." "You've certainly earned it!"

The crowd parted to let Litith come through, carrying her child. "Risa," she said, "when Nedd died you were still a stranger to many of us. But that is true no longer. You *are* our Sectuib. Let us recognize you."

She handed her baby to Dina, and pulled her house-holding ring from her finger, handing it to Risa. All over the room, Simes and Gens did the same, crowding forward to hand them to Risa—in moments her hands were full, her handling tentacles weighted down with rings as people ran for members not at the party, hurrying them into the dining hall for the occasion.

"Sergi!" Risa called.

He came to stand beside her, saying, "I know my

part, but I cannot perform it until all the members have gathered."

"Did you plan this?"

"Do you think I arranged the changeovers?"

"I don't know *what* you may be capable of arranging!" she admitted.

One of the dining tables became a platform, chairs set before it for people to step up on. The red capes were brought out, and one was draped about Risa's shoulders as with relief she put the rings down on a smaller table Loid set up on the large one. Sergi at her side, she faced the members of Keon, all now crowded into the dining hall. These people could not be choosing her to lead them—and yet their collective nager told her that it was indeed so. They wanted her. They trusted her.

Sergi brought out the length of white chain Risa had seen at Kreg and Triffin's pledge ceremony. The channels and Companions stood ready to have him fasten it about their throats, like collars. They would expect Risa to—

As she stepped back at his approach, Sergi said, "You may discard this part of the ceremony if you wish, Risa. It's your householding."

"But Keon has its traditions," she replied, eyeing the chain dubiously. "We should keep our links with the past." She swallowed hard, dreading the feel of that chain clasped tight about her throat—and suddenly she knew— "Give me that, Sergi."

She took the jewelry pliers from his hand, measured a length of the lightweight enameled chain, and made a circle large enough to slip over her head. "We are free to choose," she said. "We can wear the chain freely only if it is loose enough to remove if we see fit."

Sergi quickly fashioned the chain into lengths that the channels and Companions could put on and off easily—and all put them on, accepting the burden of their free choice.

Then Sergi took Risa's hand, saying, "As First Companion in Keon, I choose you, Risa Tigue, as Sectuib ambrov Keon. To you I pledge my life, my strength, my talent, and my future. Unto Keon, forever!"

There was silence in the room, but the ambient nager vibrated as with a huge cheer. Sergi slipped something onto Risa's finger—the ring he had showed her before. But now it was finished, gleaming gold, the ruby surrounded by diamonds, marking it as the Sectuib's ring. When had he had the time—?

Sergi held out his own ring, huge and heavy on the palm of his hand, and Risa slipped it onto his finger, not knowing what to do next. "Tell me you accept my pledge," he murmured.

"Sergi ambrov Keon, I accept your pledge," she told him. Again the silent cheer—and when Risa turned once more to face Keon's membership, the oath was repeated by every voice there.

When she had accepted the pledge, she asked Sergi, "Shouldn't I promise something?"

"You have," he replied. "In accepting us, you have accepted Keon."

People surged forward to claim their rings. Dina, who had stood silent, still wearing her Carre ring, told Risa, "If you will have me, I will send a message to Yorn at once. He is still my Sectuib until he releases me—and Carre may require my services for the winter."

"You will be welcome whenever you are free to join us, Dina," Risa told her.

Then she was surrounded by people congratulating her, finding their own rings somehow, and having her place them on their hands. People who had to hurry back to their duties were allowed to go first, but the festival mood continued.

Rikki was among the last to come forward, bringing with him the children of Keon who had never pledged, having changed over or established while the householding had no Sectuib. Loid's son Dron was there— and so was Susi Darley.

"Susi," Risa said as the girl came forward, "you

shouldn't do this without consulting your father. He wants you to live in town, with him—"

"And I will," Susi replied serenely, "as you told me at my changeover. I am an adult now, Risa—and I want to devote my life to Keon as you have made it."

Zlinning the girl's sincerity in her nager, Risa accepted her pledge, and the others'. The final ritual was complete. Music played. People burst into song.

Sergi stepped down from the platform, and lifted Risa down. She let him, feeling again the new but no longer strange link between them. Their red capes draped over their arms as he lifted her, the white chains prominent against the bright fabric—but Risa no longer felt bound. She felt freer than she had ever felt, in the midst of those she loved, who loved her. The white chains were a link with the past—and a link to the future. Her future—the one she would build with Sergi—a part of Keon, forever.